"The characters drive this novel, and the relationships between the book club members are genuine and sweet. The dialogue is fun and spirited and will please readers looking for a light-hearted, spritely mystery."   —Kings River Life Magazine

Read and Buried

"Destined to become a favorite with cozy mystery lovers everywhere. Full of Southern charm, excellent reading suggestions, and an engaging amateur sleuth named Lizzie Turner, *Read and Buried* will have readers clamoring for the next in the series even before they turn to the last page."
    —Miranda James, *New York Times* bestselling author of the Cat in the Stacks Mysteries

"A nosy book club, cozy cats, and a great whodunit!"
    —Krista Davis, *New York Times* bestselling author of the Domestic Diva Mysteries

"This book is a model for how cozy mysteries should be written. There are lovable characters, an engaging plotline, and no lack of suspects and motives that will leave you intrigued until the very last page. Erika Chase is quickly becoming one of my favorite cozy mystery authors."   —Girl Lost In a Book

A Killer Read

"This is a terrific debut! I want to join this book club, eat those cheese sticks, keep an eye on those romances, and wander around Ashton Corners. But most of all, I'd love to have Lizzie Turner as my friend. Especially if another body turns up."
— Mary Jane Maffini, author of
the Charlotte Adams Mysteries

"Who can't love a debut novel filled with mystery references and a pair of cats named Edam and Brie? And who can't adore dedicated, saucy Lizzie Turner, a literacy teacher with high hopes for her students? Readers should have high hopes for this series. And thanks to the author's fine research, readers just might find a delicious assortment of new authors to browse."
— Avery Aames, Agatha Award winner and national bestselling author of the Cheese Shop Mysteries

"Book a date with *A Killer Read*. Mystery-loving book club members will keep readers guessing as they page through clues to prevent themselves from being booked for murder."
— Janet Bolin, author of the Threadville Mysteries

Law and Author

ERIKA CHASE

BERKLEY PRIME CRIME, NEW YORK

BERKLEY PRIME CRIME

An imprint of Penguin Random House LLC
375 Hudson Street, New York, New York 10014

LAW AND AUTHOR

A Berkley Prime Crime Book / published by arrangement
with the author

Copyright © Penguin Group (USA) LLC
Excerpt by Linda Wiken copyright © 2016 by Linda Wiken.

ISBN: 978-0-425-27820-8

PUBLISHING HISTORY
Berkley Prime Crime mass-market edition / September 2015

PRINTED IN THE UNITED STATES OF AMERICA

10 9 8 7 6 5 4 3 2 1

Cover illustration by griesbach & martucci.
Cover design by Edwin Tse.
Interior text design by Laura K. Corless.

Penguin
Random
House

Acknowledgments

How can an author get any writing done with so many wonderful people in her life? It helps that they're all very supportive and understand things like having to skip an event because of edits, phone calls that sound like a mad woman calling, and not getting answers to emails, phone calls, and even missing important dates.

So, thank you so very much to all you fine people in my life, and especially to my sister Lee McNeilly, a continuing support and happy reader. Thanks also to Mary Jane Maffini, half of the wicked Victoria Abbott writing team, particularly when it comes to those phone calls and road trips. And to good friend Vicki Delany, also known in the writing world as Eva Gates. Her comments are most welcomed as is her company on many travels.

I am quite honored to be part of a very creative and caring community of writers.

Thanks also to the dynamic team at Berkley Prime Crime, especially my editor Kate Seaver, editorial assistant Katherine Pelz and publicist Danielle Dill. I continue to love my covers! And, last but definitely not least, thank you to my agent, Kim Lionetti of BookEnds Literary xxx. Who knew there were so many fabulous people in publishing!

Chapter One

◇◇◇

Won't it? Well, we'll just have to wait and see.
Won't we?

THE CARE AND MANAGEMENT OF LIES—
JACQUELINE WINSPEAR

"I'm telling you right now, sugar, I'm leaning toward bumping off Clyde Worsten rather than having to deal with him one minute longer," Teensy Coldicutt said with a dramatic sigh.

Lizzie Turner almost dropped the mini triple chocolate cupcake she'd just rescued from the serving tray on the wicker patio table next to her. She shot a glance at Molly Mathews, who started laughing, much to Lizzie's surprise.

"Don't look so distressed, Lizzie," Molly said between chuckles. "Teensy's talking about her new book, aren't you?" She shifted her glance to her childhood friend of over sixty years.

Teensy looked around at the three other women in Molly's sunroom and burst out into her own deep belly laugh. "Oh, my. Of course your mind went straight to the worst, Lizzie. Being such a great fan of mysteries, and I might add, a dynamite crime fighter, I can see as that would happen. But Mopsy is right. Clyde Worsten was going to be the hero on my latest novel, *Divine Secrets of Desire*, but he's not cooperating at all, at all. So, he's either going to be the victim, or if he gets me really riled, I'll turn him into a murderer. Serve him right if he has to spend the rest of his life in jail."

"Mopsy," Sally-Jo Baker stated with a grin. "It still takes me by surprise sometimes when I hear you use Molly's childhood nickname."

"And I didn't know you were writing a mystery, Teensy," said Lizzie.

"Goodness gracious, of course not. My forte is romance and I'm into another hot plot I want you to know, but that doesn't mean I can't throw in a dead body or two if the characters don't shape up and cooperate."

Lizzie shook her head. "I'd heard that writers talk about their characters taking over a story."

Teensy leapt up from the white wicker love seat with more energy than most women her size. Her hairstyle, a dramatic wedge, had changed since the last time her friends had seen her, from a bright orange-red to a vivid dark red with a broad white streak sweeping across her brow. The black leggings, smock-necked orange and green long-sleeved blouson, and four-inch sandals contrasted with Molly's classic cream ensemble of casual pants and silk blouse. Lizzie marveled at the many differences between the two longtime friends.

"Oh, believe me, they do," Teensy said. "And, I'm just bursting to tell you both about my news."

Molly looked up from the *Wedding Bells* magazine she was perusing. "You have a publisher?"

"Right in one, Mopsy. Remember poor Nick Jennings, the

editor at Crawther Publishing? Well, it looked like he needed someone to talk to when he was in town after that tragedy last fall, so I befriended him, and one thing led to another."

Molly wasn't able to suppress her gasp. "No."

"Oh, Molly. There's hope for you yet, but that's not what I meant. We started talking about writing, and I told him of the great success my first book had garnered around here, and he said he'd take a look at my new manuscript. So, maybe it's not a done deal but I know that when he reads the first three chapters and synopsis I've just sent him, I'll be signing on the dotted line."

Lizzie fervently hoped that would be the case. Of course, she knew nothing about Crawther Publishing and their lines, except for the mysteries they had showcased at the book fair held in Ashton Corners last fall. But, she had read Teensy's first book, which had been co-published with a local printer, and Lizzie wondered if it would have met the criteria of an established publisher like Crawther.

"We're wishing you loads of luck with that Teensy," said Sally-Jo, choosing a pecan swirl from the tray of sweets. "This is really a nice idea, Molly, having us over for a girls' afternoon while the guys are out fishing."

"I thought so," Molly agreed. "It's a wonder, though, that Bob, Jacob and even Mark were all able to find a free weekend in common to get away."

Lizzie nodded, knowing only too well that her significant other, Mark Dreyfus, didn't often take an entire weekend off from his job as police chief of Ashton Corners, Alabama. She was pleased he'd decided to go, knowing how hard he'd been working for some time now without a real break.

Teensy walked over to the table and chose a sugar cookie. Rather than eating it, she held it in her hand and started pacing. "Well, let's just hope they have lots of luck and we can indeed have that fish barbecue they're promising when they come home tomorrow."

"What has gotten into you today, Teensy?" Molly asked. "You've either got ants in your pants or you've had way too much coffee."

"I have all these ideas floating around in my head and I'm just trying to shake them into some sort of order," replied Teensy, waving her hands in emphasis. "I need to harness all this energy and do something."

"I thought writing was taking up most of your time."

"Oh, it is but that doesn't mean I can't do others things also. I think I write best if I'm under pressure and a dead-line."

"You also have the writing course you're running, I might remind you. How much more do you want on your plate? And how is the course going, by the way?"

Teensy perched on the edge of the love seat. "As well as it should, I guess. There are mostly women enrolled although I do have one elderly man. He's a bit too old for my taste, must be at least seventy-five if he's a day, but he does have a good sense of humor. Anyway, to most of the others in the class it's a social afternoon out. Oh sure, they do the home-work exercises I give them but not many are trying their hand at writing anything else. And that's what this whole course is for. I wanted to help others find themselves and explore their inner writers."

Sally-Jo leaned over to touch Teensy's hand. "I can see that you'd be frustrated, Teensy. I'd bet there's a lot of prepa-ration time that goes into it, too."

"Not really," Teensy admitted, with an embarrassed grin. "I put the outline together by looking at other courses, and then I found tips and suggestions from a whole slew of books on writing. It was easy, really. I think I'm even learning a few things, too."

"Why that's just great," Molly said with enthusiasm. "And even if you don't turn out a Pulitzer winner, at least they're all doing something they must be enjoying."

"Oh, for sure." Teensy sighed. "I guess I'm just being silly. There is one gal, though, who has lots of promise and she's working her way through writing a novel. I'm trying to help her as best I can."

She sounded a bit hesitant to Lizzie.

"Well, that's all to the good," said Molly. "Now is there anything else that's got you so bothered?"

"That's just it, I do not have an iota of an idea why I'm so antsy these days. Maybe it's a touch of spring fever. But I feel like I need something else to be getting involved in. You don't have another body hidden away somewhere that needs a heaping of justice, do you?"

Molly shuddered. "Heavens no. And don't you go jinxing us now, Teensy Coldicutt. Things have been nice and quiet with the Ashton Corners Mystery Readers and Cheese Straws Society for a while now, aside from the occasional verbal fracas with a certain stubborn retired police chief, that is."

"Pshaw. I do believe you enjoy the sparring just as much as that old dog does, Mopsy."

Lizzie turned away from them quickly before Molly could see her face. Teensy had hit the nail on the head but Molly was still in denial. Bob Miller and Molly had known each other since childhood and although their lives had taken such different paths, the ties were maybe even stronger. Much as between Molly and Teensy. That was the wonderful thing about small towns.

"What about doing some volunteer work?" Lizzie asked.

"I'm sure you'd fit right in with the reading program the school board promotes in elementary schools. You go in and read to various groups of kids. Usually they're ones having trouble with their reading skills or maybe they have short attention spans. And, you can choose the days and times you'd like to be involved. I think you'd be really good at that, Teensy."

Sally-Jo nodded. "You'd certainly be able to hold their attention, Teensy. I think you'd give very colorful readings."

Teensy's face lit up in a smile. "You could be right, girls. I'll look into that. Thank you."

"You're welcome," they answered in unison and broke into laughter.

Molly reached for the empty pitcher of iced tea. "I'm betting y'all would like some more." She paused before going into the kitchen. "Now don't say anything important until I get back."

"We'll just talk about you behind your back, Mopsy," Teensy called out. "Nothing important, though."

Molly made a face at Teensy as she came back outside. She offered to refill Sally-Jo's glass. "I know I'm real anxious to hear where you're at with your wedding plans, Sally-Jo."

Sally-Jo flipped the cover shut on the magazine on her lap and held it up to them. *Premier Bride.* "This is about as far as I've gotten. Thumbing through all these magazines. Who knew there were so many focused on wedding planning? Jacob and I are thinking small but my folks are thinking big. I'm not quite sure what to do."

"Well, I'm enjoying looking through all these here magazines," Molly said. "It sure brings back memories although we didn't go searching through catalogues for a wedding dress in my day."

Lizzie looked at her with interest. "What did you do? Go to a big city for a day of shopping?"

"Not at all. My mama had wanted me to wear her dress but it had gotten damaged over the years, despite her careful packing away of it. So, she had a local dressmaker come in, suggest a style, and take my measurements. We agreed on the material and a few months later, I had my dress. And I just loved it."

Lizzie nodded. "It looks wonderful in your photos. Maybe that's what you should suggest, Sally-Jo."

Sally-Jo had her finger marking a page in her magazine. She opened it and showed it to the others. "So tell me truthfully, what about the style of this dress?"

Lizzie leaned closer for a better look. She tried not to sound too critical. "I don't really think it's you, Sally-Jo. I somehow can't picture you in a mermaid look. I'd think something more elegant and flowing. Sorry."

"That's quite all right. In fact, I was hoping you'd say something like that. My mama, however, loves this dress. In fact, she told me to go out and buy this magazine and have a look at this particular one." Sally-Jo sighed. "It's not me but I know just how pushy Mama can be. And I'm afraid I just might end up walking or rather waddling down the aisle in this."

"Can't you just go out shopping and buy a dress on the sly?" Teensy asked, a devilish twinkle in her eye. "We'd all be as happy as a puppy with two tails to go with you."

Molly glanced at Teensy. "That's not being very sensitive to her mama's role in all this. It's as important a day for her as it is for Sally-Jo." She raised her glass toward Sally-Jo and smiled. "But, honey, we would be very pleased to help you out with this."

"Oh, no. Mama wants me to come home over Easter

break and she'll book appointments in all the bridal salons in Fort Myers. She'll summon the sisters, too. She's even offered to pre-shop for me to narrow it down and make the decision easier."

Sally-Jo looked so gloomy and defeated that Lizzie wanted to give her a big reassuring hug. "What do you want?"

A small smile crept across her face. "I'm sort of leaning to a strapless dress on the shorter side, maybe falling just below the knees and with an empire waist."

"Ah, sugar, that's so totally right for a petite gal like you," Teensy said with a giggle. "And with your skin tone, the white will look perfect. That's the only problem with being a redhead of the bottle—I admit to it—the skin tone doesn't come with it."

"I think that sounds like a wonderful choice," Molly's voice rang with enthusiasm.

"Thanks, Molly. Maybe I can get you to brainwash my mama."

"Maybe it's just the initial excitement. I'm sure she wants whatever will make you happy."

Sally-Jo shrugged. "You don't know Mama. There'll be no resting until I have a dress chosen and tucked away in my closet."

Lizzie started to say something but was interrupted by the ringing of the front doorbell. She looked at Molly, who had settled back in a lounge chair, and said, "I'll get that for you."

"Thank you, honey."

Lizzie went through to the foyer to the front door and peered through the peephole to see a young woman standing there. She pulled open the door.

"Hey. May I help you?"

The girl with the Miley Cyrus hairstyle looked to be in

her late teens or early twenties. She wore trendy skinny jeans and a silver distressed-style leather jacket along with a black shirt and multicolored beads around her neck. She tried to peer past Lizzie.

When that didn't work she crossed her arms and stated, "I'm looking for Bob Miller."

It sounded like a challenge to Lizzie.

Chapter Two

◇◇◇

"Don't underestimate me."

GRACE TAKES OFF—JULIE HYZY

Molly suddenly appeared at Lizzie's side. "Who do we have here?" she asked.

"I'm not sure," Lizzie replied. "She's looking for Bob."

"And who might you be?" Molly asked the stranger.

"My name is Darla Lyman. Who might you be?"

Lizzie stiffened at her tone. She did not like any disrespect shown when it came to Molly but before she had a chance to say anything, Molly answered, "I am Molly Mathews and this is my house."

The expression on Darla's face changed immediately. She was all smiles. "Oh, how awesome. My grandmamma Sue-Ann told me all about you and I was hoping you could tell me where my granddaddy is."

"Bob Miller is your granddaddy?" Molly's face looked as shocked as she sounded. "You're Sue-Ann's granddaughter?"

"That's right, although she passed last year. My mama is Lily Lyman." Darla suddenly looked like she would cry. "I had a bit of a disagreement with her. I need to find my granddaddy. Do you know where he is?"

Molly eased past Lizzie and put an arm around Darla's shoulder, escorting her into the hall. "Yes, I do. He's out of town for the weekend on a fishing trip but will be back tomorrow afternoon. Do you want to come in and join us? I have a few friends in for some afternoon tea. This is Lizzie Turner, by the way."

Darla glanced from Lizzie to Molly and then back again. She nodded and said, "Hey."

"It's nice to meet you," Lizzie answered.

Darla said, "The same. Maybe I'll stop by for just a short while. I'm sort of thirsty," she directed at Molly.

Molly smiled and led her through the kitchen and out to the patio. Lizzie followed, noting how Darla had a good look, although fleeting, around her as they moved along the large open foyer, through the updated kitchen, and out the back door.

"Ladies, I'd like you to meet Darla Lyman, Bob's grand-daughter."

Sally-Jo looked surprised and took a few seconds to absorb the information before she leapt up and walked over to shake Darla's hand. "It's so nice to meet you. I'm Sally-Jo Baker. Bob will be so surprised to see you."

Darla nodded. "I'm sure. We've never met. In fact, I didn't know anything about him until just before grandmamma died. Then she told me." She looked over at Teensy who had remained seated but was smiling. "Nice to meet you, ma'am."

Teensy nodded. "And you. I'm Teensy Coldicutt."

Darla stifled a laugh. She looked back at Molly, missing

Teensy's frown. But Lizzie saw it and went to sit next to her on the love seat.

"My name is not a laughing matter," Teensy hissed under her breath.

Lizzie touched her hand briefly.

Darla accepted the glass of iced tea that Molly handed her and sat in one of the wicker chairs facing the backyard. "This is such a beautiful place you have here, Ms. Mathews."

"Why thank you, Darla. And please call me Molly."

Darla smiled sweetly at Molly. "Is all that property back there yours?"

"It does go back a ways," Molly acknowledged.

Sally-Jo passed the plate of sweets to Darla and asked, "It's nice you're able to come to finally meet your grand-daddy."

Darla took two lemon-almond bars and finished one before answering, "Well, I've been curious since I found out about him. This seemed like a good time to come and get to know him."

"Why now?" asked Teensy, adding her own sweet smile to the mix.

Darla hesitated a moment. "Oh, you know how mamas and daughters can be. We had a falling out and I thought it best to hightail it for a while."

"Oh, that's too bad, sugar," Teensy said, leaning forward in her seat. "I know all about mamas and daughters. What was it about, if you don't mind my asking?"

Darla thoroughly chewed her second bar and swallowed before answering. "A guy. She didn't like my choice of boy-friend. Of course, she never liked any of them but this time I thought, I'm a grown woman of twenty-one. It's time I made my own decisions. So I decided to leave."

"You left your sweetie, too?"

"Oh, it's just a temporary thing. He understands, it's all for the good. We'll be together again. I just have to sort some things out first." She looked at her watch. "Oh, look at the time. I have to get going. I'm sorry I didn't get to see granddaddy but it was just so nice meeting all of you."

She grabbed her small backpack and was headed to the back door when Molly scurried up beside her. "I'll tell you what. We're having a barbecue here tomorrow late afternoon and Bob will be here for that. Why don't you come by and join us?"

Darla's face lit up. "Really? That's awesome. Thanks so much." She marched into the kitchen with Molly close behind her.

Nobody said anything for a few moments until Teensy broke the silence.

"Humpf. Well, what do you think of that?"

"Quite a surprise," Sally-Jo said. "I'll bet Bob will be thrilled, though."

"I'm sure he will be," Lizzie answered. She was feeling a bit off balance about it all but couldn't put her finger on what bothered her. "What did you think of her?"

"She seemed nice, for lack of more information to judge her by," Sally-Jo said.

Lizzie looked over at Teensy.

"Well, if you really want to know what I think," Teensy said sitting upright in her seat, "I'm not sure as I trust her."

Molly stepped back out onto the patio and stopped in her tracks. "Are you talking about Darla?"

Teensy nodded.

"Well, Teensy, I think that's a bit ungenerous of you. We hardly know the child and she seems so eager to see her granddaddy."

"What's the story, anyway?" Sally-Jo asked. "I mean, I

know Bob's wife left him and took their daughter but that's about it."

Molly sat back down and took a minute before answering. "Well, Sue-Ann never did like living on a police officer's salary. So much for love, etcetera. So, she planned it all very carefully, right down to finding a job in Atlanta, and then left one morning without even a good-bye. She left a note for Bob to find when he came off duty. She filed for a divorce and then up and married a banker, very snappy like. Poor Bob was still reeling from her leaving. And, she wouldn't let Bob have anything to do with their daughter, Lily, either. She treated him very cruelly."

"What a piece of work," Teensy snarled.

Molly nodded. "I think Darla is just what Bob needs in his life at this point."

"I could suggest some other things, too," Teensy said, a twinkle in her eye.

Molly blushed and filled her glass before sitting down. "We'll see."

Lizzie made sure the covered dish holding the potato salad she'd made for the barbecue sat securely in the cloth bag, then did a last-minute check on her two cats. They sat at the top of the stairs, steady as two ornaments, watching intently. "I'm out for a couple of hours, kids, but we'll have time for a cuddle when I get home. I need to get some reading done before bedtime."

That seemed to satisfy them and they stood up in unison, stretched and headed toward the bedroom. Lizzie grinned. Nice to be wanted.

She thought about the lunch she'd shared with her mama earlier in the day out at Magnolia Manor, the long-term care residence where Evelyn Turner had lived for nearly fifteen years. She hoped her mama realized how much Lizzie loved her.

Today had been a good day even though it was a shorter than usual visit. Evelyn had seemed tired and she'd actually smiled at Lizzie as she reminisced about one of their many family picnics in Glendale Park. However, the drooping eyelids and nodding head cued Lizzie that an early-afternoon nap was in order.

Lizzie hadn't missed a weekend visit, unless she was out of town, which happened less often these days. She thought back to her first years as a reading specialist with the Ashton Corners School Board. She'd made it a point to spend two weeks of her summer vacation overseas. She'd visited France, Italy and Portugal and although there were still many countries on her list, she hadn't strayed far from home since Mark came into her life. That realization came as a big surprise to her.

Lizzie pulled into Molly's driveway and parked next to Bob's old black Dodge pickup. She was pleased to see that the boys had indeed returned, although Mark had sent her a text while they were on the road so she did have a heads-up. Stephanie Lowe had picked up Andie Mason in her well-worn but new-to-her Ford Fiesta. Lizzie waited for them while they unloaded Stephanie's fifteen-month-old baby, Wendy, and all her equipment and helped carry some of it inside.

Molly met them at the door and after hugs all around, ushered them into the kitchen. "You won't believe the size of the bass the boys have caught. We're barbecuing two of the larger ones tonight and Bob has kindly brought one for my freezer."

Lizzie put her dish on the counter next to the array of salads that were already set out. Stephanie gave Wendy to

Andie to hold while she unwrapped the red velvet cake she'd made for dessert.

"Oh, my, Stephanie, you're getting to be quite the baker," Molly said, eyeing the plate.

"I'm enjoying it so much," Stephanie said. "I actually find it relaxing after a day of working at the bookstore. And I can keep an eye on Wendy in her playpen while I'm at it."

"Isn't Roger coming?" Lizzie asked, wondering how things were going between Stephanie and her new boyfriend. They'd been dating for about six months but the book club didn't get to see much of him. It seemed he was often busy whenever a social event came around although they'd all had a chance to meet him at Christmas. Lizzie had been happy that Stephanie seemed to have found a really nice, level-headed young man but she hoped they wouldn't be rushing into anything. It appeared she needn't have worried

"He's working. They were shorthanded at Walgreens and called him this morning. He sends his apologies, though, Molly."

"That was thoughtful of him," Molly answered, glancing outside to see what Bob was up to. "I think Bob has set up all the extra tables. Maybe you gals would take out these tablecloths. I'm thinking we'll do it buffet-style using two tables and then set the other two for a sit-down meal."

Sally-Jo and her fiancée, Jacob Smith, came around the corner of the house as Lizzie brought out the cutlery and napkins.

"The fish are inside," Bob called over to Jacob. "They've been cleaned and seasoned and are ready to go. I think they're looking mighty impressive."

"I'm impressed," Lizzie said. "I thought y'all might just be having too much fun to bother with fishing."

"Dang it, Lizzie. Fishing is serious business," Bob answered. "It takes a lot of concentration finding just the right spot and then waiting it out, you know."

"He's right," Jacob agreed. "It's almost like a science. And Bob here makes a masterful teacher."

"You're not a fisherman by nature?" Molly asked.

"No ma'am. My daddy didn't do too much in the way of outdoor sports. His chosen method of relaxing was sitting with a brew in hand watching a game of some sort on TV. I never did any fishing until Bob goaded me into it." He grinned.

"And you should be mighty grateful," Bob said. "You're now able to keep you and your wife-to-be in fresh fillets, if need be. A modern-day provider of meals to your family."

"Oh, no," Sally-Jo groaned. "I think a fish meal a month is enough for me."

Bob pretended to be shocked.

"I'm a once-a-week man, myself," Mark Dreyfus said as he rounded the corner, carrying a case of Coors beer.

Lizzie turned to him with a wide smile on her face. It felt more like a week rather than just a couple of days since she'd talked to him. He gave her a quick kiss, then deposited the beer on one of the tables that had been set up as a bar.

"So, you had a profitable time," she said to him.

"Yeah. It was good in many ways. Lacking in some," he added softly, giving her waist a squeeze.

She felt a flutter in her chest.

Molly came outside, a plate of ham-and-greens crostini in one hand. She was followed by Stephanie, who was carrying two dishes of appetizers, and Andie carrying Wendy. "I see we're all here, except for Teensy," Molly said. "Perhaps you gentlemen would be so good as to serve the liquid refreshment."

They were settling all down in the garden chairs, drinks and plates of appetizers in hand, when the kitchen door burst open and Teensy stepped outside holding a large glass plate of fresh fruit.

"My apologies for being late," she said, careful not to trip walking down the two stairs in her four-inch-heeled pink sandals. In fact, she wore a variety of shades of pink, all of which contrasted boldly with her red hair.

"I stopped by the Winn-Dixie to pick up this here fruit platter I'd ordered and I got to talking with Bernice Waller. Did y'all know that Frida Moreland is opening a dressmaking shop?"

"I did not know that," Molly said. "Now why do you suppose she's doing that? I thought she was happy working for Maisie. I wonder if there's enough business for another one."

Teensy shrugged and sat down beside Stephanie on the wicker settee and accepted a glass of white wine from Bob, who had jumped up to pour it for her. "Why thank you, Bob. I gather the fishing was a success?"

"You bet. You're about to enjoy the best fresh barbecued bass you've ever had."

Teensy laughed. "I can hardly wait."

Molly glanced at her watch. Bob said, "You keep checking the time, Molly. Are you planning something special?"

Molly looked over at Lizzie. "You could say that." She stood and passed around the plate of crostini. "I'm just wondering when we should start the barbecue going."

"Now, don't you worry about anything. It's all under control. Can I refresh your drink?"

"No, thank you. I'm quite all right. Should I bring out some more cheese?"

Everyone murmured that there was quite enough food all ready.

"You seem a tad jittery today, Molly," Bob observed. Molly shrugged and passed around the tray of deviled eggs.

Stephanie spread a blanket on the lawn and set Wendy down to crawl around. "She's getting to be so big," Bob said. "She'll be walking any day now."

"She's already trying," Stephanie said with a laugh. "I'm busy hiding all my breakables."

"That's just the start of it."

"How would you know?"

They all turned to see who had asked the question. Standing at the corner of the house was Darla.

"Sorry," she said with a small smile, "that didn't quite come out right. I didn't mean to accuse you. I was just trying to be funny. Sorry."

Bob stood quickly but seemed at a loss what to say. Molly hurried over to Darla's side. She slid her arm around her shoulders and said, "Now, we're all good-natured here. So don't you worry about it. Come on in and meet everyone. You already know Teensy, Lizzie and Sally-Jo."

Darla nodded but wouldn't look any of them in the eye. Lizzie almost felt sorry for her until she noticed the quick look of self-satisfaction on Darla's face.

Molly introduced the book club members, saving Bob for last. She tugged Darla over to him.

"And this is Bob Miller. Bob, you might want to sit down. This is your granddaughter, Darla Lyman."

Bob looked stunned. He couldn't seem to find his voice and indeed did sit down. At that moment, Lizzie thought he looked all of his seventy-odd years. Darla stood in front of him, stock-still, staring at him. Finally, Bob stood back up and cleared his throat.

"I'm mighty pleased to meet you, Darla. I didn't even know that Lily had herself a daughter. In fact, I don't know anything about Lily's life after she left here." He stuck out his hand and after a second, Darla slipped her hand into his. And then she smiled.

It was as if everyone had been holding their breaths, but that changed quickly and the chatter started up again.

"What can I get you to drink?" Bob asked, still in a daze. "A soda?"

She glanced over at the makeshift bar. "I'll have some white wine." She sat in Bob's chair when he went to get it for her. He pulled over another wicker chair to sit next to her when he returned.

"I just cannot believe it," he said. "How old are you, anyway?"

"I'm twenty-one, sir," she said demurely and sipped her wine.

Stephanie looked over and grinned. "I was nineteen when I came to town a couple of years ago. Are you visiting or planning on staying?"

Darla glanced at Bob then back at Stephanie. "That all depends. I wanted a time-out from my mama and I decided I needed to meet my granddaddy."

Molly came by with the plate of deviled eggs. "Darla, tell him what you told me."

Darla nodded. "Well, I didn't know anything about you either, not until my grandmamma told me last year, just before she died."

Bob sucked in his breath. "Sue-Ann is dead?"

"Yes, sir. She had cancer, which spread quickly." Darla sipped her wine. "I asked my mama to tell me all about her childhood but she said she didn't remember you." Bob winced.

"I can imagine. She was only five when they moved away."

"Well, mama said you never tried to see her."

"That's not true. I sent her presents for her birthday and cards and even tried phoning a time or two but Sue-Ann wouldn't have any of it." He sighed. "It's a long story, Darla. Anyway, I'm happy you decided to find me."

"And, we're all pleased you're here tonight with us," Molly said. "I think we'll get the fish to cooking now, and then after supper, you two can start to get to know each other."

Chapter Three

Stop harassing me. Get out of town, or else.

DAYS OF WINE AND ROQUEFORT—AVERY AAMES

Monday. Start of a new school week. And only one week to go until Easter break. Lizzie smiled at her image in the mirror. The two weeks of Easter break were always welcome even though it hadn't been a particularly taxing school year so far. As a reading specialist with the public school board, Lizzie's home base was the Ashton Corners Elementary School, an easy ten-minute drive from her house or twice that time if she walked, which she sometimes did, especially the days she chose not to go for an early-morning run.

This had been one of those days. Even though she'd not slept well and she knew the run would do her good, she decided to opt for a slow start, taking her time over breakfast, brushing both of her cats, Brie and Edam, after they'd finished off their own meals, and finally, a second espresso before getting ready for school.

While she got dressed, in black slacks and a white-and-black-striped blouse, she mulled over her reason for tossing and turning part of the night. In one word, Darla.

Bob had been delighted once they started talking, quick to get over his initial shock, and wanting to set things right with his only grandchild. Lizzie was happy for him but at the same time, she felt wary. Something just seemed a bit off about Darla although Molly certainly hadn't felt the same way. In fact, she'd been most helpful in offering Darla a place to stay when it was decided that Bob didn't have the space.

"I wasn't the only one who felt something odd going on," Lizzie told the ever-curious Edam who had a paw in Lizzie's handbag, searching for something unknown. "Out of there, baby," Lizzie said, gently pulling her cat away from the bag. She set the cat down on the bed next to Brie, who had chosen the space for his grooming ritual.

"Teensy definitely does not like the girl," Lizzie continued. "Molly knows it, too. She kept sending Teensy 'meaningful' looks all evening."

Lizzie decided she'd give Teensy a call after school and compare notes. She'd also ask for Sally-Jo's opinion if she saw her at school today. *Maybe I'm just being silly.*

She did a final check in the mirror, deciding she'd pull her long brown hair back in a clip rather than wearing it loose. She had this ongoing internal debate about whether to cut it short. Part of her longed for a cute pixie look like Sally-Jo had, but then she reminded herself that style so suited her friend's all-round petiteness. Lizzie had better stick with long or maybe go up a couple of inches to shoulder length. She stowed the continuing conversation for another time, then grabbed her handbag and ran lightly down the stairs. She found her school bag filled with her notes and some new reference books on the sofa desk in the hall, grabbed her house keys, and on the spur of the moment, her car keys and decided to drive to school.

Her first appointment was with the single mother of a second grader who refused to read. In fact, from what the teacher had been saying, Darren John Sayers refused to do just about anything these days. They agreed that something must have happened within the past two weeks to bring out the belligerent streak in the onetime cheerful child. As far as they could tell, nothing had happened in school to upset him.

His teacher, Sharlene, was hoping that Lizzie could find out in a roundabout way if anything had happened on the home front. They were reluctant to include the principal, Charles Benton, in on the process, knowing he'd be likely to get the mama's back up and then nothing would be achieved. Lizzie smiled to herself at the thought of Benton trying anything that resembled tact when dealing with a person, be it teacher or parent. Oh well, rumor had it that this first year at the school would also be his last.

Mrs. Flower Sayers sat stiffly on the chair outside Vice Principal Kim Lafferty's office as Lizzie approached the room. She recognized the woman from a brief meeting in the fall. No one knew the story about Mr. Sayers but it didn't really matter. Lizzie was concerned about the mama and child at the moment.

"Mrs. Sayers, you're early," she said, holding out her hand.

Sayers stood slowly and looked at Lizzie's hand before shaking it. "I'm sorry. I was ready early and getting jittery just sitting around. Do you want me to go away and come back?"

"No," Lizzie said with a warm smile. "Come in, but you'll have to give me a minute to get settled. Have a seat, please." She gestured to the comfortable armchair that sat across from the desk.

Sayers looked around the office as she sat down, placing her large handbag on the floor beside the chair.

Lizzie put the folder with her notes on the desk, flicked on the desktop computer and sat down, watching Flower Sayers from the corner of her eye. Sayers looked uncomfortable and jittery, not good if Lizzie wanted to have a heart-to-heart with the woman.

"Would you like some coffee?" Lizzie asked after glancing at the single-cup Keurig machine sitting on a side table.

"Uh, no thank you. I'm fine. I'm just wondering what's up about Darren John? Is he in some sort of trouble?"

"No, ma'am. I wouldn't say he's in trouble, but rather, having trouble."

Sayers looked blank.

"I'm not sure if you realize it but he's refusing to read. In fact, he's refusing to do anything he's asked. I wonder if there's something we should know in order to help him? He really seemed so eager to learn when I first met him."

Sayers shifted uncomfortably in her chair. "I don't know what's gotten into him but I'll get at the bottom of it tonight when he comes home."

"That's not what I'm suggesting, Mrs. Sayers. I know you love him very much"—she glanced at the woman, who nodded quickly—"but I think it's best if he's not confronted about this but rather we try to clear up anything that's been bothering him, if we can figure out what it is. Have there been any changes at home lately? Sometimes even a change in routine can be disrupting." Lizzie smiled again, hoping to keep Mrs. Sayers comfortable with talking.

"There's nothing," she said rather too quickly for Lizzie's liking. She glanced at her watch. "I have to go. I'll talk to Darren John when he gets home. You'll see; everything will be just fine." She stood quickly, grabbed her handbag and left the office, closing the door behind her.

"Well, I sure blew that," Lizzie said aloud, shaking her head. She hated to think that Darren John might be in for a verbal tirade tonight. She would make sure to talk to Sharlene at lunch and see if they could come up with something.

Lizzie was actually pleased to have some extra time that morning and she searched the school files on Lafferty's computer, making some notes, before moving to her cubbyhole in the library. She spent the rest of the morning finishing a term-end report to be handed in at the school board office before the end of the week.

At noon she headed for the staff room and found Sharlene already eating at one of the long tables. She sat down beside her and recounted the early-morning meeting. "I sure hope I didn't make things difficult for Darren John," Lizzie ended.

"My impression of Flower Sayers is that she's fairly wishy-washy. I seriously doubt she'll say anything to her son. I'll keep a keen eye on him tomorrow, though. What do you think our next step should be? I hate to mention it to Benton."

Lizzie shuddered. "Me, too. I wonder if I could find a book at his level that might deal with talking about problems. I don't know, something that he can relate to and maybe will take to heart."

Sharlene's face lit up. "That sounds like a good solution, Lizzie. Do you have the time to look for it?"

"Sure," Lizzie said, wondering how she'd find the time. "I'll get right on it and check with you tomorrow." She grabbed her uneaten sandwich and headed back to the library. She'd check the school board database first of all and see if anything sounded like it fit the bill. Her next step would be to consult with the children's librarian at the public library. But that would have to wait until after school.

By the time the final bell rang, Lizzie had almost forgotten the trip to the library. She was anxious to get over to Molly's and see how day one with a houseguest had gone. However, as she parked in front of the library, she made a quick call to Teensy to see if she had heard from Molly.

"Why, sugar, I was just thinking about you," Teensy said once Lizzie had identified herself. "We just have to get together to talk about this Darla business. You know, I'm still upset about it. That little waif just wove both Molly and Bob around her little finger. But of course, it really wasn't any of my business so I couldn't say anything. But I had the distinct feeling you had the same thoughts."

"I'm uncomfortable with it all," Lizzie admitted, "but I don't have any real reason. Just a feeling, as you say. Have you heard from Molly today?"

"No, I haven't and I did call earlier but there was no answer. I left her a message but she hasn't returned my call. Do you think we should be worried?"

Lizzie tried to make light of it. "Probably not. You know that Molly has a lot going on. She's probably running around doing errands. Or she might even be at the bookstore." *I wonder what Darla's doing?*

"Tosh. I bet you're right and I'm just making a mountain out of a molehill again. But I'll be keeping tabs on that girl just in case she's planning to make off with the silver or something."

Lizzie grinned. She could just picture Teensy to the rescue. "Good idea. I'm planning on stopping by Molly's after I take care of some business at the library."

"I feel better knowing that. Thank you, Lizzie. Bye, bye."

Hearing someone else worry about the situation helped to put it into perspective for Lizzie, she thought during the short drive to the library. She admitted she probably was overreacting and she'd just leave the worrying to Teensy. She locked the car and walked up the stairs to the front door. The afternoon sun reflected in the glass of the door, making Lizzie wish she hadn't left her sunglasses in the car. She glanced back at the car and noticed two people moving quickly across the town square and walking at an angle toward the stores along Main Street, to Lizzie's left. They didn't give her a glance and she hadn't gotten a very good look but she thought it was Darla, and it looked like she wasn't happy about being shoved ahead by the man at her side. Lizzie lost sight of them as they slipped around the corner into the first alley, next to the florist shop.

Lizzie quickly ran back down the stairs and down the street, pausing at the entrance to the alley to peer around surreptitiously. The woman was indeed Darla and she'd been backed against the wall, with the man shaking a fist at her. Lizzie couldn't make out what he was saying, except the fact that he was angry. And a stranger. *I should yell and make a scene.* Before she had a chance, the man looked like he might hit Darla but instead, he started backing away, toward Lizzie.

Lizzie backtracked into the doorway of the Up'sa Daisy Flower Shop and pretended to be closely examining the window display. The stranger walked right past her without glancing her way. *If looks could kill*, Lizzie thought with a shudder, watching his reflection in the window. From what she could see, he appeared to be around her age, maybe even a bit older, in his early forties. The New York Yankees baseball cap he wore didn't quite cover his black hair that matched his thick moustache.

Lizzie wondered if she should let Darla know she'd seen what had happened. At least check on her to make sure she was okay. Before she could, Darla appeared and turned in the opposite direction without looking Lizzie's way, walking at a jaunty pace. *What on earth was all that about?*

Well, at least she knew where Darla was. Not with Molly. And, who was the guy? Definitely nobody Lizzie had seen around town.

Lizzie puzzled about it as she went back to the library. Once inside, she spotted Hailey Pratt, the head of the children's department, standing at the front desk and flipping through a catalogue. She looked up as Lizzie approached.

"Hey, Lizzie Turner. It's nice to see you," Hailey said.

"And you. I was hoping you'd have some time to help me find a particular book for a second-grade student with a particular problem. At least, I think he has a problem."

"Happy to. Come on over to my desk." She led the way and after hearing Lizzie's plan, checked her computer and then went over to the shelves in the children's section, returning shortly with two books.

"I think these might be just what you're looking for. It sounds like a very good idea. See what you think."

Lizzie read the jackets and flipped through both books. "These look perfect. I'll check them out on my card. Thanks for your help, Hailey."

"A pleasure. See you at choir on Friday?" Hailey had recently joined Musica Nobilis, the community choir that gave Lizzie so much pleasure.

"For sure," Lizzie said and went to the front desk with her books.

Chapter Four

◇◇◇

Yes, she would ask her.

THE SATURDAY BIG TENT WEDDING PARTY—
ALEXANDER MCCALL SMITH

During the drive to Molly's, Lizzie continued to puzzle about what she'd seen in town. She wondered if she should mention it to Molly and then decided not to. After all, she didn't have any real details and she didn't want to worry Molly. She'd just keep an eye on Darla and if anything else came up, she would share what she'd seen at that point.

Lizzie found Molly in the kitchen, setting the table for two for dinner. "Would you like to join us?" Molly asked.

"That's nice of you, Molly, but I've got some school work to get finished for tomorrow." Too bad, she thought. It would have been a good opportunity to find out a bit more about Darla. She watched as Molly puttered around the kitchen. "Can I help you with anything?"

"No, honey. I've got it all in hand."

Lizzie helped herself to a handful of almonds from a dish on the table. "Where's Darla?"

"Oh, she said she was going into town to poke around a bit. She spent part of the day with Bob and he's coming over for dessert, after he finishes doing some more work on that boat he's building."

Lizzie smiled at the thought of Bob finally having found a project that so totally engrossed him. As far as she knew, he'd been a dabbler in do-it-yourself tasks since he'd retired from being chief of police. But she'd suspected he had a tough time of it, especially after the new chief, Mark, had become so entwined in their lives. The boat kept him occupied and would be put to good use, if it would actually float when done. Now, Darla was a different matter.

"What's she like?" Lizzie asked.

"Darla? Well, we haven't really had a chance to talk much. She turned in fairly early last night, in fact just after y'all left, and slept late this morning. Over breakfast, she did tell me a bit about her childhood. It seems Bob's daughter Lily was a very social being and liked to have a lot of people around."

"What about her daddy?"

"She never knew him. Apparently, he left town shortly after Darla was born. She seems to have a good head on her shoulders, though. And that would be no thanks to Sue-Ann."

"Why do you say that?"

"Sue-Ann was always flighty. Never could take responsibility for things, like the time the high school mascot, our wild turkey, got lost."

"You had a real wild turkey as a mascot?"

"Oh, gracious no. It was a stuffed toy but he was our good-luck charm and had to be at every team game. Sue-Ann begged to be in charge of him and one day, she *said* he disappeared from his spot in the cupboard at back of the homeroom."

"You didn't believe her?"

"Not since I knew she often *borrowed* him to take and parade around at parties where she wanted to impress the boys. Anyway, and then there's the way she treated Bob, running out on him and not letting him keep in touch with his own child. Harrumph."

Lizzie wasn't quite sure what to say to that. She went back to the starting point of their conversation.

"What does her mama do? How did they live?"

"Probably with a lot of help from Sue-Ann and her rich banker hubby." She sighed.

"Sue-Ann was no good for Bob but it sure did throw him for a loop. She could be very cruel, especially not letting Bob have any contact with Lily. That's what really broke his heart." Molly sighed. "Darla did say that Lily had a job as a hostess. And that could have lots of connotations although I'd rather not think that." Molly sat down across from Lizzie at the table. "It's really such a shame that Sue-Ann wouldn't let Lily get to know Bob. Things may have been very different for her, and her daughter, if he'd been in their lives."

"How does Bob feel about all this?"

Molly sighed. "I think he's really torn up about it. He's spent a whole lot of years worrying about Lily and just feeling so badly that he was cut off. So, here comes Darla and while he's delighted to have this opportunity to get to know her, and hopefully Lily, too, it's also bringing back all those guilt feelings."

"That's so sad. I feel for him."

Molly leaned across the table and patted her hand. "That's sweet of you, honey, but I think if we're all here helping him focus on the good aspect of this, the other will fade, which it is meant to do."

Lizzie sat silent for a few minutes watching as Molly went back to the stove to stir something that smelled entirely delicious. She wondered just how frank she should or could be with Molly about this.

"Molly, do you get the sense that Darla is really sincere about all this?"

"Why of course, Lizzie. Why wouldn't she be? It's not every day a young girl gets to meet her long-lost granddaddy. Family ties are so important. I believe she's really grateful to have found him."

"I hope so," Lizzie said under her breath. She couldn't quite shake the uneasiness though. "So, she doesn't know anyone else around here?"

"Not a soul."

"That was awfully nice of you to invite her to stay here, Molly."

Molly turned to look at her. "Why, it was the right thing to do. Once we found out she was staying at that dreadful Mountain View Motel, I couldn't let her go back there. Not Bob's grandchild. And it's for sure she couldn't stay at his place. He barely has enough room for all his belongings in those three rooms. Now, how about pouring us each a glass of iced tea. I just made it fresh."

Lizzie nodded and after taking the pitcher out of the fridge, had just filled their glasses when Darla came strolling in.

"Hey, Molly," Darla said and looked over at Lizzie. "Lizzie."

Lizzie nodded.

"Did you have an interesting day?" Molly asked.

Lizzie wondered how much she would tell.

"I guess. The town sure is small."

"Well, that stands to reason, seeing as you've lived in Atlanta all your life," Molly answered pleasantly.

"Yes," Lizzie added, "and it's not like you know many people here." She watched closely for a reaction.

Darla shrugged.

Lizzie continued, "I'd imagine Ashton Corners pales in comparison, if you're looking for excitement. What kind of things do you like to do?"

"Me? Uh, dancing with my BFFs. Clubbing a lot. Are there any here?" she asked, sounding hopeful.

"It's not really my scene," Lizzie admitted. "I'm sure there's something, though. I know a couple of the bars have dance floors and live bands on the weekends."

Lizzie shrugged slightly when she noticed the look Molly was giving her. *She asked; I told.*

"Do you like reading, Darla?" Molly jumped in.

Darla stared at Molly a minute. Lizzie mentally filled in the imaginary dialogue bubble above her head—*What's that?* Lizzie shook her head. *Not nice.*

"Uh, sure. I could spend all afternoon looking through fashion magazines and hairstyle ones, too."

Molly stood a bit straighter and smiled. "That's nice, dear, but I was wondering if you might enjoy reading mysteries? The reason I ask is we have a mystery book reading club and your granddaddy's a part of it. So are Lizzie, Sally-Jo, Andie, Stephanie and Jacob, all of whom you met yesterday. Our next meeting is this Thursday night, right here. I wonder if you'd like to join us. I know there isn't a lot of time to read the book but you could thumb through it, read the first and last chapters if you'd like. You can use my copy."

Darla looked in shock. "I . . ." She paused, unable to come up with an answer. "I guess."

"Well, you don't have anything else lined up for Thursday,

do you?" Lizzie asked, wondering if the mystery man was still around.

"No. No, I don't. Sure, I'll come."

"That's so good," Molly said. "I know Bob will be pleased and I think you'll find we're a lot of fun to be with. Especially since Stephanie and Andrea are closer to your age. We call ourselves the Ashton Corners Mystery Readers and Cheese Straws Society."

Darla seemed at yet another loss for words so Lizzie explained further. "Bob came up with the name. I'll bet he'd get a real kick out of it if you made a big fuss over what a great name it is."

Darla nodded and in a few moments she smiled. "Yeah." She stretched her arms out above her head and tilted her head to each side before lowering her arms again. "I think I'll just go on up and have a nap before supper. I've done a lot of walking today." She nodded at them both and left them watching her leave.

"Nap?" Lizzie asked when she was sure Darla was out of earshot.

Molly shook her head. "She seems to be resting a lot. I hope she doesn't have something, like mono or some such. Or maybe it's just that she doesn't want to spend a lot of time with me."

"Well, you don't really have a lot in common if you ask me, unless you've taken up hip-hop," Lizzie added, a mischievous smile on her face.

Molly looked taken aback. Lizzie stood and gave Molly a small hug. "It's her loss."

Chapter Five

◇◇◇

Even if the curiosity tugged at her brain until she was cross-eyed.

FREEZER I'LL SHOOT—VICTORIA HAMILTON

Lizzie paused to watch the final stages of the sunrise the next morning during her jog. She looked down the embankment at the reflection in the Tallapoosa River and took a deep breath. Some mornings everything felt right. She tried to hold that feeling for the remainder of her run but felt the tension start to build up again as she walked into her house.

She had a long day ahead of her at school and then, what might feel like an equally long session with her literacy class tonight at Molly's. She loved both her jobs but sometimes, dealing with too many upset parents in one week could take its toll. And since Christmas, at the literacy class, she seemed to be constantly butting heads with Madona Currant, a high school dropout at seventeen who had recently decided it would be to her advantage, monetarily, to get her GEDs. Lizzie had a feeling it was more that her daddy had made the decision and tough love had taken over the Currant household.

She was all for that, if it motivated Madona to make the grade, but she couldn't tell if there was any sincerity in place. What made it even more irritating to Lizzie was the fact she knew that here was a smart girl who could do the program with flying colors, if she'd only decide to do that.

Lizzie sighed. She'd recently made a pact with herself that some hours of the day were special, when she wouldn't let the worries of work intrude her space. Early morning was one of those times as were weekends, and any time spent with Mark. She wondered where he was at that moment. At work, getting ready to go to work, sleeping in? She knew it wouldn't be the latter. Mark Dreyfus took his job as police chief very seriously. Just one of the many things she loved about him. Love. Hmm, she'd used that word a lot lately when thinking about him. They'd just never really said it aloud to each other. She wasn't sure if she was even ready for that.

She glanced at the wall and snapped into hyperdrive. A power shake would have to do for breakfast and she quickly threw together a tuna wrap for lunch. After showering, she dressed in a tan pencil skirt and red floral blouse, lay down on the bed beside her cats, Brie and Edam, giving them a pep talk about what a great day was in store and finished with a kiss to the top of each head. She grabbed her school bag and car keys, took a final look in the mirror at the front door, and left.

Lizzie filed the final notes from the last meeting of the day in the one section she'd been allotted of the vice principal's locked cabinet behind the desk. The day had felt long, as predicted, and she was more than ready to head out into the sunshine and try to clear her head. She made it as far as the parking lot when her iPhone rang.

"Lizzie, it's Molly. Can you come right over, honey? It's really important."

"What's wrong, Molly? Are you all right?"

"Yes, I'm fine but I'd rather wait until you're here to talk about it."

"I'm on my way," Lizzie said, sticking the keys in the ignition. She was about to stuff her phone in her purse when she noticed she had voice mail. Molly's voice gave her the exact same message she'd just said a few minutes ago. Lizzie must not have heard the ring that would alert her to this when she switched her phone on after her last meeting.

She drove as quickly as possible, worried about Molly. She felt protective toward her, knowing that Molly was always there for her when needed. It had been that way since Lizzie was a young child. Molly had been her grandmamma Beata's friend, an easy entry into the family where she'd remained ever since. And when Lizzie's mama was moved into Magnolia Manor, the assisted living facility, Molly had been right there for them both. And she continued to be.

She hit the brakes as she approached Molly's driveway. Two police cars were parked on the street and one more, along with Mark's Jeep, were at the top of the drive, in front of the house. As well, a hearse from the Sunset Funeral Home sat at the opposite end of the house.

Lizzie felt her heart pounding in her ears as she parked her Mazda and sprinted up the driveway. She reached the front door just as it opened. Officer Amber Craig of the Ashton Corners Police walked out and almost collided with Lizzie.

"It's all right, slow down," Craig said. "Molly is just fine, although somewhat upset."

"What happened?"

"A body was found out in the backyard earlier today by the gardener."

"A body! Not someone we know, I hope."

"It's a man and he's not a local."

Lizzie took a deep breath. "Okay. And Molly is fine?"

"Yes. You can go in if you want. She's in the living room." Craig held the door open for Lizzie and then closed it as she left.

Lizzie rushed into the living room and found Molly sitting on the love seat facing the front window. She glanced around for Darla but Molly was alone.

"What happened, Molly?" Lizzie asked, crouching in front of her. "Are you sure you're all right?"

"Just a bit overwhelmed and shocked. In fact I'm in total shock. There's a body in my backyard and I've no idea who he is or how he got there."

"You didn't go out and look at him, did you?" Lizzie clutched Molly's hand.

"No. Mitchell came to do my gardening today and he found him. Mark took a photo of his face and showed it to me." She shook her head. "I don't know him and I cannot imagine what he's doing back there."

"Where's Darla?"

"Oh, she's been in town most of the day again. I would expect she'll be back shortly. She doesn't know about this."

Lizzie stood and put an arm around Molly's shoulders. "Can I get you some sweet tea or would you like something hot?"

Molly nodded. "Some hot tea would be lovely, thanks."

"Okay. You just stay here and I'll get it ready."

Lizzie went into the kitchen and right over to the back door to take a look at all the activity. Her initial shock had worn off and her curiosity had taken over. She was itching to know what was happening and the identity of the victim. Also, just how he had died. She opened the door and a couple of officers turned toward her. Mark looked over from where he'd been examining the ground. He strode over, meeting her before she'd taken more than a couple of steps outside.

"I'd rather you didn't come out here," he said, squeezing her arm. "It's a crime scene."

"Was he murdered?" Lizzie held her breath.

"It looks that way."

"Who is he? Molly said she didn't recognize him."

"He doesn't have any ID on him but we do have a lead on who he is."

"Can I have a look at the photo you showed Molly?"

Mark pulled his cell phone out of his pocket and brought up the picture on the screen. Lizzie took it from him and held it at an angle away from the glare of the afternoon sun.

She knew that face. She thought. Finally it hit her and she gasped.

"What is it? Do you know him?" Mark asked.

"I'm pretty sure I've seen him in town but I don't know anything about him."

"Just tell me what you do know. Where did you see him?"

"He was going into the alley that runs alongside the flower shop on Main, close to Garrett Street. I noticed him when I was on my way to the library yesterday afternoon. He was with someone. They were going into the alley and it looked like they were arguing."

"Who is 'they'?"

Lizzie glanced at the hall door and said in a soft voice. "He was there with Darla Lyman."

"You mean Bob Miller's granddaughter? The one who just arrived in town?"

Lizzie nodded. "Oh, boy. I was worried when she just showed up after all this time. But I hadn't imagined anything like this. How did he die?" *And, who is the killer?*

"He was hit over the head from behind with a heavy object."

"Yikes. Did you recover the murder weapon?"

Mark looked at her speculatively before answering. "We have what we believe might be the weapon."

"What was it? Can you get DNA from it? Fingerprints?"

"That's all I'm willing to share with you, Lizzie. And you're not getting involved. Got it?"

"Yes. But what if Bob's granddaughter is involved?"

"I think I know how to handle this, Lizzie. Now, what you need to get to work on is finding somewhere else to hold your literacy class tonight because this entire area is off-limits for several more hours."

"But nothing happened in Molly's house."

"Not that we know. And, I don't want any of your students getting curious and walking around too much before we've seen everything we need to."

Lizzie looked around the backyard. It was such a beautiful place of serenity and peace to her. This was almost obscene to have happened here. "What was he doing here anyway?"

"Good-bye, Lizzie. I'll phone you later tonight if I get a chance."

"Uh-huh." Lizzie took one last look at where the body lay, hidden from view by a tarp. "Good-bye, Mark."

She knew when to beat a tactical retreat.

She went back inside and finished brewing the tea and took it, along with a plate of sugar cookies, to Molly. Lizzie poured a tea for each of them and insisted Molly have something to eat, too.

Molly's smile was small. "Are we switching roles here?"

"Only temporarily. What a terrible thing. Did they tell you anything at all about what happened to him?"

Molly shook her head. "And I didn't ask. It's just too soon to be finding another body around here. It's been only a year and a half since the first one. Remember, at our first meeting of the book club? The body in the car outside my house?"

"Oh, I remember all right."

"Not that there's any amount of time in between finding bodies that would be acceptable. I wonder who this fellow is and what on earth he was doing in my backyard."

"I wonder when he was murdered. You said the gardener found him early afternoon?"

"Yes, just after he got started. I haven't been out back at all today. Otherwise, I would have seen him, I'm sure."

"Well, thank goodness for that. What about Darla?"

"You don't think she's involved, do you? I can't imagine that. She's just arrived in town."

Lizzie took a seat across the ottoman they were using as a coffee table. She sighed. "I might as well tell you because I just told Mark. He showed me the photo of the guy and I recognized him, although I don't know his name or anything else about him. But I did see him and Darla having an argument in the lane just down the street from the library yesterday afternoon."

Molly gasped. "Darla knew him? Are you certain it was them?"

"Yes, I am. I got as close as I could without being seen but I couldn't hear what was being said. I hate to say this, but I wonder if she might have an ulterior motive for coming to town."

"Oh, Lordy, I hope nothing illegal is going on. That would break Bob's heart. It would be bad enough if she was using him as an excuse to be here." Molly stood and walked over to the window, pulling the sheers aside to peek out. "Where is she anyway?"

"You shouldn't mention any of this to her, Molly. The police will want to talk to her and they should be the ones to bring it up, to see her reaction."

Molly turned to Lizzie and sighed. "I guess you're right. But I feel we need to do something. But how can we if we don't know what's happening?"

"Well, if you want to do something you can help me call the students that would be coming here tonight. Mark said we'd have to relocate. I'll call the community center first and see if they have space." She pulled out her iPhone.

"Of course." Molly headed for the kitchen while Lizzie searched for the phone number and then punched it in. She joined Molly in the kitchen after a few minutes.

"We're in luck. They have two small rooms available. And having the students reroute to downtown shouldn't be a problem for any of them. Would you mind giving Sally-Jo a call and let her know? She'll have to get in touch with her class, too."

"I have Sally-Jo's class list here. It was a good idea to leave me a copy in case of an emergency. I'll let her students know; that will give me something to keep busy. You'd better talk over the logistics with Sally-Jo."

Lizzie smiled. Molly was in charge again. "Will do."

They heard the front door open and Darla's voice raised in argument with Officer Craig. Darla was obviously not pleased to encounter her. Lizzie followed Molly down the hall in time to see Craig, holding Darla's right arm, escorting her around the side of the house.

Chapter Six

✧✧✧

If you know anything more than what you're saying,
it's important that you tell us.

MURDER WITH GANACHE—LUCY BURDETTE

Lizzie turned around on the spot and led the way back to
the kitchen, where she opened the kitchen window closest to the crime scene, as quietly as possible. She boosted
herself to a sit on the kitchen counter and leaned against the
open window to hear as much as possible.

She couldn't make out the conversation too well, except
that Mark was using his serious interviewing tone. When
Darla let out a yelp, Lizzie almost fell through the window.
The movement caught Mark's attention and although Lizzie
had scrambled down from the counter and was casually
leaning against it by the time he walked in, he said, "You'd
better come out here, Lizzie. I don't want you falling out and
breaking something."

She winked at Molly as she followed him outside.

He turned to her as soon as the door had closed behind

her. In a low voice, he said, "You can listen but don't say anything. Understood?"

She nodded and gestured that her lips were zipped shut. He grimaced and walked back to where Darla and Officer Craig were standing. Lizzie followed a few feet behind and stood to the side, hoping not to be intrusive. She knew a gift when she saw one and realized, even though Mark had told her not to get involved, he wanted her to have some information. Maybe it was his attempt to keep control of the situation, realizing that she'd probably be involved at some point. Whatever, she was pleased.

"So, you say you don't know this man?" Mark continued. "But we have a witness who saw you with him in an alley in town yesterday afternoon. Would you like to change your story?"

Darla glanced quickly at Lizzie but Lizzie knew she hadn't been spotted. Maybe Darla was hoping for some backup or just plain moral support.

"I guess he is the guy I was talking to but I didn't know him," Darla finally answered.

"So, if that's the case, would you please explain how you happened to be with him?"

"I was walking down the street and he, he accosted me. That's it. He pulled me into the alley."

"Did you scream?"

"No. I was so shocked."

"Did he try to hurt you?"

"He had grabbed a hold of my arm really tight. It was hurting a lot."

"What did he say to you?"

Darla hesitated a moment. "He wanted money but I didn't have any."

"He was trying to rob you?"

"Yeah. But I didn't have money so I yelled at him and told him to get lost."

"That was very brave, or foolish, of you."

"Yeah, well I got over being scared really fast and then I got angry. I'm in desperate need of money, too. Why would I give that creep any?" She stuck her hands in her jeans pockets.

"So what happened then?"

"He looked like he was going to punch me in the mouth so I twisted out of his hold and hightailed it back to the street."

"He didn't follow you?"

"No. I guess he realized I didn't have anything for him."

"You were very lucky in that case," Officer Craig said. Lizzie glanced at her. Something in her voice. But her face retained its usual cop bland expression and she wouldn't catch Lizzie's eye.

Darla glanced back at the body. "I guess so. Who would want to kill him, though?"

"Does the name Rafe Shannon mean anything to you?" Mark asked.

Darla looked startled but quickly reverted back to normal. "No. Should it?"

"You tell me. That's the name of the victim."

Lizzie looked over in surprise. When had they discovered the victim's name?

Darla shrugged. "I told you I didn't know him," she said in a whiny voice.

"You can see it's looking a bit suspicious," Mark said. "You having an argument with him and the next day he's found dead here at Molly's, the place you're staying."

Darla looked frightened. "But, I didn't do it. I told you that. I promise, I didn't kill him."

Mark looked at her a minute without saying anything.

Darla looked like she was trying hard not to fidget. He finally said, "Where are you staying?"

"Right here, with Molly. If that's still okay with her."

"I want you to go with Officer Craig down to the station and write out a statement. And, I don't want you leaving town anytime soon. Especially not without checking with me first. Do you understand?"

Darla nodded and swallowed hard. "Yes, sir," she answered, her voice a whisper.

Craig motioned for Darla to follow her.

When they were out of sight around the corner, Mark said to Lizzie, "I want you to go over again what exactly you saw and heard in that alley."

Lizzie went over the details again, stressing that although she hadn't heard the conversation, it wasn't until near the end when the dead guy had looked like he might hit Darla.

"Was what she described consistent with what you saw?"

"Basically, except that they were crossing the town square when I first saw them together. I thought it was Darla but I wasn't positive until I went over to see what was going in the alley. It looked like they were arguing and then the guy stomped off."

Before Mark had a chance to say anything, Bob rounded the corner. "What's going on? I thought I just saw Darla in the backseat of a police cruiser driving off."

Molly had come outside and quickly walked over to Bob and put her hand on his arm. "There's been an incident here." Molly sighed and pointed to the body in the background on the lawn. "Someone's been murdered."

Bob peered around her. "Who?"

Mark answered. "Male, around forty years old. He's not from around here although we believe his name is Rafe Shannon. Does that ring a bell?"

Bob shook his head. "So what's it to do with Darla?"

"She was seen talking to him yesterday in town. Craig is just getting a statement from her and will drive her right back here."

"So what are you saying? Did Darla see this happen? Is she in any danger? You've gotta protect her if she is."

"We just want to find out what she knows about this guy."

Bob glanced sharply at Mark. He opened his mouth to say something but instead, shook his head and walked over to the body, and bent down for a closer look. Lizzie watched him, trying not to look at the dead man's face when Bob pulled the tarp back. After a couple of minutes, Bob replaced the cover and stood. "That's a nasty head wound. Any idea what happened? Did anyone hear anything?"

He looked at Molly, who shook her head. "We didn't hear anything at all outside."

"We don't have a time of death as yet," Mark stated.

"Who saw Darla with this guy?"

Lizzie answered. "I did. I spotted them walking into an alley off Main Street. It looked like they were arguing."

Bob nodded. "Did you hear what was being said?"

"No, I didn't. I thought at one point he might hit her but instead, he stalked off leaving her standing there."

"Did you ask her about it?" Bob asked.

"I thought it prudent not to let on that I'd seen them."

Bob looked at her quizzically. "Why?"

Lizzie shrugged. "I don't really know. It just seemed like the right thing to do."

Bob let out a deep sigh but Lizzie could tell he was upset. "You don't seriously think she's involved in this, do you Mark?"

"It's too early to say, Bob. You know that. I'm keeping an open mind here. We'll go with that until we hear anything different but we don't really know the girl. None of us do," he said pointedly.

"She's my grandchild," Bob said, his voice flat. "I have to believe her."

"I understand but I hope you'll stay out of this," Mark answered. He looked at Lizzie. "All of you."

Bob gave a curt nod. "I'll just go down to the station and then bring her back here after she's finished."

Mark watched him walk away. "I have a feeling this isn't going to be easy."

Lizzie looked at him. "Least of all for Darla."

Chapter Seven

◇◇◇

I was probably worrying over nothing.

NAUGHTY IN NICE—RHYS BOWEN

"Of course there's something she's hiding," Molly agreed with Lizzie.

They were sitting in Molly's kitchen at the banquette, where they could keep an eye on the progress out in the backyard while waiting for Bob and Darla to arrive. Lizzie studied Molly's face, noting there were probably just a few more lines added around her mouth and forehead. But for someone in her midseventies, she looked great. Of course, her sense of style and knowing how best to wear her shoulder-length hair helped.

"She doesn't know us so she won't trust us. But I'm pretty certain there's more to her story of why she's here," Molly was saying. Lizzie realized she'd been daydreaming.

"I didn't know you thought that," Lizzie said with relief. "I thought I might be a bit too suspicious."

"Well, whatever it is, I don't think it's the fact she's a murderer. That child doesn't have it in her."

"I hope you're right, Molly. But I did see her with that Shannon fellow. And it looked like they knew each other not that she'd just been accosted."

"Perhaps you've—we've all been reading too many mysteries?"

Lizzie shook her head. "Anyway, I just hope whatever it is she's hiding won't hurt Bob."

"You're so right, honey. That's why we have to find out what's going on and try to keep Bob on the sidelines."

"Easier said than done."

"I know. But if he sees we're all trying, maybe he'll back off a bit. I'm going to call all the members of the book club right now and see if they can come over tonight."

"Tonight's the literacy class, remember?" Lizzie glanced at the wall clock.

"I really did have my mind in working order earlier today," Molly said with an embarrassed laugh.

"There's been a lot happening. It's easy to forget things. Why don't Sally-Jo and I come by after that and let's wait until Thursday night for the book club? It's our regular meeting night, after all. And we may have more information to go on by that time."

"That sounds like a very good plan."

"I should make up a sign for your door, though, in case I can't get hold of everyone."

"Don't worry about that. I can do it."

"Thanks, Molly. I guess I'd better get going home." Lizzie gave her a quick kiss on the cheek. "Try not to worry."

She left without saying good-bye to Mark and drove home quickly. She made an espresso, thinking she'd need the extra energy, and pulled out her class list to inform them all of the change in plans. She managed to contact most of her students by five P.M. but had to be content with leaving a message for one of them, just as the cats came strolling into the kitchen.

"Dinnertime, I guess." In answer, Brie jumped onto the counter and nudged Lizzie's arm. After a few minutes of stroking the silky chocolate coat, Lizzie filled both cats' dishes and then looked in the fridge for something quick and easy for herself. Leftover stir-fried veggies and some slices of deli ham would do the trick.

Lizzie arrived half an hour before the class time, wanting to check out the room and to put a sign on the main counter informing her students of the temporary location. After being satisfied the space would work just fine, she went in search of Sally-Jo.

She had to duck into an open doorway to avoid being knocked over as two male staff members led another man toward the front door. They looked like they meant business, each hanging on tightly to both arms of the guy. Nothing was said but the guy looked over at Lizzie, a smirk on his face.

"What was that all about?" Lizzie asked another staff member coming up behind them.

"He's a drug dealer. Tries hanging out around here, dealing to the kids. We've issued a No Trespass for all the good that does."

"Why don't the police handle it?"

"He's smart. We've called them but he's taken off before they've arrived. Usually he doesn't come inside, though." He shook his head and walked off.

Lizzie felt some anxiety, wondering if her students could be a target. She needed to find Sally-Jo.

"Hey," Lizzie said as she pushed open the door after a

quick knock. "I just witnessed something unnerving in the hall." She went on to explain what had happened.

Sally-Jo looked shocked. "There are young kids using this facility. Not to mention our own students."

"Yeah, I know. Well, I guess we just keep an eye out for him and hope not to see him again. Is all well with this?" She gestured around the room.

Sally-Jo glanced around, too. She tried tucking a stray bang behind her ear, something not easy to do while her hair was at that growing-out length. Lizzie had bet Stephanie that by the wedding date, Sally-Jo's hair would be back to its usual pixie style.

"It's good. Not as comfy as being at Molly's but at least it's clean and bright. Have you heard anything more about Darla or what's happening?"

"I gave Molly a quick call and she said neither Darla nor Bob were back yet, and that a police officer had remained in her backyard even though the body has been removed. Teensy was with her, which is a good thing. I thought we should stop by after class."

Sally-Jo nodded. "Poor Molly. Another body outside her house. I'd think it's very unnerving. Do you think there's anything we can do to help this time?"

"I'm not sure. We don't really know any of the details."

"I thought you'd seen Darla talking to the victim."

Lizzie nodded. "But I have no idea why except for what Darla said."

"You think she's lying about that?"

"I hope not but it seems sort of strange. She's new to town and so is he."

The first of Sally-Jo's students entered the room. Lizzie nodded at the young girl and told Sally-Jo, "I'll see you later."

Lizzie was pleased to see three of her students sitting at

the rectangular table when she got back to the room. Noelle Ward, Tyler Edwards and Priscilla Ingersoll looked expectantly at her as she joined them, pulling over a chair to the end nearest the door.

"I'm sorry about this last-minute change of plans but I'm happy you're able to make it. I'll just pass out your essays from last week while we wait for Madona Currant. I hope she got the message I left her about the change of venue. Have any of you heard from her?"

Nobody answered, so Lizzie continued. "If you have any questions, I'm happy to answer them."

Tyler tipped his chair back, leaning precariously. "What's up at the mansion? Why the change?"

Before Lizzie could answer, Priscilla jumped in. "I heard on the radio that a body was found somewhere around there? Was it at the mansion, miss?"

Lizzie hadn't expected the question, although she realized now that she should have and come up with a ready answer. "I don't have any details but we were asked to find a different location for tonight." She knew that wouldn't satisfy Priscilla.

"So, was there a body or not?"

"She just told you, lamebrain, she don't know," Tyler said, shaking his head.

Priscilla jumped out of her seat. "You are such a dumb a . . ."

Lizzie loudly cleared her throat and Priscilla glanced at her before continuing.

"Aardvark. I'm allowed to ask questions so just back off."

Lizzie thought it best to let the standoff of glares play out before saying anything. Priscilla finally sat back and made it obvious she was ignoring Tyler. A wide grin spread across his face. *Oh boy.*

Time to get back on track. Lizzie pulled the homework she'd assigned last week out of her bag. The assignment had been to choose their favorite mode of transportation, to take out a book from the library about it, and to write a short three-hundred-word essay. She hadn't been at all surprised to read that Tyler wrote about motorcycles while Priscilla fantasized about a Porsche.

She'd decided that each week would include a short in-class test to get them more comfortable with writing them. That was next on her list and while they attacked the questions, Lizzie tried to focus on tonight's class and not let her mind wander to the murder. It was a struggle, though.

When the timer she'd set on the table went off, Lizzie went over the answers to the test and then ended with a question period, questions from the three of them, that she hoped would give her better insight into what assignments to prepare for future classes.

"This is it until after Easter break," she finally said, wrapping up the evening. "I hope y'all have a good two weeks and we'll see you back at Ms. Mathews's house when we resume."

Lizzie left her classroom at the same time as Sally-Jo. "They were really curious as to why we changed location. What about your kids?"

"The same. I tried to deflect a lot of the questions and finally, they gave up. You can bet they'll make up for it next time once the news really gets out."

Lizzie nodded. "Lucky us. Now, if they'd just apply that amount of inquisitiveness to the school work, all would be fine."

Sally-Jo chuckled. She shrugged her shoulders up to her ears. "I hope Jacob's around when I get home and that he's in the mood to give me a massage."

"I'll ask the cats to walk around on my back for a while. Not as effective but at least it's something."

Sally-Jo smiled. "I think I'll pass on Molly's, if you don't mind, though. I want to help if I can but the last thing I need right now is more stress in my life."

Lizzie stopped and waited until Sally-Jo had stopped moving and turned to look back at her. "Is it mainly the dress?"

Sally-Jo shrugged. "At this point, yes. But I guess I'm also gearing myself up for much worse to come. You know my mama. It's her way or no way, and I get all tied up in knots thinking about how Jacob's taking this. If I were him, I might reach the point of no return and just bail."

"Don't be silly. You're projecting your desperation on Jacob. He's tough. He can take it and I know he'll be there for you. Now, if you want to worry about something other than Jacob, who doesn't need you to worry about him, then you can worry about me and my dress. I don't have a clue what to wear to your wedding."

Sally-Jo burst out laughing. So much so, she was almost in tears by the time she pulled herself together. "You're wonderful. Thank you for that." She gave Lizzie a long hug.

As Lizzie watched Sally-Jo walk away, she just hoped her friend could do a lot more laughing over the next several months.

By the time Lizzie parked in Molly's driveway, it was just after ten. A police cruiser was parked on the street and Bob's old pickup sat in front of the double garage. Lizzie knocked and then walked inside, following the voices out to the kitchen where she found Molly, Bob and Darla seated at the banquette.

"You look tired, honey," Molly told Lizzie and got up to get her a glass of tea.

"It feels like a long day. How are you doing?" Lizzie asked Darla. She glanced at Bob at the same time and noticed he looked totally exhausted.

Darla yawned. "I've been better. I don't think your police friend believes me." A flash of anger crossed her face. "This is so dumb. I didn't kill the guy. You believe me, don't you, Granddaddy?" She looked at Bob, almost in tears.

He reached across the table and patted her hand. "Of course I do, Darla. But the police do have to thoroughly examine all links to any case. It will help clear you faster, you'll see."

Darla sounded angry this time. "You used to be police chief, didn't you? Grandmamma told me so. Why can't you tell them to stop it?"

"I'm afraid that's not how it works."

Darla stood up. "I can see what Grandmamma meant." She stomped out of the room.

The others were silent as they listened to her heavy footsteps going upstairs. Then Molly said, "Don't take it to heart, Bob. She's tired and she's lashing out because she's also afraid."

Bob sighed. "I know, Molly, but this isn't helping me get into her good books any." He ran a hand through his already disheveled gray hair.

Lizzie sat on her hands so she wouldn't reach over and pat the wild wings back into place. "We all know how murder investigations can shake things up," she said. "Let's just hope something useful shakes loose real quick."

Chapter Eight

<>

That's a convenient coincidence.

TOP SECRET TWENTY-ONE—JANET EVANOVICH

Lizzie's first appointment at the school the next morning wasn't until eleven o'clock. She debated about going to Molly's but thought she needed more information about the investigation before tackling Darla again. A phone call to Mark was in order.

She tried his cell phone and after the third ring he answered with, "No, I'm not about to share any information with you, Lizzie."

"Huh. And good morning to you, too. Just for that, Mark Dreyfus, you're going to have to allow me to buy you a coffee."

Mark laughed. "You're on. How about tonight?"

"How about in an hour?"

"I can't get away."

"I'll come to you bearing gifts."

Mark sighed. "A short visit and no questions."

"A short visit with not too many questions but a large latte."

"Sweet."

"I always am." Lizzie hung up and hummed while she dressed in a short black skirt with a tangerine T-shirt. She found the cats lazing on top of the love seat backrest, in the sun streaming through the window. She grabbed a comb for Edam and the brush for Brie and tried to do a two-handed grooming session. She gave up after a few seconds and gave Edam a thorough combing, luxuriating in the soft warmth of his fur. Then it was Brie's turn. He was more playful and ended up chewing on the edge of the brush. Lizzie finally gave up and left them to enjoy the sunbathing.

By the time she'd picked up two lattes and a couple of chocolate biscotti at the Cup'n Choc down the street from the police station, it was nine thirty. Mark stood at the front desk in the waiting room, speaking to the volunteer on desk duty when she walked through the doors. Lizzie stayed close to the door she'd just entered, watching Mark. He still managed to take her breath away. She'd never told him how sexy she found the fact that he'd chosen to go bald. And he still had the physique of the high school football hero he'd once been. But most of all, it was his dark chocolate eyes, so expressive and yet so liquidy deep, that most times when he looked at her, she felt herself melting.

Mark finished giving instructions to the older woman and ushered Lizzie into his office. He gave her a quick kiss and then removed the lid from the coffee container.

"I do have sweets," Lizzie said, holding out the small brown bag.

"You may stay," Mark said with a smile.

"That's good, because that was my plan." Lizzie sat on the upholstered chair at the side of Mark's desk, while he pulled his leather swivel chair over beside her and sat. He took a long drink of his coffee before talking.

"I'm afraid I really don't have long so just tell me what you want to know."

Lizzie grinned. "I thought I couldn't ask any questions."

"I know how this plays out so I'm just skipping to the end. Shoot."

"Do you have any more details about the murder?"

"Not much and not much that I can share."

"Seriously?"

"It's all technical stuff, Lizzie. I do know though that the victim is Rafe Shannon and that he's from Atlanta."

"We knew that yesterday."

Mark grimaced. "Can I continue? Furthermore, we now know that he is known to the police there. It seems he has ties with some local hoods in Atlanta. He's worked as a bouncer at one of the casinos and he also likes to do odd jobs for bookies."

"Yikes. Sounds like bad news. Which begs the question, how did you find out his name? I thought he didn't have any ID on him."

"He didn't."

"So how?"

"Not going there." Mark sounded stubborn but he did allow her a small smile.

"Okay, so how come Darla knows someone like that?"

"According to her, she doesn't."

"She's still saying that? You didn't beat it out of her?" Lizzie asked, eyebrows raised in question.

"No. My rubber hose is out for repairs at the moment." Mark got serious. "I don't believe her but I'm not going to accuse her of lying just yet. I want to get some more facts from her hometown first."

"Good. That should speed things up."

"Glad you approve." He leaned back in his chair and enjoyed another sip. "Has she told Molly anything about her home life or more about why she's here?"

"Not as far as I know. What if there wasn't a blowup with her mama? What if there's a more sinister reason she's here?"

"Something to do with our dead guy?"

"I was thinking more something to do with Bob. But he's not rich so it's not likely she's ingratiating herself into his life for his money."

"You really don't like her, do you?"

Lizzie thought for a moment. "It's not that I don't like her. I just don't trust her. And I'm worried that Bob will get hurt in some way."

"He's a grown man, Lizzie. He can take care of himself."

"This is his granddaughter we're talking about. It's not like he's chasing the bad guys or choosing a new car."

"Ouch. Okay, I get it. You are concerned, and I also don't like the idea that she might be playing him. But like you said, he doesn't have any money so that doesn't make sense. Maybe she's a young girl who wants to get to know her family. And she's also in trouble." He looked at his watch. "Sorry but I've got to get going. There are some people I need to talk to."

Lizzie finished her latte and tucked her untouched biscotti back in the bag and placed it on his desk. "For snackies." She grabbed her handbag.

"I'll call you tonight," Mark said as she opened the door. "And thanks for the treats."

Lizzie thought about their conversation all the way to the school. If Darla was in some serious trouble back home, had it followed her to Ashton Corners? She tried to come up with some scenarios that might work but nothing seemed to fit.

At least, nothing she thought about. There were some places she just didn't want to go with this.

After school, Lizzie drove over to Molly's, anxious to find out more about her houseguest. She found Molly out front, clipping back the boxwoods that grew along the sides of the porch. Although Molly's gardener came in regularly, she enjoyed keeping a hand in it, too. As Lizzie got out of her car, Teensy's yellow Cadillac pulled in beside her. Teensy bounced out of her car and gave Lizzie a quick hug, on her way over to Molly, who got an even longer hug.

"I'm glad you're both here," Teensy said before anyone else had a chance to talk. "I've just been going over this here incident in my mind and I'm thinking you shouldn't be staying here alone, Molly."

"But I'm not alone," Molly pointed out.

"Humpf. That child in no way is protection for you." She glanced at the front door and lowered her voice to a whisper. "And who's to say she's not the cause of all this?"

"What a thing to say," Molly answered, in a shocked voice. "Why would you even think that?"

"Because she just arrives in town, nobody knows anything about her and a couple of days later, a guy who she's been seen to have contact with is found dead. You do the math."

"There's no reason to believe any of it is more than coincidence," Molly stated and went back to her clipping.

"Is she at home?" Teensy asked.

"Yes but she's been staying in her room all day. She's upset, which is understandable."

"Of course she's upset. She knew the guy." Teensy threw up her hands in exasperation.

Lizzie thought it was time to step in before tempers started to flare. "There's no real reason to think she's involved in anything, Teensy."

"But you're the one who saw her with that guy."

"Yes, and what I saw sort of reinforces what she said happened. She did try to get away from him."

"And now he's dead. And why in your backyard, Molly? What was he doing there in the first place if not here to see her again?"

Molly dropped her clippers to the ground and stood up to face Teensy. "Not so loud, if you please. There's no need to be upsetting Darla even more than she is." Molly took a deep breath. Lizzie could tell she was trying hard to hold her temper in check. Molly reached out and grabbed Teensy's hand. "I appreciate the fact that you're concerned about my welfare, Teensy, but it really is misplaced. You have to trust me on that."

Teensy sighed and her shoulders hunched forward a fraction. "You're right, I suppose. But you're also right that I do worry about you, Mopsy. Now don't go getting mad but I want to know if she's given you any further explanation about the guy."

"No, she hasn't wanted to talk about it at all. And I take that to mean nothing more than she's upset by the whole thing. Who wouldn't be? Accosted by this stranger one day and the next, he's found dead almost outside her door?"

"Your door," Lizzie said quietly. "He must have followed her to your house, Molly. Why else would he be here?"

Molly shrugged. "I don't know. The police don't know. So for now, let it be. Come on. Let's go around back and have some tea. Enjoy the afternoon sun."

Lizzie and Teensy waited outside, seated on the wicker patio chairs, while Molly went in to wash up and get the tea. She came out several minutes later with a tray holding three glasses, a small pitcher of iced tea and a plate of lemon melt-away cookies.

"I asked Darla if she'd like to join us but she declined," Molly said as she poured the tea. "Now, better get it all off your chest, Teensy. And Lizzie." She sat down and angled her chair to face them both.

Lizzie looked at Teensy, who raised her eyebrows. Lizzie decided to take that as an invitation to take the lead.

"Has Darla said anything more these past few days about what happened at home? Why she came here?"

Molly looked thoughtful. "No, not really. She's mainly been asking questions and of course, wanting to know more about Bob. That's natural, don't you think?"

"Of course. Have they been spending a lot of time together?"

"I think they should be spending more time but Bob's moving slowly."

"Why do you think he's doing that?"

"Because he's scared. Here he hasn't had any contact with any of his family all these years and now this bright young girl comes along. He's not sure what all she's been told about him, although I'll bet he's thinking it's not very nice, and he's worried about scaring her off. So, it's been good that she's been staying here. I've tried to do things with her, show her around town and the like, but it hasn't been easy. So, I finally thought I'd just let her set her own pace about it all."

The back door opened with a small creak and Darla asked, "Have you ladies been talking about me?" She had an odd smile on her face.

Lizzie was quick to reassure her. "More like talking about Bob and how happy he is to have you here. You really can't imagine."

Darla shrugged and walked over to join them. She held

a glass of red wine in her right hand and a pack of cigarettes in the other. She sat downwind from them. "I'll try not to blow smoke in your faces," she said after setting her glass on the table and lighting a cigarette.

She's surveying the place like she owns it. Where did that thought come from, Lizzie wondered.

"Have you had a chance to walk the maze yet?" she asked, trying to dispel her own discomfort.

Darla didn't bother looking at Lizzie. "No. It really is a big place, isn't it?"

No one answered. They just sat watching Darla, who finally turned slightly so that she could see the others. "What's it like, living in a small town?"

"I was born and raised here," Lizzie said, "but I went to college in Auburn and after that, worked in Montgomery for a short while. They were big in comparison but not a large as Atlanta."

Darla smirked. "Atlanta's a real city with lots going on, day and night. I think I'd go antsy living here."

"I didn't realize you were contemplating doing that, sugar," commented Teensy, her voice dripping Southern, a tone Lizzie knew meant Teensy had reached her saturation point. Next stop, speaking her mind.

"Were you working?" Lizzie asked quickly.

"Sometimes. I didn't have a permanent job, if that's what you're asking. I couldn't find what suited me. My last job was as a server at a bar." Darla drank some wine and looked pensive. "Mama wasn't too happy about that, either."

"Every mama wants what they think is best for their children," Molly said.

"I suppose. But not everyone can marry a rich banker, like my grandmamma. And as for my mama, she's never even told me who my daddy is. The story always was that he had to go out of town on business and died in a car accident before they could get married but I think that's just another load of crap. She married Jack Lyman when I was three. What a loser. He did adopt me though and then, he took off, too."

Molly looked a bit shocked and Teensy said, "I think maybe I'll have me some of that wine." She stood and asked Lizzie if she wanted some. Lizzie shook her head and wondered what next to ask Darla. She was dying to ask about her argument with her mama but not with Molly around. Maybe she should offer to show Darla the maze and have a little talk out there.

Before she could, Sally-Jo came bounding around the corner of the house. She looked surprised to see them there but before anyone could say anything, Sally-Jo explained, "I am so fed up, Molly. I just needed a sane person to talk to. If I don't sort this out soon, I think I'm going to kill my mama."

Chapter Nine

✧✧✧

No. I needed a plan. Well. Two plans.

THE BUSY WOMAN'S GUIDE TO MURDER—
MARY JANE MAFFINI

Teensy stopped as she came through the door. "I think you need a glass of wine, sugar. You just sit yourself right down and I'll get it." She turned and went back into the house.

Sally-Jo looked around, a bit bewildered, and finally settled on Teensy's chair. Lizzie knew that something was really wrong for Sally-Jo to take the chair she knew that Teensy always chose. The one with the view of the kitchen door. Of course, the comment about her mama had been a clue, also.

"What's happened?" Lizzie asked.

Teensy came back and put a glass down in front of Sally-Jo. "I thought I might as well bring the whole bottle," she said, holding it up for all to see. "And, here's a glass for you, Lizzie in case you change your mind. This sounds like it's going to be a heavy session."

Lizzie accepted a glass of wine this time but set it down, waiting to hear what Sally-Jo had to say.

After downing half the glass, Sally-Jo took a deep breath and looked at her hands, clasped in front of her, on her lap. "Mama has put a deposit on that dress she so likes and has brought it home for me to try on as soon as I get down there next week."

"Sounds like you'll have a busy Easter break," Teensy said.

Sally-Jo nodded. " I've told her two days was all the time I could take to visit, so I guess it's my own fault. Again. But she's really pushing me on this." She finished the rest of her wine. "I really want it to be a wedding I'll remember with happiness." She sounded almost in tears.

"Wow, and I thought my mama was meddling," Darla said with a low whistle.

Lizzie shot her a glance hoping Darla would stop talking. She didn't get the message.

"Like, is she paying for this wedding or something? You're working at a good job, aren't you? Teachers must make big bucks, so you could pay for your own wedding, couldn't you and then she couldn't say a thing."

Sally-Jo shook her head sadly. "That's not how it works. Jacob and I are paying for the wedding but she's still my mama and I'm her little girl, and next thing I know, she'll probably refuse to show up if I don't do it her way."

"Well, my mama was all against me marrying John," Teensy ventured, "so we just eloped. Of course, they never wanted us to visit them anytime we came back home, after that."

Molly shot Teensy a stern look, which Teensy acknowledged with a shrug and questioning look.

"It's not the same thing," Molly told Sally-Jo. "Your mama is a very strong-willed woman but I don't think there's anything you could do that would make her refuse to see you again."

Sally-Jo let out a slow breath. "I'm sure you're right, Molly, but that doesn't really give me any clues as to how I'm supposed to deal with her next week."

"You could agree to the dress," Teensy suggested, "and then just accidentally set it on fire."

Sally-Jo's jaw dropped and then, on seeing the look on Teensy's face, burst out laughing.

Lizzie was pleased the tension had broken, and took a sip of wine. She noticed that Darla's look of disdain hadn't changed.

"You really don't like me, do you?" Darla suddenly threw out at Teensy.

Lizzie heard a light gasp from Molly. It took Teensy a few seconds to compose herself. She sat forward at the edge of her chair and drew herself up to look as tall as her five feet would allow, chin at a slight tilt and fire in her eyes as she answered, "It's not that I dislike you, child. It's that I distrust you. And that silly Sue-Ann didn't do a whit when it came to instilling good manners in you."

She held Darla's gaze and didn't flinch. Finally, Darla stood, although a bit unsteadily, making Lizzie wonder how many glasses of wine she'd had before joining them.

"I can take a hint." She stomped toward the kitchen but paused when Teensy said in a loud voice, "I do apologize for speaking despairingly of your late grandmamma."

The screen door slammed behind Darla, leaving Molly to look bewildered and Teensy to help herself to another cookie.

Lizzie was having a hard time concentrating on the book she was reading, *The Wolfe Widow* by Victoria Abbott. She decided to give it a pass at the moment, preferring to spend time with her favorite author when she could pay more attention to what was going on between the covers of the book.

She still couldn't get over what had happened earlier at Molly's. That was quite the scene and while she silently was rooting for Teensy, she couldn't help but feel a bit sorry for Darla. If she hadn't already felt unwelcome, that would surely do the trick. Molly had been horrified by the behavior of both of them. And fortunately, Teensy knew when to make a strategic exit, before any more words were said.

Was Darla merely a misunderstood young woman who knew it and had her back up? Or was there more to it? Her mind kept playing with the Darla conundrum.

She knew this was something stemming entirely from her own conjecturing. Aside from Teensy, everyone else seemed to be accepting Darla at face value, believing her motives to be pure. *Why can't I believe that, too?*

Best to go through the encounter in the alley yet again, Lizzie decided. She told herself to sit back and relax, breathe deeply, picture a watch on a chain swinging in front of her eyes. Wasn't that what hypnotists did? After a couple of minutes, she decided she was spending too much time trying to relax and focus. *Just relax.*

She pictured the alleyway, visualized Darla wearing her torn black denim jeans and green hoodie, with the man, now known as Rafe Shannon, dressed in dark leather jacket and jeans. He had hold of her upper right arm and pulled her along with him. So she was right about that. She hadn't wanted to go.

However, when Lizzie next visualized them in the alley standing next to a large green garbage can, Darla was leaning back against the wall facing Shannon. He looked frustrated more than threatening, until he grabbed her left arm and pulled his right back as if to punch her. It was Darla's face that Lizzie focused on. She didn't look afraid; it looked like she was sneering. Taunting him even.

Lizzie opened her eyes and sat straight up on the love seat. Darla had lied. She did know Shannon. Otherwise, why would she dare provoke him like that?

She reached for the phone to share her insight with Mark but heard the familiar beep of a message waiting. It was Mark making his excuses. Okay, good excuses but still the bottom line was he couldn't come over. What she had to tell him would have to wait until morning, unless he called her later. He had said he would. But she also knew, after all this time, that she shouldn't really count on things like phone calls or even dates when he was on a case.

She made a face and picked up her book again, hoping she'd be able to spend the rest of the evening with Jordan and Vera and maybe even finish reading *The Wolfe Widow*. If she couldn't have Mark, at least she could enjoy a good read.

Chapter Ten

✧✧✧

I'll let you know, Andie. Although I really hadn't
thought the book club would get involved in a real
murder.

A KILLER READ—ERIKA CHASE

Lizzie had to be content with leaving Mark a message at
his office the next morning since he didn't answer his
phone. She rushed to get out the door to school. She'd over-
slept, something that rarely happened, especially since she
usually had her clock radio set to switch on to her favorite
NPR station and awaken her to the sound of classical music.
Last night, she'd forgotten to set it. *How strange.*

She made it through a morning of meetings, wondering
where her brain was, and then finally settled into a routine
while sitting in on two classes in the afternoon. She made
notes as she listened in, aiming to turn them into construc-
tive suggestions for the teachers in the morning.

Her iPhone rang as she walked to the car after the final
school bell. Molly sounded breathless as she spoke quickly.

"Darla has just left with her boyfriend. You know, the

one her mama doesn't like? There wasn't anything I could do to stop her, although I'm not even sure that's my place to be doing that. Anyway, I was hoping you could stop by for a visit. I do need to talk this over with someone. In fact, I'll make you supper and you can just stay on for book club. Is that okay?"

"How about if I just stop by home first and feed the cats. I'll grab my copy of the book, too. I'd love to stay for supper."

"All right. I'll see you shortly then."

Lizzie wondered if Bob knew about this boyfriend incident. But what was the harm in it, as long as she didn't leave town? Maybe Mark was the one Molly should have phoned. She absentmindedly fed the cats, who wound around her legs in anticipation, even though it was early for them.

"My lovelies, I'm out tonight. We'll cuddle at bedtime," she told them as she grabbed her necessities for the evening. She quickly pulled the door shut behind her and locked it.

Her neighbor and landlord, Nathaniel Creely, was locking his front door at the same time. "Hey, Lizzie. How are you doing?"

"Just great, Nathaniel. I haven't seen you around lately."

"Been busy, young lady. You know that Lavenia is always on the go. I might stop by for a while on the weekend, though. Want to talk over something with you."

"That's fine, Nathaniel. I'll be running errands on Saturday and seeing Mama on Sunday but mostly home."

He nodded and gave her a big smile before getting into his car.

Lizzie thought about the exchange on her drive over to Molly's. He was right about his special friend, Lavenia Ellis. She seemed to be involved in a lot of things around town, involving him right along with her. Lizzie was happy to see him so active and cheerful. She knew Lavenia was like a tonic for him. But, she was dying to know what he wanted to talk about.

She pulled into Molly's driveway and was surprised to see Mark's Jeep there. Maybe Molly had alerted him after all. She found them out on the back patio, enjoying the late-afternoon rays of sun. It had been unusually warm for mid-March this year but it was welcome after an odd winter of colder-than-usual temperatures. In fact, they'd even had a couple of days of light snow, much to Lizzie's delight.

Mark saw her approaching and smiled, then looked back at Molly, who was talking. "That's about all I can tell you about him," she said, then turned around to greet Lizzie.

"Mark just stopped by to talk to Darla. I was telling him all about her boyfriend."

Lizzie glanced at Mark, whose face remained passive. No telling what he thought of this latest development.

"She hasn't left town, has she?" Lizzie asked.

"No, fortunately. He's staying at the Mountain View Motel and she's gone back to stay with him. I don't think Bob's going to be too pleased at this turn of events."

"That's tricky, but I think he'd be wise not to object since he's just getting to know her."

"So true. But you know Bob. I wonder if she'll remember about book club tonight and come by."

Lizzie looked at Molly incredulously. *Why would she do that?* She hadn't been too keen on the idea to start with. Molly didn't notice the look but jumped out of her seat and headed for the back door. "Where are my manners? I'll just get us all some nice freshly made tea, shall I?"

Lizzie sat next to Molly's chair. "What are you thinking?" she asked Mark.

"That there goes my theory the murder victim might have

been her boyfriend. There was the possibility she'd been running away from him."

"Don't you think she would have said that since he was dead and she wouldn't have to run anymore?"

"Not if it gave her a motive to murder him."

"Huh. There is that. Any new theories?"

"Not at hand." He leaned back in his seat and shoved his notebook into his shirt pocket as Molly came back out with a tray.

Lizzie leapt up to help her.

"Oh, do sit down, honey. I can manage this just fine." Molly placed the tray on the wicker table and poured a glassful for each of them. "I heard Lizzie's question. You don't have any information about what the dead man was doing here?"

Mark took a long drink of the tea before answering. "Nothing more than since the last time I questioned Darla."

"Excuse me if I'm asking what I shouldn't, but she hasn't told me anything about what's going on and I do want to know, as much for Bob's sake as my own."

Oh-oh. That's her persuasive stare. Mark's gotta tell her all.

Mark shifted in his seat. "What I can tell you is that he was from Atlanta as I said before, and had a police record, also some connections to some thugs who are tied into one of the casinos. I'm waiting to hear more, which may give us a clue as to what he was doing here."

"What on earth could a man like that have to do with Darla? It doesn't make sense. It must be as she stated, he just accosted her on the street. Maybe he was thinking of something, you know, intimate in nature."

"Anything's possible at this point." Mark quickly finished

his tea and grabbed his hat as he stood. "I've got to be going. Thank you for the tea." He touched Lizzie's shoulder as he left.

"That was totally unhelpful," Molly said after a few minutes. "Do you think he's going over to the motel to question Darla?"

"Probably. Well, at some point, anyway. What's her boyfriend like?"

Molly gathered her thoughts before answering. "I don't think he has much money, especially since he's staying at the Mountain View Motel. But he was concerned enough about Darla to follow her here so I guess that says a lot in his favor. I just hope Bob sees it that way."

Lizzie nodded but didn't say anything.

"I can see you're in deep thought, honey. Where are you going with all this?"

"I'm just back at the thought of a big-city thug being here in Ashton Corners. It seems coincidental that three visitors appear within a few days of each other."

"We do have visitors to this city all the time," Molly said with a smile. "Just playing the devil's advocate."

"Okay. But these three have a connection. Atlanta. And the incident in the alley, so that's two. And, Darla obviously is connected to her boyfriend. So, three. She's tied into both guys."

"What are you suggesting?"

Lizzie shook her head. "I don't know if I'm suggesting anything. Just pointing it all out."

"Well, I really don't see how this means anything other than the obvious. Coincidences do happen. And I'm not ready to believe there's a big conspiracy going on here." Molly sighed. "I was so hoping we wouldn't get involved in another murder. At least not quite so soon."

* * *

Lizzie was tucking the last of the supper dishes into Molly's dishwasher when the front doorbell rang. She yelled out to Molly, who was upstairs getting changed, that she'd answer it. She was surprised to find Sally-Jo on the porch.

"Are we late in eating or are you early in arriving?" Lizzie asked, holding the door open for Sally-Jo.

"Oh, I'm early. I grabbed a quick bite and then ran away from my computer and phone. I didn't even bring my cell phone along. All I ask is just one evening without having to do verbal jousting with my mama." She led the way back to the kitchen and plopped down onto a red wooden chair. Molly's eclectic mix of chairs, each one painted a different color, and a banquette newly upholstered in a paisley pattern that captured all the colors, made it a cozy setting that drew everyone into it.

"What's the latest or would you rather not talk about it?"

Sally-Jo gave a weak smile. "My head is bursting with all the back-and-forthing we've been doing about that dreaded dress. And now, she's trying to convince me to have a chocolate fountain, pouring out of a peacock no less, at the reception. You can understand now why we wanted to have a small, intimate wedding."

Lizzie just about burst into laughter. *Not good.* "That's really too bad. This should be a happy, exciting time for you."

"Yes, it should be. But in order to make it so, I have to get all this out of my system before I go down next week with her, otherwise we'll be butting heads all the time. So, I hope you don't mind, but you may be hearing a lot more of my troubles in the next few days."

"Anytime."

"I'll second that," Molly said as she joined them. She gave Sally-Jo a quick hug. "But for tonight, try to put all that business out of your head and just enjoy being with your friends and talking about Janet Evanovich."

Molly looked so expectant and cheerful that Sally-Jo nodded and followed up with a smile. "Tonight belongs to Evanovich."

They heard some voices in the foyer. "It sounds like we have company," Molly said.

The three of them left the kitchen and found Stephanie and Andie followed by Bob, who was just closing the front door.

"It's such a pleasure to escort two beautiful young gals to our book club meeting," Bob said.

Andie grinned from ear to ear while Stephanie blushed a bright pink. *She's still not used to getting compliments*, Lizzie thought, remembering how quiet Stephanie had been at that first meeting of the book club a year and a half ago. As a newcomer to town, Stephanie had taken a while to make new friends, especially difficult since at nineteen, she was already several months pregnant with her first child. Lizzie had met her first at her job as a waitress in the Oasis Diner and then when Stephanie joined her literacy class. And the book club members had enveloped her, making her part of the family of friends. Now she was the mother of fifteen-month-old Wendy, manager of A Novel Plot, and an independent young woman.

"I'm so excited to have it be my book tonight," Andie said, hugging Molly and then Lizzie.

"Yes, I'm so excited, also," Bob said in a droll voice and everyone laughed.

"You're so cool to read Janet Evanovich, Bob. You know, I think it makes you more of a stand-up kind of guy."

Bob's coloring verged on pink, but he shucked off the

comment with a grumpy noise. "I'm here mainly for the cheese straws, as y'all know."

Jacob was the last to arrive.

"Are we going to have to move the talking into the kitchen? I don't think so," Molly said as she shooed everyone into the library. Lizzie grabbed a plate of shrimp and one filled with an assortment of crackers and cheese. And Sally-Jo followed with a plate of cheese straws and a two-tiered server featuring chocolate shortbread on top and an assortment of cookies on the bottom.

Lizzie noticed Molly lingered along with Bob in the kitchen for a few minutes before joining the others. She'd bet they were discussing Darla. When they did join them, Bob was carrying the tray with a pitcher of iced tea and the glasses.

After everyone had settled with a full glass and plate of sweets, Molly turned the floor over to Andie, who'd been shifting about on the love seat she shared with Stephanie.

"All right, then. I'm just dying, so to speak, to get into talking about this, because *Top Secret Twenty-One* is so awesome. Okay, so I'm totally blown away by every one of her books. But this one just hit the right spot. Y'all know what I mean?" She looked around the room hopefully.

"Blown away? That's very appropriate for a Janet Evanovich book," Lizzie said with a laugh. "But I do know what you mean. Sometimes a book talks to you like it was written especially for you."

"That's it! I mean, in a way. It's not like I get into all the messes she does. But I sure think her life is cool. In this one here"—Andie pointed to her copy of the book on the coffee table—"Stephanie Plum is hot on the trail of a skip—she's a skip tracer y'all know that, I'm sure—and he's on the trail of this guy Briggs, who used to be his accountant. And the bad guy's aiming fire bombs at Briggs all over the place."

"That's the thing about Stephanie Plum or actually Janet Evanovich," Stephanie jumped in. "You can always be sure there's going to be a car bombed or an apartment, usually Stephanie Plum's."

"Yeah, but that isn't a bad thing. I think even the Agatha Christie books that Molly likes so much get to be same old a lot of the times. Sorry, Molly," Andie added after a quick look at Molly's face.

"I didn't meant that in a bad way," Stephanie answered. "In fact, there are other ways these books are sort of like an Agatha Christie book." She glanced at Molly, whose face had taken on a noncommittal look.

"Right on," Andie came back with. "You know this thing is going to happen but you wait to see how and what because they all change. They are a lot alike."

Lizzie sat back to enjoy the discussion. She was impressed that Andie had put so much thought into it. But she wasn't really sure how Molly was taking it all or where it was going.

"In what way?" Molly asked.

"Well, Poirot has his Captain Hastings and Miss Lemon. Stephanie Plum has her pal Lulu and Connie in the bail bondsman's office." Stephanie sat back, obviously pleased with herself.

Andie chortled and leaned forward on her seat. "Right on. And there's Inspector Japp. Stephanie has Morelli and, of course, Ranger."

"Oh boy, that Ranger gets my heart to pitty-patting every time I read about him," Stephanie added, fanning herself with her napkin.

"I understand what you're saying." Molly's voice was a bit louder than usual. "Of course, Agatha Christie focused on the details of the crime rather than going into so much detail about their private lives."

Lizzie tried to hide a smile by taking a sip of her tea. This was getting very interesting.

"I might point out," Molly went on, "that there were bombings in some of Christie's books, too. In *The Big Four*, the murderer set a bomb to go off at the end but then disarmed it when Poirot appealed to his attraction to a young woman. And in *Postern of Fate*, the house of Tuppence was bombed, although that was due to the war. But there are others—*Taken at the Flood, The ABC Murders.* . . ."

The front doorbell rang, interrupting her. Molly looked startled and then quickly said, "I'll get that," beating Bob to it. He'd just sat back down with two more cheese straws on his plate. He made to get up but Molly put up her hand to stop him. He shrugged and settled back to eat.

In a couple of minutes Molly returned with Darla in tow. "We have a guest at our meeting tonight," she said, indicating a wing chair next to Bob for Darla to sit in.

Bob searched Molly's face and seeming to find an answer, said, "It's sure good to see you, Darla. I'm happy you decided to join us after all."

Darla looked startled. "I'm not joining y'all. No way. Just sitting in and visiting tonight."

Bob looked taken aback but then laughed. "That's what I meant. Now, what have you been up to?"

Molly spoke before Darla could say anything about her afternoon exploits. "I'm glad you could make it, too, Darla. Now, what can I get you to drink? Some sweet tea? There's a fresh pitcher here."

Darla nodded and also accepted a small plate, choosing a couple of crackers, slicing a sliver of Edam cheese from the serving dish Andie had brought over. Lizzie looked over at Molly, who merely raised an eyebrow.

"You missed the fun part, the part when everyone gives

their opinion about the book and Molly digs her heels in since it's not by Agatha Christie," Bob said with a chuckle.

Everyone laughed, but Darla looked confused.

"Don't let him tease you, Darla," Molly said. "We've just finished discussing tonight's book but since I hadn't really expected you'd have time to read it, you didn't really miss anything. We're glad you can join us for some socializing instead."

Darla looked hesitant. "My boyfriend, Wade Morris, dropped me off while he goes and does something. So as soon as he's finished, he'll be picking me up."

The doorbell rang as if on cue. When Molly returned from answering it, she had a young man in tow, towering above her at around six-foot-four, with black hair shaved around the bottom and the top standing straight up with the help of some powerful product, Lizzie bet. He wore a black T-shirt and a black leather vest enlivened with colorful reptile artwork, and black straight jeans. The tail of some type of creature tattooed to his right upper arm slithered down toward his elbow. A matching one but in a variety of colors adorned his left arm. When he finally removed his sunglasses, Lizzie noticed the bushy black eyebrows. She also noted he didn't smile, not until he saw Darla. Then he produced a sexy smirk. Lizzie hoped Bob hadn't noticed. It was not a smile for granddads.

Darla jumped out of her chair and rushed to his side. She slipped her arm through his and pulled him over to Bob. "This is my granddaddy."

Bob stood and stuck out his hand. Eventually Wade did the same. Darla gave him a small nudge and he smiled. She then turned him around to face Molly and did the introductions. Lizzie noticed that this time his smile grew wider at the mention of Molly's name.

Darla didn't bother with individual introductions for the rest of them, eliminating them with a wave of the hand and saying they were the book club.

"Have a seat," Bob demanded. "There's some awfully good sweets here."

Darla pulled Wade over to where she'd been sitting and let him take the chair while she perched on the arm. Molly homed in on them with a tray with two glasses of freshly poured tea. They each took one but nobody said a word.

Molly looked at Bob and raised her eyebrows. He cleared his throat and asked, "What brings you to town, Wade?"

He finished chewing and swallowed. "I came to take Darla back home."

Molly stopped in her tracks as she passed the sweets along to the others. "Surely, not so soon. Bob and Darla are just getting to know each other."

Darla smiled sweetly at Bob and then focused on Molly. "I know. I am so much enjoying getting to know my granddaddy, and you also, Molly. And I want Wade to get to see some of Ashton Corners and all. But we don't have hardly any money between us to pay for another night in the motel, so we'll get going tomorrow morning. I guess I need to go crawling back to my mama, tail between my legs, and beg her forgiveness. Although I know I'm not at all in the wrong here."

Bob looked stricken. Molly took one look at his face and spoke up. "Why I think you should both move in here with me. I have plenty of space, as you well know. And I think you could probably put up with an old fussbudget like me." She directed the last comment at Wade.

Bob looked relieved, although Wade's face hardened. Darla was beaming, but one look at Wade and she quickly deflated. "Oh, that is so sweet of you, Molly, but Wade doesn't believe in making a nuisance of ourselves. We really do need to stay on our own and not take advantage of your hospitality." Lizzie thought she'd added that last bit as if remembering lines from a play.

"Well, I'd be happy to pay for your motel for a few more days," Bob said. "I think it's the least I can do. That will give you time to sightsee and we'll also get to spend a bit more time together."

Molly looked about to say something but had second thoughts.

Wade jumped on it right away. "We'll take it." Darla nudged him. "Uh, thanks," he added. He stood and grabbed her by the arm.

"We've really got to get going now," Darla said. "Thanks for the food."

Bob walked them to the door, pulling out his wallet as he did so.

None of the others said anything for a minute after they left the room, and then Andie spoke up. "That guy gives me the creeps."

Molly shushed her. "Don't let Darla hear you say that. She could come back into the room, you know. I'm glad Bob will have more time with Darla, though. Now shall we get back to talking about books?"

"We should," Lizzie agreed, "but could we give some collective thought to the real murder first?"

Andie's hand shot up. "Internet search."

Lizzie chuckled. "Not a surprise. I guess we should try to get more information about the victim, Rafe Shannon, if we want to figure out why he was here in town, and more importantly, here at Molly's house."

Bob came back into the room and went straight this chair, sat down and crossed his arms. "I'm not so sure I like where this is heading."

"What? The Internet search?" Lizzie asked.

"What Internet search? No, I mean Darla's leaving with her boyfriend. I haven't had any experience in this grand-daddy business, but my gut tells me to do something about it."

Molly leaned across and touched his arm. "You know what that would lead to, don't you? She's likely to pull away and maybe even leave town. I hate to say it, but you don't know her well enough to be sticking your nose in her life. I know you have good intentions and she'll know it, too, soon enough. But it's still too early on in your relationship. Trust Darla to know what she should be doing. For now, anyway."

Bob shook his head. "I feel so useless."

Lizzie jumped in. "Then put your investigative skills to work and let's try figuring out why a corpse was found in Molly's backyard. Remember, there's still a tie-in to Darla, so we need to be helping her, too."

"All right. That is something I can help with. What do we know about the guy? Has Mark told you anything about him?"

"Just that he's from Atlanta . . ."

"Same as Darla," Bob interrupted.

"Yes. He's also got a rap sheet." *That'll get a reaction.*

"Rap sheet? You've been watching way too much TV, young lady." He paused and started laughing. "Okay. He's known to police. For what?"

"He's a tough guy, does dirty work for others, and he also has connections to one of the smaller casinos and some bookies."

"An enforcer maybe," Jacob said.

"Yes, Mark did think that. So, why would he come to Ashton Corners?"

"I'll bet it wasn't for a vacation," Stephanie threw in.

"A meeting with someone?" asked Sally-Jo.

"We know of only one meeting he had and that was with Darla," Lizzie pointed out.

Both Molly and Bob looked at her sharply. "I'm sorry but that's true. So how do we find out if he also met someone else? That mystery person could be the killer."

Nobody spoke for a few minutes. Andie nudged Stephanie and pointed at the plate of cheese straws. When she'd chosen one, she munched on it, her eyes cutting from one person to the other. "Maybe my Internet search will turn up some clues."

"I'll help you with that," Stephanie chimed in.

Bob nodded. "And I'll start asking around town, try to find out when he arrived and where he stayed. Someone must have seen him. Lizzie, maybe you could sweet talk Mark into telling you if they've found out about any local contacts he might have had, as in the unsavory kind."

"That's good," Jacob said. "An old classmate of mine has a criminal practice in Atlanta. I'll give him a call tomorrow and see if he knows anything about Rafe Shannon."

"Molly, you seem to be the closest to Darla," Lizzie said. "Maybe if she stops by on her own you could sort of nudge some more information about the encounter out of her."

Molly sighed. "I don't think she's at the confiding point with me. But if the opportunity arises, I will try my best. Now before y'all wrap up and disappear, I need to tell you the title of next month's book."

Lizzie ignored the groaning noise Bob made.

"Some of you will be pleased to hear that it's not an Agatha Christie novel this time."

"Three cheers," said Bob, clapping.

Molly favored him with an indulgent smile before continuing. "It's *Queen of Hearts* by Rhys Bowen. I'm not going to say anything more about it but I think y'all understand when you read it why it's something I'd suggest."

"May I just add a loud groan at this point?" Bob asked.

"You mean another one?"

Everyone chuckled. Except Bob.

"Getting back to the investigation," Sally-Jo broke in, "what can I do to help?"

"I think you've already got a lot on your plate, honey." Molly smiled at her. "You need all your strength to deal with that mama of yours."

"Amen," Jacob muttered, then gave Sally-Jo a quick hug.

Chapter Eleven

◇◇◇

Good Lord, now what?

PEARLS AND POISON—DUFFY BROWN

L izzie listened to the soprano practice CD in the car on her way to work the next morning. The spring concert was still a month and a half away, but there were three new pieces they'd been practicing since January and one in particular, a full-length mass, was giving her a lot of problems. She'd hoped to ace the soprano line, including words, in the credo of the *Celtic Mass* by the Canadian composer Scott MacMillan for tonight's rehearsal, but she admitted to herself that wasn't the case. She loved the rhythm and found herself "dancing" in the driver's seat but couldn't quite get the Celtic pronunciations right.

She parked her Mazda next to Sally-Jo's Kia and sat singing along softly until the current track ended. As she got out of the car she noticed that the pink azalea bush marking the sidewalk path from the lot to the school had been squashed and tire tracks were gouged out in the lawn surrounding it.

She shook her head, already missing the splash of color the bush added through the seasons. She stopped in at the main office once in the school and spotted the secretary, Diane Kelly, leaning on the counter, talking on the phone.

Diane nodded at Lizzie, so she waited until the conversation ended. "Hey, Diane. Not off to a good start this morning?"

Diane shook her head. "Already there have been three phone calls to the principal from unhappy parents and I just got off the phone with the police. We've had a visit from vandals last night."

"I saw the azalea. What else has happened?"

"Oh, the usual. Graffiti on the back wall and doors. Nothing that can't be fixed or painted over, but it's all the grass that's been dug up by some idiot racing around the back playing field that really riles me. I just hope it wasn't former students." She grimaced.

"What can be done?"

"Well, the police will do a few extra overnight patrols around here for the next while, but the little creeps will just wait awhile and then start all over again."

"We haven't had much of a problem before, have we?"

"Not here. I admit I'm thinking about what happened at my last school. Like to have given the principal a heart attack. Anyway, that's taken care of. Is there anything I can do for you? And I hope it's something good, if there is."

"No, nothing. I admit to giving in to curiosity about the azalea."

"You know what they say about curiosity."

"Hm. You have a good day, Diane." Lizzie shivered as she wandered down the hall to the library, where she'd be working most of the morning. It was more than curiosity that made her want to call Mark and find out if he was any further with the murder investigation. She hadn't talked to him all day yesterday, which wasn't unusual during an investigation. That was a good enough reason for a quick call.

She set her books and a couple of student file folders out on the desk and dialed her iPhone, leaving a short message for Mark when he didn't answer. She looked at the file folder on top. This one required a meeting with the teacher. She'd try to set that up over the lunch hour. The second file was something she could work on right away. She started reading and didn't look up until a shadow blocked the sunlight shining through the side window. By the time she looked up, the shadow had vanished and bright sunlight filtered through once again.

She stood and stretched, checking the clock on the wall. At the same moment, the recess bell rang. She went looking for Sally-Jo and found her on playground duty.

"Sally-Jo. How are you feeling today?"

"Frazzled. Still. I expect to be in this state until the day after the wedding." She crossed her arms and hugged herself. "I used to be so laid-back and happy and . . . and I even looked forward to visiting my parents. Who knew that instead of Bridezilla there would be a Motherzilla-of-the-Bride?"

Lizzie chuckled softly. "Wow. I can't begin to know how stressed you are. You sure there's nothing else I can do for you? Offering moral support seems hardly enough."

"Believe me, it's great. Even Jacob is getting a bit exasperated. He tried not to show it but I can tell. I try to make the planning fun when it's just the two of us but lately, I end up dissolving fairly quickly. I had to stop talking about it on the way home from Molly's." She turned to face Lizzie. "What if he decides it's not worth it and calls the whole thing off?"

Lizzie grabbed her arm. "Now, don't go there, Sally-Jo. You know that's not going to happen. Jacob's allowed to get a bit uptight, too. But that certainly doesn't mean he'll back out. He's an amazing guy. You know that. Trust yourself on this."

"You're right." Sally-Jo sighed and burst into a bright smile. "You see, you're doing a lot to help out. Thank you, Lizzie."

"Glad I could help. Now on a more mundane topic, are you going to the teacher luncheon today?"

"I'd thought about it. I usually enjoy potlucks but we really don't have a lot of time at lunch. Who thought of that anyway?"

Lizzie shrugged. "I think it was Patti. She can be pretty efficient when she wants to be. I'll bet she has us eating and tidied well within the hour."

"One word. Indigestion. No, I think I'll stick with my little brown bag at my desk and then hotfoot it downtown to check out Norman Jewelers. I know there's plenty of time but a shopping trip might be a fun diversion right now. I was thinking about cuff links for Jacob as a groom's gift. Cool, right?"

She took a look at Lizzie's face.

"All right. Sounds pretty boring, doesn't it?"

"Uh, yeah. Unless they happen to be very creative cuff links."

"Oh boy, like what?"

"What does he love the best, besides you, of course?"

"Hmmm. Golf." Sally-Jo was quiet for a minute and then broke out into a wide smile. "You may be onto something. Will you come with me, please? Please? Or do you desperately want indigestion?"

Lizzie laughed. "When you put it that way, I'll come with you."

"Oh, thank you again, Lizzie. You're a charm."

The bell rang and both women stepped aside as the children surged toward the double doors. Lizzie sent Sally-Jo

ahead to her classroom while she waited until the last child
had reentered the school. As she closed the final door behind
her, she sighed, worried about Sally-Jo and wishing she could
wave a magic wand to make the ideal wedding just happen.

Lizzie put her iPhone on vibrate and stuck it in her right
pant pocket before she went to take her chair at the choir
rehearsal. She'd put in another call to Mark and was hoping
he'd get back to her, even if it meant she'd have to duck out
of the session to take the call. She'd been unable to reach
him all day and she needed to ask some questions about
Rafe Shannon. It had been bothering her all afternoon at
school, and her mind had gone back to the puzzle when she'd
been trying to concentrate on drafting a workshop for the
next teachers' professional development day. It was not a
good thing when murder impinged even on her work life.

She'd had an eventful lunch hour, without thoughts of
murder, helping Sally-Jo shop. Although they'd gone back
to school empty-handed, Sally-Jo had a short list of possibilities, one of which was a set of sterling silver golf ball cuff
links, and she felt a bit more at ease about the wedding plans.
Although any talk about her trip back home could send her
to the brink. Lizzie had to concentrate to prevent the words
"Fort Myers" and "your mama" from escaping her lips.

The choir director, Stanton Giles, looked up from his
score and happened to lock eyes with Lizzie. She immediately felt more guilt for bringing outside thoughts to choir,
especially those having to do with murder. She silently
vowed to give him her total attention and even challenged
herself to try singing without using her score. Giles was
often asking the members to take a chance and see just how

much they'd memorized by repetition. She'd always worried that she'd flub the singing but tonight she'd give it a try.

After the warm-up and partway through the first movement, Lizzie realized how irrational that was. Not only did she not know the words by heart, she also didn't know the notes as thoroughly as she'd thought. She tried to discreetly open her score and find the right page while the altos were running over, yet again, their line in the credo.

Krista Barlow, standing next to her, gave her a quick jab with her elbow and grinned when Lizzie looked at her. Lizzie tried not to look too sheepish but was grateful when Krista leaned closer and pointed out the bar of their entry. *Right. Concentrate.*

At the break, Lizzie decided to have a coffee, something she usually avoided during rehearsals. However, she needed the blast of caffeine to keep her on track. She'd found it far too easy for her mind to drift back to the murder and those two questions: What was Rafe Shannon's connection to Darla, and why was his body found at Molly's?

"Were you trying to show the rest of us up back there?" Krista asked with a smile, suddenly appearing at her side. "Me in particular. You know how I hate memorizing lyrics."

"Absolutely. You'll notice how I aced that."

"Well, it was a noble effort, I'm sure. You do look distracted tonight, though. Tough day at work?"

"Not really. Just a lot on my mind."

"Well that's not so great. You know what I usually do, which of course might not work for you but you never know. I just park it when I come to choir. I tell myself, Krista, you cannot deal with two things at the same time and do a good job. So just put it out of your mind and let your subconscious deal with it. Put your whole being into the singing, which is good for the soul. And then when you're ready to deal with it, pull it out and you may find there's an answer that comes right out with it."

Krista sat back with a self-satisfied smile and opened her music.

The second half of the rehearsal went more smoothly for Lizzie. She even managed not to lose her place in the score, all thoughts of murder having been temporarily banished. The minute she turned on her car's ignition, though, she was right back in the middle of her quandary.

Chapter Twelve

◇◇◇

With a grin that came across as a leer, he said, "I think it's a marvellous idea."

GRACE AGAINST THE CLOCK—JULIE HYZY

Lizzie looked up from tying her shoelaces as the back door opened and the bell rang. Mark stood there, dressed in black shorts, faded gray T-shirt, and running shoes, with a Braves ball cap on backward. He grinned at her expression.

"What are you doing here this early and dressed like that?" she said, agape.

"I've spent the last two days tied up in investigations and meetings, so today I'm taking at least a couple of hours to get my head straight. Patchett and I thought we'd join you in a run." His smile slipped. "If that's all right? You haven't gone and are back already, have you?"

Lizzie stood and went into a crouch, stretching her calf muscles. "No, I haven't. Just getting ready and I'd love the company. I'm just not used to seeing you out for a run."

"Never too old to learn new torture."

"Humph. You're in better shape than I am. You won't have any difficulty with this. And just to get some ground rules straight, if you feel the need to eclipse me, then just keep on running at your speed. We'll meet up somewhere."

Mark leaned against the kitchen counter and grinned.

"Are you enjoying this? Shouldn't you be stretching also?" Lizzie asked, head down against her right knee.

"Already did that before I got in the Jeep. I'll just go let Patchett out and we'll meet you in front since you don't like an audience."

Lizzie made a face and concentrated on the remaining warm-ups. She grabbed her keys and joined them outside. Patchett did his version of a happy dance when he saw Lizzie approach. She bent down to scratch him behind his loppy left ear and then straightened, turning to check out the street.

"How about down to the pathway along the river and out to the park?"

"You might just outrun us. Patchett might just have a field day nosing around there."

"I'm surprised you can get him to run."

"He likes it. Keeps him in good shape."

"And how often does he take part in this activity?"

"This might be his second time. But don't worry. I have lots of treats." He pulled up his T-shirt to reveal a fanny pack.

"Let's just see if that works," Lizzie challenged and took off at a slow jog. She could hear Patchett's dog tag flopping against his collar just behind her, but she didn't look back. By the time she reached the riverbank, she didn't hear him any longer. She jogged on the spot and turned to watch them approach from a distance.

"How's the running partner working for you?" she asked as they got within hearing distance.

Mark had slowed to a jog and was coaxing Patchett to

pick up the pace. "Not one of my better ideas, I admit. Now, if he had the scent of something, say a coon or rabbit even, we'd be leaving you in the dust."

"Huh. Do you want me to bring up the rear with him while you turbo ahead? We can take turns."

"Thanks, that's thoughtful, but I'm ready to admit defeat. It's just good to be outdoors and not thinking about the murder all the time. You go on ahead, though."

Lizzie shook her head. "Naw. I think a walk will do me just fine."

They continued along the path in silence until they reached the arm that would take them back up to Glendale Park and the center of town. Lizzie had been reluctant to try to get Mark talking. She knew he had a lot on his mind and counted herself lucky to be the one he wanted to share the walk with.

Patchett jerked at his leash and pulled Mark over to a fallen log.

"Must be something awfully exciting under that log," Lizzie commented. "Just as long as it doesn't slither out."

Mark grinned and called Patchett. When the dog responded, Mark gave him a treat and kept walking back to Lizzie. "Remember another Saturday morning? I was lying flat on the ground trying to take pictures of a bird, and you tripped over my feet?"

"I remember. Boy, did you give me a scare. That was almost a couple of years ago. A lot has happened since then."

Mark stood right next to her. "It has. Both good and bad." He turned to face her. "But the best part was meeting you again." He bent over and kissed her, then pulled back and watched her face a moment before saying, "I love you, Lizzie."

She sucked in her breath.

"Don't say anything," Mark said. "It doesn't require an

answer. I just wanted you to know. Now, let's try to get some more running time in." He tugged at Patchett's leash and started jogging.

It took Lizzie a couple of beats to close her mouth and shake herself out of the trance. *He loves me!* She had heard him right. And to think that in high school she'd mooned over the then football star, the guy who had all the girls chasing after him, the one she was so certain didn't know she existed. She'd been stunned when they'd met again so many years later, Lizzie involved with the book club and a murder outside Molly's house, and Mark, the chief of police. When he had let on that he'd noticed her way back then, she'd been blown away. Lizzie gave her head a small shake, bringing her back to the present.

She started after him and kept apace until they had passed the offices of the Ashton Corners Historical Society. The library was next up on their right. She slowed and looked across the street at the alley where she'd seen Darla and Rafe Shannon meeting.

Mark followed her gaze and stopped. "It's hard to get away from it," he said with a shake of his head. "Why don't you walk me through what you saw, again?"

They started walking down the alley and stopped partway.

Lizzie looked around before answering. "This is where they really got into it. I was by the corner of the building back there. I thought he was going to hit her but he gave her a slight jab in the arm."

She stared at the spot they'd stood without speaking.

"Lizzie, what is it?"

"I was just picturing it. Darla did look frightened but I don't think it was because she thought it was a mugging.

She wasn't clutching her bag close to her or anything like that. And then she just sort of seemed to switch gears. She wriggled out of his grasp and started getting in his face. That's odd, don't you think?"

"It is if she was afraid for her life. Or very foolish."

"Have you learned anything else about him?"

Mark tugged her arm and they walked back to the street. "It seems he did know someone here in town."

Lizzie looked at him and waited, wondering if he'd share the information.

"I will tell you, Lizzie, but I don't want you to go bothering her trying to find out any details. All right?" Mark locked eyes with her.

Uh-oh. "All right."

"He's Amber Craig's cousin."

"What?" Lizzie lowered her voice and continued. "You've got to be kidding. She didn't mention that at the crime scene. Did she?"

He shook his head. "That's not necessarily something she wanted the world to know. But she did tell me. She hasn't seen him for years and in fact, had broken all ties with him and that side of the family when she became a police officer. She confirmed that he's had a lot of run-ins with the law ever since he was a kid and he's been in prison a couple of times."

"For what kind of things?"

"Mainly assaults."

Lizzie shuddered. "No wonder she wanted nothing to do with him. So, she didn't know he was in town?"

"He hadn't tried to get in touch with her. He might not even have known she lived here. I have had to take her off the case, though."

"That's too bad. I'll bet she's not a happy camper."

"You've got it. I've made her liaison with the mayor's office, which will help free me from the weekly meetings with him and let me concentrate more on solving this case."

"Yikes. I know how she feels about meetings. So, is Officer Yost your second in command?"

"I don't have a second in command, but he is the one doing a lot of the legwork on this."

They started a slow jog back toward Lizzie's. After a couple more stops for Patchett to sniff out scents, they reached her place, and Mark put Patchett in his Jeep.

"Do you have time for a coffee?" Lizzie asked.

"I was hoping you'd ask." He followed her into the kitchen. "I'm also hoping to be able to take you out to supper tonight. That is, if you don't have any other plans?"

"I was saving tonight for you," Lizzie answered, giving him a light kiss. "But I have another idea. How about we stay in, I cook, and we can enjoy a quiet evening together, alone."

"Sounds perfect." Mark grinned and Lizzie felt that familiar tingle in her toes.

She put a K-Cup in her new Keurig for Mark and ground some espresso beans for her brew. When they were both ready, she put them on the kitchen table and sat across from Mark.

"So do you have any idea why he came to town given that it probably wasn't to see Amber?"

"He's not the vacation-type of guy so it must be business related. Amber is going to make contact with her relatives to see if anyone has any information."

"Could he have followed someone to town?"

"Who? Darla?"

Lizzie shrugged. "Possibly but she doesn't seem to be big enough fish, doesn't she?"

"Big enough fish? You come out with some of the hokiest sayings sometimes, and I mean that in the nicest of ways," he hurried to add.

"Thank you. But don't you agree?"

"Possibly. Ashton Corners may be a small town in some ways but when it comes to standing out, as in a new man in town maybe asking questions, it's suddenly a very big place."

"And that's why you have a job."

Mark grinned. "You've got that right, babe."

It took all of Lizzie's willpower not to stop in at the police station as she drove by at noon. Mark's Jeep was not in the lot but Amber Craig's black CRV was. However, Lizzie had less than five minutes to get to the Mellow Yellow Eatery for her lunch date. Teensy Coldicutt had phoned her after Mark had left, and asked if they could meet for lunch. Lizzie knew what she wanted to talk about. Darla. And that was more than fine with Lizzie.

She found Teensy at a table for two, off the main room in a recent addition to the popular restaurant. Teensy sat facing the entrance, beneath a painting of the old fairgrounds. It's like she dressed for that particular seat, Lizzie thought as she threaded her way to the back. Teensy's bright fuchsia and purple top with flowing sleeves brought out similar colors in the artwork. She even looked a tiny bit like the carousel canapé behind her. Lizzie almost mentioned it but decided better not. As she sat down, Teensy pushed a small basket of rolls toward her.

"These are real yummy. They'll tide you over until we get our lunch. It's so busy here today, it might be a long wait."

They didn't have to wait long for a server to appear,

despite the lunch-hour crowd. They each ordered ice tea with lemon while they scanned the menus, and placed their food orders when their drinks arrived.

Teensy took a long drink and then leaned forward, her arms crossed on the table. "I'm so glad you were able to meet me, sugar. I know you're just as worried about Molly as I am, so we have to come up with some way of dealing with Darla."

Lizzie made a face. "That's not going to be easy, Teensy. We both know that Molly feels she needs to help Bob out here and since Darla is his grandchild, nothing we can say will change her commitment."

"What if Darla isn't his grandchild?"

"Do you know that for a fact?" Somehow Lizzie couldn't believe that Darla would come up with such an audacious plan. Surely the threat of being found out would prevent her from lying about it.

"No. Just thinking out loud. I do think she's trying to pull a fast one, though, and I'll bet money is at the root of it."

Just what Lizzie had been thinking. "But Bob's not wealthy."

"We all know that, and once Darla saw where the dollars lay, that would be when she took a gander at Molly's home sweet home, she latched onto Molly's emotions right quick. I'll bet your boots that's what that girl is after. Money. Not family. It was never about family."

Lizzie sat back and took a deep breath. Teensy certainly was on a roll and had clearly taken a deep disliking to Darla. Was that the basis of the distrust? Or could Teensy sense deeper goings-on?

Their orders arrived and Lizzie made busy with buttering a roll and checking out her field greens salad, giving her time to think things through. Teensy's face had lit up at the sight of her biscuit-topped chicken potpie, and she had already tucked into it by the time Lizzie came up with an answer.

"I don't know if I totally agree with you, but what do you propose doing about it all?"

Teensy finished eating her mouthful and then put her fork down, leaning forward and lowering her voice. "We need to either confront Darla about it or that boyfriend of hers. Now"—she held up her hand before Lizzie could speak—"I'm sure all Darla will say is that we're plain loco and that boyfriend . . . I'd rather talk to a baboon."

"Okay, are there other options?" Lizzie asked hesitantly.

"How are your breaking and entering skills?"

Lizzie's mouth dropped open.

"Just kidding. What I am seriously thinking of doing is taking a little trip to Atlanta and having a chat with Darla's mama. Get the lay of the land, so to speak. Maybe, if they are at outs like Darla claims, her mama may be willing to answer a few questions."

"She might not know anything about this. Darla did say she'd left home abruptly."

"I'm not ready to believe anything that girl says. Besides, her mama may have an idea of what's up and she might be willing to share it with someone who can do something about it."

"What if, as you suggest, Darla is after some money? Maybe her mama is in on it, too. Maybe she thinks a grandchild has a better chance of getting something rather than the daughter who has ignored her daddy all these years."

"Girl, you are cooking. I hadn't thought about that. I obviously have to come up with a cover or some sort of story to test the waters first and then decide how to handle mama."

"As intriguing as that all sounds, I'd think twice about doing it. You know that Molly will be awfully upset if she hears about it. Bob, too."

"Only if I'm wrong. If I'm right, surely they'll thank me. I'm doing it for their own darn good."

Lizzie thought about it as she ate some more of her salad. "Maybe Bob doesn't really care what the reason is. You could see how emotional he was about meeting Darla. Even if he doesn't say too much, it's easy to see it affected him."

"Of course it affected him. He's getting on in years, as we all are, and that's when you wish you had kids around. I know I sure regret not having any. It was fine while John was alive. We were so wrapped up in each other and doing things." She paused and blushed. Lizzie wondered if it had anything to do with their nefarious activities. "Anyway, I'm just saying that whatever his reason, I think it will hurt him much more if he finds out she's only after his money. Not that he has any. And Molly. Why she's got you but there are no children for her, either. And even though she won't admit it, even to herself, she's attached to Bob and so anything he wants, she's for it."

Teensy stopped talking long enough to take another long drink. "It's touching but in this case, it's foolish."

"I don't know what to say, Teensy."

"Well, don't say anything then. To anybody. If I do decide to go to Atlanta, I'll give you a call and let you know. Now, you're not to blow my cover with Molly. There's no reason she should ask you for any details anyway. So just don't volunteer any. Okay?"

Lizzie nodded. She didn't know what else to do. She'd have to give it some serious thought once she was away from Teensy's web of enthusiasm. One thing did trouble her, though. What if this put Teensy in danger?

Chapter Thirteen

◇◇◇

What are friends for?

THE WOLFE WIDOW—VICTORIA ABBOTT

Lizzie tried to avert her eyes as she retraced her drive along Main Street after lunch. But the police station was like a magnet that drew her gaze to the parking lot as she passed by. Still no sign of Mark, but Amber Craig was definitely at work.

She found a spot half a block along and parked. She wasn't quite sure what approach she should take but she knew it had to be done. She hoped their bonding the Christmas before last, over the attitude of some of the male officers to female attendees at staff parties, would guide them into shared confidences. Since that time she had been pleasantly pleased with Amber Craig's friendliness. The officer had even gone out of her way last summer to keep Lizzie posted on the changing focus in two murders involving Bob Miller.

Lizzie nodded at the volunteer at the front desk and peeked around the corner, spotting Craig at her desk.

Amber must have sensed she was being watched because she looked up from her computer screen and after a moment's hesitation, which Lizzie thought also contained a grimace, she waved Lizzie in.

Lizzie glanced at Mark's office as she walked by just to make sure he wasn't in. She knew he could appear at any minute but short of finding out where Craig lived and visiting her at her home, there would always be the possibility of being outed.

"How are you?" Lizzie asked as she sat in the straight-backed chair to the right of Craig's desk. She sat in that chair a few times, usually when giving a witness statement. This time she tried for a more congenial opening.

"The chief told you."

"Uh, yes, I guess you could say that."

Amber slumped back in her swivel chair. "Can't say I'm surprised. And now you want to quiz me, right?"

Lizzie tried to read her face for a hint of how to proceed. Nothing. She was a cop, after all. "I'd hoped you would fill in the blanks. I'm really only interested in what Rafe Shannon was doing in town and whether it had anything to do with Darla Lyman."

"Priority questions for the police, also." Amber stood and walked over to the drip coffee maker on the counter top on the side wall of the room. "Would you like some?" she asked, holding the carafe up for inspection.

"No, I'm fine."

Amber grunted and poured a cup, adding three spoonfuls of sugar and a hefty dose of milk.

Lizzie tried not to make a face. "How do you stay so slender with all that sugar intake?"

"Stress. Makes the calories vanish. And besides, it's the only way to drink this crap. Now, what specifically do you want to know?"

"What do you think he was doing in town?"

"I have no idea. I haven't seen nor heard from him in close to fifteen years. I have heard things, though, at family gatherings. Hard not to. He's been keeping on his collision course with the law in all the years I've been away. Had two short-term stays in prison. And now, apparently, he was back to his old ways." She leaned back again. "He always did play the heavy. No talking through a problem. Of course, being a girl, I never felt his full wrath but a couple of my male cousins ended up with bloody noses over the years. After one of those encounters ended up in the ER for stitches, for another cousin, not Rafe, he was discouraged from attending family gatherings."

"That can be tricky. What about his parents?"

"My aunt Wanda and her idiot husband, who goes a long way in explaining Rafe's behavior. All her siblings felt sorry for her but that was the extent of it. She eventually stopped coming but still kept in contact with my mama and her other sisters until she died a few years ago."

Lizzie hadn't had what she considered to be the luxury of a large extended family and even though she often wished that had been different, it was stories like this, and sometimes Sally-Jo's tales, that made her grateful she'd been an only child with few cousins.

"Hmm. How sad for her. Can you think of any possible connection he might have to Darla?"

"Not unless she worked for thugs or was someone's mistress and ran out on him."

"Then he sent Rafe to bring her back?"

"Could be. Or if she took something this fictional guy wanted, Rafe might be here to collect it. That could be why he was at Ms. Mathews's house. He could have gone there to search for it."

"Like money."

"Yes."

"But we know it's not that because Darla doesn't have any. That's why she stayed with Molly and I'll bet that's why she came here in the first place."

"To hit up her granddaddy for some money?"

Lizzie shrugged. "It's as likely a reason as any."

"You don't think she's here for sentimental reasons?"

"She doesn't come across as being that type of girl."

Amber smiled. "Is this instinct talking?"

"Yes. I'll admit it. But back to Rafe, what's being done to check all this out?"

"I'm afraid I'm not privy to many details about the case, Lizzie. You'll have to ask the chief."

"Huh. Fat lot of good that will do me."

"Well, putting on my police officer cap for a moment, that's a good thing. I'm sure he's already told you to not get involved in the case."

"Perhaps."

"Yeah, as if that will do any good. Look, I'm as interested as you are in finding answers and as much in the dark. I do know that whatever brought him to Ashton Corners is what got him killed."

"I'm sorry for your loss, Amber. He might not have been a nice guy, but he was your cousin and he didn't deserve to die like that."

Amber took a deep breath. "Amen."

Chapter Fourteen

◇◇◇

"And now, seeing you in action, I think that she's right."

MURDER ON BAMBOO LANE—NAOMI HIRAHARA

Lizzie felt anything but refreshed the next morning. She and Mark had enjoyed a leisurely meal of grilled tuna with tomato spaghetti in the evening, which had taken Lizzie what was left of the afternoon to prepare. The romantic nestling on the love seat was the ideal ending to what Lizzie considered to be a perfect evening and would have continued into a cozy breakfast except for Mark's being summoned to the scene of a bad fire around three A.M. He had taken Patchett along with him, planning to head on home later rather than waking her again. Sleep eluded her, though, and she found herself thinking about Darla.

By the time her eyes did close, she'd concluded that going directly to the source for a frank talk was probably a good course of action. If she confronted Darla without anyone else around, and that included the boyfriend, maybe she could convince her to give some straight answers. The worst that could happen was Darla refusing to talk. She'd be no further ahead but at least she would have tried.

To get her energy level up, she took a long run the same route as the day before but at a much faster pace. It still allowed her to enjoy the neighborhood and the array of spring flowers popping up. If there was one thing to be said about Hagan Road it was that the residents loved their flowers. From the brilliant colors of the camellia and peony, to the summer wisteria and hydrangea, the fall hues of the petunias and mums, and then the surprising colors of potted roses and poppies in late winter, this stretch of Ashton Corners could be the poster street for floral beauty throughout the year.

She slowed at the corner of Colonel Drive, to allow herself to enjoy the new landscaping the Bartonnis had just finished having installed. The tiny white picket fence surrounding the mini wooden bench and equally small round table hinted at a fantasy garden, since no one under the age of sixty lived here.

She picked up the pace again and made it over to Glendale Park in record time, doing a loop and heading back into town. As she passed the Cup'n Choc, the aroma of freshly brewed coffee assailed her when the door suddenly opened. If only she'd brought some money. By the time she reached her house, she was ready for an espresso, a shower and breakfast, in that order, before really getting on with her day. She realized, much to her surprise, that she hadn't thought about Darla all morning and now that the thought had appeared, she quickly shoved it back down into her subconscious.

After a shower and breakfast of waffles topped with fresh strawberries and another cup of espresso, Lizzie dressed in a long, lime green lightweight cotton pullover and cream skinny pants. She planned to visit her mama around eleven

and stay for lunch with her today. The cats were roughhous-
ing on the bed while Lizzie dressed, until Edam, the older
Siamese, put an end to it all with a series of serious growls
and hissing. Brie, as usual, took a few minutes and extra
swipes to his face before getting the message.

Lizzie pulled into the long driveway leading up to Magnolia Manor. Not too many cars here today. Where were all
the visitors? Maybe those with younger kids or grandchildren
were already heading out of town for the Easter break. She
parked next to an old Austin-Healey, hunter green, in mint
condition. It was here every weekend. She must find out whom
it belonged to. Although Lizzie didn't consider herself a car
buff, the sight of the Healey brought back some memories
from college days and a carefree, too much so as it turned
out, young man from the English faculty. They'd enjoyed
some adventuresome months and wild drives in that car, until
he'd moved on to his new conquest. Lizzie had, after a much
shorter period of mourning than she'd believed possible, put
him out of her mind. Until now. No way would it be the same
guy. Although, it was a rare car. She shook her head, no way.

She found her mama outside around back, sitting on one
of the swings but not moving. Lizzie sat across from her for
a few minutes, talking about the weather and her week, and
slowly got them rocking. She noticed very quickly Evelyn
seemed to relax once the swing was in motion.

She was wearing a blue and white floral jersey dress and
a delphinium blue cardigan that Lizzie knew was a gift from
Molly. The color enhanced Evelyn's eyes, which had once
sparkled but grown dull over the years.

Eventually, Lizzie turned the talk around to Darla's grandmamma. She was hoping to glean some information that came
from neither Molly's nor Bob's perspective, although Bob
certainly hadn't said much about his ex-wife.

And, of course, Lizzie knew it was almost hopeless to think her mama would tell her anything. It had been many, many years since they'd carried on a conversation. She often found, though, that talking it out to her mama helped to sort through a problem.

"Did you know Bob Miller's wife, Sue-Ann?"

Evelyn kept looking straight at Lizzie but the expression on her face didn't change.

"The reason I'm asking is that their granddaughter is here in Ashton Corners, visiting. Her name is Darla Lyman. Her mama is Lily. Do you remember Lily Miller, Mama?"

Maybe not, but Lizzie proceeded to tell her a bit about Darla but was careful not to mention the murder. She didn't really know what information Evelyn processed and didn't want to take a chance of getting her upset.

"So, Teensy thinks Darla's here strictly for money. I'm tending to believe that, too. But I don't know what to do about it except for asking her straight out. Do you think that's the thing to do, Mama?"

Evelyn's eyes closed. Lizzie took that as a sign of agreement. A few minutes later, she woke her mama and escorted her into the dining hall for lunch.

Lizzie's phone was ringing as she closed the back door to her house behind her. It was Molly inviting her over for Sunday dinner, along with Mark if he was free.

"I'd love to but I'll have to check with Mark. I have no idea about his schedule these days. I guess Darla and her boyfriend will be there, too?"

"They've been invited. Darla didn't say if Wade could make it. Bob is hoping for another chance at grilling him, though."

"I'll bet. The boyfriend didn't make too good of an impression on anyone the other night. Can I let you know about Mark?"

"I'll make plenty. Tell him he can just turn up if he's able." Molly chuckled. "We're getting used to his routines."

Lizzie smiled, happy to be part of such a warm and loving group. "Thanks. See you later."

Maybe Lizzie could suggest this time that she and Darla take a walk through the maze and then she could grill her. Of course, that wouldn't work if the boyfriend was there. He seemed to be the hovering type and there's no way Lizzie wanted him in on this conversation.

Lizzie decided she had time to run the vacuum around the main floor, which might also lead to an idea or two on the Darla question. She often found that doing housework had that effect on her, and the bonus was something got cleaned. Finally.

The cats disappeared as soon as she dragged her aged Hoover out of the closet. She put a John Lee Hooker CD in, even though she knew she'd miss large portions of it, plugged in and set about it. By the time she'd finished the living room and hallway, she'd decided to stop by the motel where Darla was staying and ask if she wanted a ride. She could say that Molly had been uncertain about whether Darla was going alone. If Darla was alone, she could have that talk. Better still if it took place in the car.

She realized she hadn't yet told Mark about dinner and shut off the machine while dialing his home number. No answer. She next tried his cell and ended up leaving a message when he didn't answer. Maybe he was still tied up with the aftermath of the fire. She hadn't thought to turn on the radio this morning to find out what had burned. She had a dread of fires, ever since she'd been a little girl and trapped by a fallen flaming electrical cord in a small cabin her parents had rented for a week's vacation. Her mama had rushed through the flames and scooped up Lizzie, carrying her to safety. It was only many years after Lizzie realized her memory had embellished the story, adding height and density to the flames. However, her mama remained the hero of the hour and her fear of fire had also remained.

By the time she finished cleaning, she had to hurry to get ready. She chose a bright red sweater set and cream-colored pants, fed the cats, and pulled a package of Cajun frozen fried okra out of the freezer, and from the cupboard, a jar of homemade citrus mayonnaise she'd bought at the indoor market just the week before. It wouldn't take long to heat up the okra, and she was dying to taste the mayo. Even though Molly had said not to bring anything, sometimes she remembered her Southern manners.

It took about ten minutes to drive out to the Mountain View Motel on Highway 2. Lizzie pulled into the parking lot and surveyed the five cars and one pickup parked there. She had no idea what Wade Morris drove, so looking around wouldn't help. She parked close to the motel office and went in to ask about a room number.

Back outside, she got her bearings and found number six to be in the far right hand corner, as far away from the office as possible. She heard her footsteps crunching over the gravel that seemed to cover more space than the pavement did. The place gave her the creeps, probably from watching too many cop shows, she thought. As if in one of those shows, she paused before knocking on the door and put her ear to it. She heard music inside but not voices. She took a deep breath and pounded on the door.

"Darla, it's Lizzie Turner."

After waiting for a minute, with no response, Lizzie tried again, this time adding some vigor and volume.

The door was finally pulled open a crack and Darla slid through. "Oh, hey Lizzie. Why are you here?"

"I didn't have a phone number for you or anything and I just wondered if you might need a ride to Molly's tonight, just in case Wade isn't planning to go."

The door was yanked open behind Darla. "Who said I wasn't going?" Wade Morris stood in the doorway, bare chested with his jeans riding low and a challenge in his eyes. "We're both going to be there and I'll bring Darla."

Darla looked like she might be blushing, or else she'd applied a lot of blusher, Lizzie wasn't sure which it was. "Uh, thanks anyway, Lizzie. We're going to be a bit late. See you there."

Wade grabbed Darla's arm and pulled her back inside. He glared at Lizzie before shutting the door.

What was that all about? Lizzie shivered and hurried back to her car. She was getting bad vibes from the guy but she wasn't at all sure why. Did he think she was prying? Okay, maybe she was but she hadn't thought she was that obvious. Although, if Darla had told him Lizzie was the one who put the cops onto her and a connection with the dead guy, maybe he was angry about that. But as far as Lizzie knew, Darla had no idea it was Lizzie who had seen them together.

Lizzie glanced at the motel room window before driving off. She still wanted to talk to Darla. It sounded like the maze was out, too. She'd just have to bide her time.

By the time Lizzie pulled into Molly's driveway, she still hadn't heard from Mark. She parked next to Bob's pickup and pulled out her iPhone, trying to call him once more. It still went to voice mail and she left one saying she'd arrived at Molly's. Either he'd come when he could or he wouldn't. She was getting used to the unpredictable hours of a police chief.

Bob pulled the front door open before she could knock

and walk in. "Uh. Just about ran you down. Sorry. I've got to make an emergency run to the Winn-Dixie for some half-and-half." He hustled down the stairs as Lizzie went in search of Molly.

She found her in the kitchen, peeling carrots. "Can I help?"

Molly scanned the counter top. "I don't think so, honey. It's all in hand. And speaking of which, what's in yours?"

"Oh, I had a bag of frozen okra and just thought I'd bring it, along with some really yummy mayo I've just discovered." Lizzie looked at the counter top and table. "I thought this was a small Sunday supper."

Molly shrugged. "I got a bit carried away. I thought, why cook for six when you can cook for twelve?"

"Twelve? So, Sally-Jo and Jacob, right?"

Molly nodded.

"Stephanie and Roger?"

"That was the plan but she just called to beg off. It seems little Wendy has a cold, or the start of one, and Stephanie thinks it best not to bring her out. She doesn't want to leave her with a babysitter either. I can certainly understand that. Now, I was just going to reset the table."

"I could do that."

Molly shook her head. "Not to worry. I'll get to it and if I don't, well there's way worse things than having too many plates out."

Lizzie shrugged. "Okay, that explains some of the settings but I give, who else?"

"Well, I invited Teensy and she asked if she could bring someone along. I don't have a clue as to who it could be, so don't bother asking. Now, I guess there is one thing you can do and that's take care of your okra." The doorbell rang. "Or rather, would you mind seeing who that is? And I'll just set the okra in the microwave."

Lizzie nodded and went to answer, opening it as the second ring sounded, wondering who it might be as everyone knew to just walk in.

"Hey, again."

Lizzie looked from Darla to Wade, who managed a wide, if not sincere, smile.

"We thought we might as well come early and see if we can be of any help to Molly." Darla led the way inside. "Is Granddaddy here? I don't see his car."

"He's running an errand and will be back any minute. Come on out back."

Lizzie puzzled over this change in plans. From late to early. What was that all about? Molly looked pleased to see them both.

"Can we be of any help?" Darla asked her. Darla looked from Molly to Lizzie and then to Wade. Lizzie noticed he made a subtle movement of his head toward the door.

"I'll bet you've already been helping a lot, Lizzie. Why don't you go outside and relax and take Wade with you so that he's not in the way. Now, Molly, what can I do for you?"

Lizzie wasn't quite sure what to make of that. A new, concerned, helpful Darla? And what had that look from Wade meant? Did he want her out of there and she just refused? Lizzie glanced at him to see his reaction. He looked okay with it all. *Odd.*

"There's nothing that I can think of," Molly said. "Why don't y'all just help yourselves to a drink and go outside, enjoy this great weather, while I finish this up. It won't take but a few minutes."

Wade helped himself to a beer, not bothering to ask the women what they wanted. He was taking a drink out of the bottle when Lizzie heard a knock and the front door opened. Sally-Jo and Jacob appeared through the hallway door and greeted everyone.

"I've brought a pecan pie I baked this morning," Sally-Jo explained as she cleared a spot on the counter for it. "I've been baking up a storm this weekend." She giggled. "It helps to keep me calm."

Jacob grimaced but Sally-Jo didn't notice.

"You leave tomorrow for your mama's, don't you?" Molly asked. She put the pot of carrots on the back burner of the stove and walked over to Sally-Jo. "How are things going in that department, honey?"

Sally-Jo shrugged. "I guess I'll find out tomorrow. As of this minute, we're still at an impasse and I'm no way any wiser as to what to do about it."

Jacob put an arm around Sally-Jo's shoulders. "I'll just bet when you get down there and are talking to her in person, she'll feel more included in the plans and then go along with what you want. I'm sure she wants what will make you happy."

"I'm sure any mama feels that way," Molly added. "She would be feeling a bit out of all the planning excitement we've been lucky to share. I'm sure Jacob is right. Once you're there and possibly asking for her input on some of the other items, she'll be more likely to give way when it comes to your dress."

"You think so?" Sally-Jo sounded a bit more optimistic.

Lizzie noticed Wade shake his head and pull Darla toward the door.

"I do," said Molly. "Now, I want all you young people to go outside and sit and enjoy some drinks and starters—Sally-Jo, you'll just pull them out of the fridge, won't you—and let me get on with what needs to happen indoors. Scoot, now."

Lizzie was about to follow the others outside when Teensy arrived, dressed in a vivid red caftan trimmed with shimmering gold, and an older man in tow. Lizzie almost dropped the plate she was carrying when she realized the man was Stanton

Giles, her music director. He noticed her at the same time and grinned, a little embarrassed, Lizzie thought.

"Y'all, I want to introduce Stanton Giles," Teensy said, adding Bob, who'd just slipped into the kitchen behind them, to the sweep of her arm. "Of course, you would know him, wouldn't you, Lizzie? He's the wonderful, accomplished director of Lizzie's choir and I do so love classical music, as y'all know."

Lizzie avoided looking at Molly, certain she wouldn't be able to keep a straight face. First time she'd ever heard of Teensy's passion for music. Oh well, Stanton was a grown man, Lizzie told herself. And he was probably in for a very good time or a bumpy ride. She wasn't quite sure just which it was and probably would never find out, she realized. Not that she wanted to.

"It's very nice to see you, Stanton," Lizzie said. "We're just starting with drinks out on the patio."

"Oh, yes, let's join them," Teensy said, "or do you need my help, Mopsy?"

"No, you go on out and meet the others. You, too, Bob. I need some space and some quiet to perform some magic."

After Teensy had done the rounds of introductions, she accepted a white wine spritzer from Bob, much to his surprise, and sat down very close to Stanton on the wicker love seat. "How long have you lived in Ashton Corners, Stanton?"

Lizzie leaned a little closer. She didn't know very much about the guy either, and now that he might be entering their little group, she was curious. She was just about to ask him something herself when Mark Dreyfus came out the kitchen door, carrying a tray of white wine spritzers.

"I guess I'm the official booze server," he said, winking at Lizzie.

Sally-Jo leapt off her seat and took the tray from him. "I

hate to see a member of law enforcement having to moon-light."

"You never say that to me," Jacob said in a pseudo-whisper.

Everyone burst out laughing. Lizzie noticed Darla rolled her eyes at Wade, who made a cutting motion against his throat. She suddenly felt chilled.

Mark pulled up a chair beside her and gave her hand a squeeze. "I'm afraid it's another eat and run night."

"No matter. I'm glad you're here. Molly is, too."

After about twenty minutes, Molly appeared at the door. "Y'all come on in."

They settled in their seats quickly with Bob and Molly as anchors at each end of the large dinner table. The pale peach damask cloth served as the perfect backdrop to the large cen-terpiece of cut flowers from Molly's garden. Almost the entire top of the table was covered with serving dishes, cutlery and everyone's plates. It looked like Molly had worked all day but Lizzie knew from experience how efficient she was when it came to entertaining large numbers of hungry people.

Lizzie was pleased to be seated next to Teensy. She hoped to quiz her about how she came to know Stanton Giles well enough to ask him to dinner. She'd just have to wait for her chance. Partway through the meal, it presented itself. Stan-ton was in deep conversation with Jacob, so Lizzie leaned into Teensy. "Okay, spill. How do you know Stanton?"

Teensy giggled and looked over at Stanton. "He is quite a catch, isn't he, sugar? Why that mane of white hair. It makes him so artistic looking, so virile."

Lizzie almost choked on the sip of wine she'd just taken.

"It's quite romantic, the way we met. I was at the Valley Gardening Center, struggling to load a bag of peat moss into the trunk of my car, and he assisted me."

"Romantic?"

"Yes. Chivalrous. I like that in a gentleman, especially one so handsome. Well, one thing led to another and he asked me out to dinner. This is our second date." She sounded very pleased with herself.

"And you didn't think to mention this? You know he's my choir director."

Teensy patted Lizzie's hand. "I didn't want to jinx it, sugar. He's my first beau after the disaster last summer with our former mayor."

She looked so hopeful that Lizzie gave her a quick hug. "Fingers crossed."

As Andie set the dessert in front of everyone, Bob asked Darla what her plans were now that Wade was in town. Molly looked at the pair seated to her right, a fork in her right hand held at half-mast.

Darla squirmed in her chair. "Well, I hadn't planned this to be so public but I'd kind of like to stick around a while longer. And get to know you better, Granddad. But we've still got this problem of not having enough money to stay on. And we can't keep mooching off you forever." She sounded sincere.

Lizzie looked sharply at Darla, trying to detect any subtext but she seemed truly apologetic. *Maybe Molly is right. Cut her some slack.*

"We're sort of in need of some cash for food and stuff. There's a microwave in the motel and we're trying to save money by eating in as much as possible. But then there's the rent."

Molly cleared her throat, drawing everyone's attention. "I have a suggestion."

Darla's face lit up.

"We're planning a gigantic book sale to raise funds for

the literacy program here in town. Both Lizzie and Sally-Jo teach classes that meet here in my house. The other book club in town, Readers Are Us, has taken on a book sale as their main community project this year and they're donating the funds to the literacy program. So, I volunteered our group to help out. The more hands the better, you know." Molly looked at Lizzie, who nodded. "Anyway, Darla, long story short, we're collecting donations and sorting them starting next week at the community center during Easter break. Maybe you and Wade would help out and we'll pay you a salary."

Lizzie glanced at Wade in time to see the shocked look on his face before it was replaced by something more neutral. Lizzie knew that Molly would be paying that bill but at least it would get them more help and also put an end to the handouts.

"And, maybe we could also talk about you doing some shifts in my bookstore, A Novel Plot, Darla."

"Uh, sure." Darla glanced at Wade and narrowed her eyes. "That makes me feel a whole lot better. I sure do hate asking for money."

"Great idea," Wade added, not sounding at all like he meant it, and took a large drink of his beer.

Molly beamed. "That's set, then. Lizzie is in charge so she'll tell you when you're needed and what to do. Now, coffee anyone?"

Lizzie kept looking toward the door into the activity room at the community center the next morning. She had five volunteers helping sort the books that had been dropped off at the center over the past few weeks, and she was waiting for Darla and Wade to arrive. She'd asked them to be there at ten. It was half past and still no sign of them. She sighed. She knew they wouldn't work out.

Andie hauled a box of books over to where Lizzie stood sorting through her own large one. "These look to all be big picture books, you know the kind my mama leaves around for everyone to see? The ones that scream, 'I have excellent taste.'"

"Coffee-table books. Let's have a look." Lizzie grinned as she pulled out a couple of home decorating hardcovers and two travel books on Italy. "These are in great condition. If all the rest of them are also, we'll just put them in the individually priced section. Why don't you put the box over at the end table for sorting?

"Okay. I thought the dream team were coming and helping to pick up boxes that are being donated. I have the list ready to go."

Lizzie sighed. "I know. Hopefully they'll arrive soon. Do you need a map?"

"Naw. I know most of these streets. They've been divided up so that all five stops are in the same area." Andie tugged at the silver ring attached to her lip. Lizzie cringed, hoping it wouldn't start bleeding. "They're not the most reliable, are they?"

"No. But I'm hoping they'll get into the swing of things once they get started here."

"Do you think she's out to fleece Bob?"

"Why do you say that?"

Andie shrugged. "Well, it's like she just shows up and Molly takes her in. Then he shows up and Bob pays for their motel. And now, they're being paid to do, what? Nothing, by the looks of it."

"It's hard to turn away a grandchild, and Molly wants to help as much as she can."

"Yeah, but like, those two don't even seem to be grateful. They take the money and that's it."

"Interesting observation."

Andie shrugged. "I don't like them."

"Stephanie seems to like Darla."

"That's because she feels sorry for her. I guess she can relate a bit. She came here with no money and no friends a couple of years ago. But she wasn't looking for a handout."

"It's really not up to us what happens moneywise."

"I know. And then, there's this murder. I think something fishy is going on there, too. Like, this stranger is going to just show up and get killed right after another stranger shows up and gets taken in."

A small part of Lizzie was just a tiny bit pleased that someone else agreed with her, but she quickly banished that thought. She also knew this wasn't the kind of talk that should be getting around. "We can't jump to conclusions."

"No and that's why we should be doing more to find out what happened to the guy."

The door banged noisily against the wall as it was pushed open. "Here they are now." Lizzie went over to meet them, with Andie close behind.

"Sorry we're late," Darla mumbled. "What do ya want us to do?" she asked as she looked around at the activity in the room. Wade stood watching but not saying anything.

"I'd like you to drive around to some homes and pick up their boxes of donations. It's nice to have a guy to help with this. Andie will go with you. She knows the streets, and of course, you'll be paid for your gas."

Darla shrugged. "Hokay." She glanced at Andie. "Where to?"

Andie grabbed her jacket and led them back through the door. Lizzie breathed a bit easier. She'd been wondering if there'd be resistance to the task, although Wade didn't look any too pleased. He was Darla's responsibility, though. If he wanted money, he'd have to do what was asked of him. It was that easy. Although Lizzie had imagined it would be hard.

She went back to the box she'd been sorting and kept at her task until the three returned an hour later.

"Did you have any problems?" Lizzie asked.

Darla answered. "Nope. Where should we put these boxes? Wade got the dolly and is bringing in some of the heavier ones."

Lizzie pointed out where the girls should leave their load, then she looked out into the hall for Wade. Darla and Andie were chatting away as they opened the boxes. Lizzie went out to look for Wade. She opened the back door to the parking lot and pulled back before stepping outside. Wade stood hunched over, deep in discussion with a shorter male over at the corner of the building. When the second guy turned slightly, Lizzie recognized him. The same guy who had been issued a trespass notice the night of the literacy class last week. He'd caused quite a commotion. Eddie Riser. That was his name. Now why was Wade talking so intently to him?

Chapter Fifteen

◇◇◇

I couldn't begin to guess.

SPEAKING FROM AMONG THE BONES—
ALAN BRADLEY

"Why would Wade Morris be talking to that guy?"
Lizzie asked Mark later that evening when he called.

"Maybe just asking about the town or maybe he was trying to buy some drugs. I'll have the guys keep an eye on the parking lot if Eddie Riser is back to ignoring trespass notices. That's been one of Riser's favorite haunts in the past."

"Why don't you just arrest him?"

"We're trying to find his boss. Arresting Riser would just be a minor setback for him."

"I wouldn't put it past Wade to be buying drugs."

"You don't like him either, do you?"

"No and for the same reason as my feelings about Darla. I think he's trying to take advantage of Bob and Molly."

"But he was there working today, earning his keep?"

"Yes," she admitted reluctantly. "He did go and pick up the

boxes of donations and then schlep them inside. Mind you, they arrived late and left much earlier than the other volunteers."

"Well, you could mention it to Molly. She's paying them after all."

"No I can't. It wouldn't do any good, anyway. She's sure this will ensure they stay around awhile and don't keep borrowing from Bob. She's probably right about that. Do you have any more news about the murder?"

"Nothing that I'm about to share. And, I'm glad to see you're keeping your investigative instincts under control."

Lizzie flashed briefly on the fact that Jacob had just called with word from his lawyer friend about Rafe Shannon. She knew Mark already was aware of the fact that Shannon had been recently released from prison after serving three years for extortion. And, that the Lucky Roller Casino had him on the payroll as a bouncer. But none of that explained what he was doing in Ashton Corners.

"Is Darla still a suspect?"

"She's involved in some way but I don't think she killed him. I know she's hiding something, though. I thought Bob might get her to confide in him but so far that hasn't worked."

"She's friendliest with Stephanie. Maybe we could ask her to do some probing."

"*We* will not. I don't like the idea of involving a citizen in a police investigation, as you may be aware. Besides, my investigation is proceeding as it should. Amber Craig is on a visit to be with her family in Atlanta. She plans to look into Rafe Shannon's dealings while she's there, of course."

"Some holiday."

"It was her idea."

"I don't doubt it, because you'd have her on desk duty otherwise, wouldn't you? I know all about this notion of not being involved when you're connected to the victim. Or suspect," she added, thinking back to her own recent dance with the police, and Mark's removing himself from questioning her.

Mark cleared his throat, then asked, "Now, how about we talk about something else for a change, like when can we get together?"

"That's entirely up to you. It's your murder investigation that's intruding on our plans. Which is why I thought you'd like a little help."

Mark chortled. "Nice try, Lizzie. I think I might just be able to tear myself away for a cup of coffee later."

"I'm holding you to that."

Lizzie checked her email before going to bed. A couple of the digests she belonged to had come in and she scanned the topic headings, choosing the items of interest, rather than reading the entire digests. She was just about to close down the computer for the evening when a chat message pinged. She checked. It was from Sally-Jo.

> I've been here 12 hours and have already tried on three dresses. All DREADFUL!!! My mama is driving me nuts. Missing the gang already. I'd rather be talking about solving a murder than planning a wedding. How bad is that???

Lizzie shook her head and messaged back.

> Nothing new in murder department. Hope dress department does better tomorrow. We miss you, too. Look on the bright side. Once you get through all this you'll be a happily married woman.

> Hah. If I live that long. Over and out. Xoxo

Lizzie looked at the clock. After ten already and no sign of Mark. He must have headed home instead. She shoved the feeling of disappointment aside and grabbed a glass of water to take upstairs. The phone rang as she was about to start up the stairs. *Mark!*

She checked the call display as she answered. Teensy. Awfully late for her to be calling.

"Hey Lizzie, I know it's late and I do apologize, but can I stop by tomorrow morning? I'd like you to take a look at some chapters one of my students in my creative writing class has turned in."

"Uh, sure. Why do you want me to read it?"

"I value your opinion, that's why. I do have some concerns, though. Look, it might be nothing but I just want to see what you think."

"Uh, nice and mysterious Teensy."

"Sometimes."

"Why don't you come over around ten and I'll have the coffee ready?"

"Lovely. And I'll bake up a fresh batch of my delicious lemon cranberry scones in the morning to bring over, shall I?"

"Uh-oh. More calories."

"As if you have to worry, sugar. Nighty-night, now."

Lizzie wondered what that was about but she was happy Teensy had been deflected from heading to Atlanta to confront Darla's mama. She'd just reached the top of the stairs when the phone rang again. Mark this time.

"I'm sorry, babe, but I just woke up. I took Patchett for a walk when I got home and then sat down to read the paper and well, look at the time."

"Don't worry about it. I was just heading to bed myself."

"Maybe I should come over in that case."

"And fall promptly back to sleep? I think not. Why don't

you rest up and we'll continue this conversation another night?" she suggested playfully.

"I'm on it."

Lizzie flipped through the four chapters that Teensy had just handed her. "What are you hoping I'll find or not find, Teensy?"

"I don't want to say. Why don't you take a few minutes and read it over. It won't take long. Is that okay?"

"Sure." Lizzie shrugged. She'd been planning to do some housework this morning but she always took advantage of a reason not to. She topped up both their coffees and carried her mug and the papers into the living room, with Teensy trailing after her. She sat in one of the taupe wicker chairs and watched while Teensy made herself comfortable on the green-striped love seat in front of the window. Teensy lifted her mug toward Lizzie, as if saluting her or daring her, and took a bite of a scone, then a long drink of coffee. Lizzie started to read.

Teensy had been right. It was a fast read. When she'd finished, Lizzie tidied up the papers and sat back to look at Teensy. "What do you want to know?"

"Where do you think this story is heading?"

"An abusive husband. A woman who finally, after years of being under his thumb has started to think of a life for herself. Maybe she's going to eventually leave him?"

"Fannie, that's the writer, Fannie Hewitt, told me it was going to be a murder mystery. So who's your best bet to be the victim?"

"It looks like it's the wife's story, so it won't be her. My money is on the husband, at the moment anyway."

"Uh-huh. That's exactly what I thought. And who do you think is the best candidate for the murderer?"

"Well, the way it stands now, either the wife or someone she hires to do the job, or someone, maybe in her family, who is sick and tired of what's going on and decides to remedy it. What's this all about, Teensy?"

"You think like a writer, Lizzie. All those possibilities. You should try your hand at it someday."

"Probably not but thanks for the suggestion. Now, what's gotten you so fired up?"

"She's a good writer, don't you think?"

Lizzie nodded and tried not to show the fact that she was getting tired of the twenty questions game.

"But she's a first-time writer and she's so into the character's head, I think that's because it's her own head. I think she might be writing her own story and she's planning to kill her husband."

"That's quite a leap, Teensy. Do you know if she's being abused at home?"

"She does have the odd bruise, now that I think back on it. And that one really hot day we had last month? Remember, we all said the weather gods were teasing us? Well, she actually wore a turtleneck to class that day."

"You know, you could be reading things into her behavior now that you've read this story."

Teensy pushed herself off the love seat and started pacing around the small room. "I know. I've told myself that. But it's what you might call a gut instinct, a writer's instinct, and it's telling me that something else is happening here."

"A writer's instinct." Lizzie hid her smile. "If you were writing the story, what would happen next?"

"Exactly what is happening. Fannie would be going to the library to research methods of murder."

"How do you know that's what's happening?"

"I've seen it with my own eyes. I ran into her in the library last week and I asked what she was doing. She said she was doing research for her book. She was in the medical section, Lizzie. You know, poisons and such."

Lizzie stopped to think about it. She was sure Teensy was raising the alarm bells where none were needed. It would be just like her to let her imagination run away with her.

"Well she wouldn't be so dumb as to write the actual story of a murder she's about to commit, would she? You'd think someone, like the police, would clue in and there's the evidence of their killer."

"We haven't read the end of the story yet. She may have figured a way out of being caught."

Lizzie leaned back in her chair and sighed. "I understand what you're saying and why you're saying it, but I really do think you may be reacting a bit too soon or too drastically."

"Would you meet with her?"

"What?"

"I'll set you up to have a coffee with her and just get to know her a bit. See what vibes you get from her."

"Don't you think that would look strange?"

"Well, maybe," she hedged. "I know, I'll invite her for coffee, say it's to talk about her manuscript and then you just stop on by. That would work, don't you think?"

"It would but I'm not sure to what avail. Don't you think you're maybe relying a bit too much on your instinct?"

Teensy sat down again, her back ramrod straight. "As you are with your distrust of Darla?"

"Ouch." Lizzie managed a small smile. "I guess you're right about that. But what if Fannie is writing this story as a cathartic relief? She deals with it all on paper and then can move on. Maybe she'll even leave the guy, if this is a true story. Murder is really an extreme reaction and I'm not entirely convinced that it's a reasonable option for most people."

"You can say that with so many people being murdered around here in the last few years?"

"Well, there is that."

"Look, I'm just saying, come by the house, talk with her awhile. Just get a feel for the woman. All right?"

Lizzie sighed. "Sure. Fine. You can let me know when it's arranged."

"Tomorrow at three."

"What? You were awfully sure of yourself."

"Of course I am, sugar. The class ends at two thirty and I invited her over right after, so we can talk about her book. She was very eager to accept." Teensy pulled her cell phone out of her pocket as she stood. She checked the screen. "I'd better get going. I have a dentist appointment in half an hour. Not my favorite thing. Thanks for the coffee, sugar."

"Well, thanks for bringing those delicious scones."

Teensy linked her arm through Lizzie's as they walked to the door. "My pleasure, for sure. You know, maybe you should think about this murder at Molly's as a novel. Write your own story for it and see if it helps figure out what happened. Anyway, see you tomorrow."

She squeezed Lizzie's arm and left. Lizzie thought about the suggestion as she tidied up. If the murder of Rafe Shannon were a novel, she'd need to know what he was doing in Ashton Corners. That had to be part of the reason, at the very least, as to why he was killed. She had been planning to stop by the community center and check on how the sorting of the books was progressing. She'd include a stop at the police station, on the way.

* * *

Mark put the papers he was thumbing through into a neat pile on the center of his desk and gave Lizzie his full attention. "Do you have some new evidence that I should be aware of? Is that why you're back in here with more questions about Rafe Shannon?"

"No, it's just that I thought you might have some new answers. Like, why was he in Ashton Corners? Surely, that's why he was killed."

"Do you not think I'm good at my job?"

Lizzie hesitated. Where was he going with this? "Of course, I do. You're an excellent police chief."

"Then why don't you trust me to do it? When I have a murder suspect in custody, I will let you know."

"Because Bob is still worried about Darla. That's why, although I really do trust you. Is she still a suspect?"

"She hasn't been eliminated but I don't think she did it, as I already told you."

"So, you think she's involved in some way?"

"Perhaps. And that's the best I can do for you at the moment."

"So his boss didn't send him?"

"He had many bosses."

"What about the casino."

"That boss says no."

"And have you heard from Amber Craig? Does her family have any news of him?"

"Nothing we don't already know. It seems he didn't keep in touch with his relatives a lot lately."

"Why lately?"

"That's just a figure of speech. I didn't mean that specifically." Mark leaned back in his chair with his hands folded behind his head. He looked to be enjoying this.

"What about his belongings? Any clues in them?"

"Nothing suspicious."

"Where was he staying?"

Mark thought for a moment. "I guess it won't hurt to tell you. The Mountain View Motel."

"That's the same place that Darla and her boyfriend are staying," Lizzie pointed out.

"Could be because it's the cheapest one in town."

"True."

"Shannon checked in one day after Darla appeared and by then she had checked out of the motel and moved in with Molly. And Wade Morris didn't show up until another two days later."

Lizzie studied the calendar on his desk. She sighed. "So, no overlap at the motel."

"No. Good try, though. By the way, have you heard from Sally-Jo?"

"We connected on chat message last night saying she was already driven to distraction. Hopefully, she'll get back to me again tonight."

"Good. Now, why don't you put all this thinking of yours to finding a way to help her with her problem," he said, standing and walking over to Lizzie, turning her toward the door and giving her a slight nudge in that direction. "I have to get back to work. Not that this hasn't been fun." He gave her a light kiss on the lips and opened the door for her.

"Likewise, I'm sure."

Chapter Sixteen

◇◇◇

Tomorrow morning, she'd find out. Whatever was true was good.

THE WRONG GIRL—HANK PHILLIPPI RYAN

Lizzie drove home trying to think up plots in order to get more information on Rafe Shannon's stay in Ashton Corners. The best she could come up with was going to the motel and trying to get some details from the clerk there. But she knew she shouldn't go alone. Maybe it would be a good idea to get some more input first. As soon as she arrived home she called Molly first to make sure it was okay, then called the other book club members, hoping to have them all stop by Molly's that evening. For drinks. But really, to talk murder.

Jacob was the only one who couldn't make it because of a meeting with a client that evening. The others arrived at Molly's at the usual time.

"What did you have in mind?" Molly asked, as she passed around a plate of cheese straws. Bob helped himself to three and turned to Lizzie.

"Does this have anything to do with the murder?"

"Yes, it does. As far as I know, it's not solved and Darla is still a suspect. Is that right?"

Bob nodded. "I've been trying my darnedest to get in on the investigation but I'm being stonewalled. I know in my heart and my brain that Darla is not a murderer. I say that not only because she's my grandchild but I've gotten to be a pretty good judge of character over the years. So, what did you have in mind, Lizzie, because I'm all for it."

Lizzie took a sip of her tea and then explained her plan. "So, I think I should find out who was on at the front desk around the time that Rafe Shannon may have checked in, then ask that person if he said anything or asked any questions, anything that might give us a lead. Because I'm pretty sure the reason he came to town is the reason he was murdered."

"That makes sense to me, but you're not the best person to get that information. I think I should go," Bob said.

"But what if Darla or Wade spots you? They're staying in the same motel that Shannon did, after all."

"They are? How do you know that?"

"Mark admitted Shannon had a room at the Mountain View Motel. So, I should go."

"And me," Andie said quickly.

"Oh, no," Bob said adamantly, shaking his head. "Way too dangerous for you, young lady."

"Why, because of my age? That's just it. They won't suspect anything, whoever they are, if they see me with Lizzie. We're just two chicks asking about a guy."

"Well. When you put it that way, I definitely say 'no.'"

"All right, maybe that wasn't the best way but still, it should seem less threatening, don't you think?"

Bob looked at Lizzie, who smiled back. "I guess. But I'm going to be sitting out in my car parked on the street in front of the motel and the first sign of trouble, you two get out and get back to my car. Deal?"

"Deal," Lizzie and Andie said at the same time.

"In fact, if the clerk even becomes a bit suspicious about why you're asking questions, you hightail it. Right?"

They both nodded.

"Okay, then." He finished off his cheese straw and reached for another.

"Has Darla mentioned anything to you, Stephanie?" Lizzie asked, holding the plate of cheese straws so that Stephanie could choose one without having to lay Wendy down. It had taken just over twenty minutes of walking around Molly's library to get Wendy to sleep.

"Thanks. We haven't really had a chance to talk much since Wade came into town. At first, I thought Darla and I might be able to spend some time together after work. But we only did that once."

"What did you do?"

"Umm, we met for a mocha latte at the Cup'n Choc. We'd planned to then go to see a movie but I was so tired having been up with Wendy most of the night that I begged off. It's too bad. I would have liked to get to know her better."

"You still might have that opportunity," Bob offered.

"I hope so. But I tried calling her and Wade answered. He told me she was busy and she never called back, even though I asked him to give her a message. I think he didn't do that."

"That's too bad," Lizzie said. *In more ways than one.* So much for getting Stephanie to ask some probing questions of Darla.

Molly served a fresh round of tea. "I worry about her with that Wade."

Bob nodded. "So do I, but I'm at a loss here. I just don't know what to do. How much to interfere with her life."

Molly touched Bob's hand. "I guess we just wait and hope for the best."

Bob picked up Lizzie at nine A.M. on the nose the next morning, but they had to wait a couple of minutes at Andie's house. She ran down the front steps and hopped into the backseat, all apologetic.

Lizzie turned around to take a closer look at the outfit she wore. An orange and black T-shirt with denim shorts, complete with ragged hemline. *Not very nondescript.* She didn't say anything, though.

Bob dug into his jacket pocket and pulled out a photo. "Now, here you go. You'll probably have trouble establishing a date he stayed, but just flash this picture around and it might jog some memories."

"Where did you get this?" Lizzie asked. "Or shouldn't I ask?"

"Let's just say, a few favors are owed. Now then, if you gals are ready, let's get going."

Lizzie drummed her fingers on the armrest. She was itching to get going and finally find out some answers. She looked over at Bob. "Do you happen to know what Wade drives?"

"Why? What are you planning on doing, sticking a tracking device under it?" Bob asked with a chortle.

"Hadn't thought of that. No, I just wondered so that I'll know it when I see it."

"Well, it's pretty nondescript from head-on. A red Ford pickup from the late nineties, I'd say. The paint's dulled by the sun. But on the driver's side there's a stick-on of a lizard. Looks much the same as that one crawling down his arm." Bob grinned.

Lizzie shuddered. "Yuck."

"Exactly." He turned right at the next corner onto Highway 2 and took the short drive to the Mountain View Motel. He pulled up to the curb on the street across from the motel and slipped a ten-dollar bill into Lizzie's handbag as she exited the car. "I've found this is a good memory refresher, too."

Lizzie nodded and together with Andie, crossed the street and entered the small office at the front of the motel. She glanced around the small, somewhat dingy room. The walls were an off-white, probably more from the dirt than any decorating plan. A couple of old vinyl kitchen chairs flanked an end table with some yellowing magazines on it. The calendar hanging on the wall across from it was from 2009.

The front counter had some menus from a pizza delivery down the street and a bell but no clerk. She hit the bell and they waited while hearing noises from a back room, sounding like someone struggling to get through a mess of stuff. Finally the door opened and a glowering middle-aged man appeared, with a few strands of dark hair held down to his scalp with some kind of product, the only hair on his head. His face actually lit up when he saw who awaited him. Lizzie wished he would close his mouth so she wouldn't see his yellowed teeth. The top four buttons of his blue short-sleeved shirt were open to reveal a mass of gold chains in varying widths around his neck.

"What can I do for yourselves?"

Lizzie pasted a pleasant smile on her face to cover her unease. "We're sorry to bother you but we have a couple of questions we hope you don't mind answering." She smiled brightly and gave Andie a gentle nudge with her foot to do the same. "We have this person's name, Rafe Shannon, and we know he stayed here a few days last week." She pulled out the photo and showed it to him. "We're just wondering if he gave you any hint as to what he was doing here. Maybe he asked about someone or something?" She smiled again.

"Are you cops?" His scowl was back.

"No. No, we're definitely not cops. In fact, I'm sure they'd be upset if they knew we were here asking these questions." She hoped full disclosure might help.

"So, why are you asking them, then?"

"We're just trying to help out a very dear old friend, old being the operative word here," Lizzie answered with as much sincerity, and a touch of begging, as she could muster.

The clerk sighed, looked at the picture again and put it back down. "What's in it for me?"

Andie said, "Look, mister. Wouldn't it just feel good to do something that would be a big help to someone in trouble?"

"I only have your word for that, kid. And besides that, I'm in trouble all the time, too. The money kind, as in, I don't have any."

Lizzie pulled out the ten that Bob had given her and tucked it under the photo.

The clerk folded his arms and stared at her.

She knew when she was beaten. She dug into her wallet and pulled out another ten. "That's all I have. I'm in need of money, too."

He grabbed it out of her hand and scooped up the bill from the counter. "He checked in last Sunday. Said he'd be here for two, maybe three nights depending on how long it took him to do his business."

"Had Wade Morris checked in by that time?"

"Nope. Only person from Atlanta was that young chick he shacked up with later. "

"Darla Lyman?"

"That's the one."

"When did she arrive?"

"Saturday."

"And she moved out on Sunday so she just missed Rafe Shannon."

"If you say so. 'Cause she never totally checked out."

"She'd kept the room even after she moved to Molly's?"

"How do I know where she went?"

"But she held on to her room all week."

"That's what I just said. In fact, she still has it. Same one she's sharing with Wade Morris."

Andie leaned her arm on the counter and narrowed her eyes. "How do you remember so much? All their names and dates and all that?"

"'Cause the cops asked me the same thing." His grin looked more like a leer.

Of course they did. "Did Rafe Shannon say anything about what brought him here?" Lizzie brought the topic back to her original plan.

"The next morning, he asked if the food at the Red Spot a few blocks over was any good. That's it."

"That's close to the community center. Did he ask any questions about the center?"

"Nope. That's the only thing he asked. The missus was here with me and that night he stopped in and asked for a city map. She asks him how he liked the food at the Red Spot. He says that it was okay. In fact, everything was falling into place and would be okay. That's what he said. That's it. The next day the cops come by and tell me he's dead."

"What happened to his stuff?"

"It's locked in a storage room here until someone comes to claim it. Some relative or something. I'm to keep it for a month, that's the law, then I can do whatever I like with it."

"I don't suppose you'd let us have a quick look through it?"

"I don't suppose you've got another twenty in that purse of yours?"

Lizzie shook her head. He shook his in return.

"Thanks, anyway," she said as she grabbed Andie's arm and pulled her out of the office.

"Twenty bucks," Andie snorted in disgust. "What a racket."

"I didn't like the idea of spending any more money on this. The police have gone through his things so I'm sure they know if anything suspicious was in there. I wonder who'll claim it." *Amber Craig?*

They waited until three cars had driven past and then made a beeline for Bob's truck. Lizzie told him everything that had happened, except for the bit about Darla never really checking out, and waited for a response.

"That doesn't give us much that's new," he finally said.

"Well, it does put him in the vicinity of the community center, and if that guy who's dealing drugs was hanging around then, that could be a clue."

"What guy?"

Uh-oh. Lizzie remembered too late that she hadn't filled Bob in on having seen Wade talking to Eddie Riser, the suspected dealer. She'd wanted to keep that from him but now she had to tell all. When she'd finished, Bob grabbed onto the steering wheel. "I knew there was something fishy about that Wade Morris guy. I can always trust my instincts and this time they're telling me he's no good for Darla. But how to make her see that?"

"You can't just tell her that," Andie ventured. "You know she'll get all defensive and maybe not even talk to you anymore. Isn't that why she moved away from her mama?"

A look of pain crossed Bob's face. "You're right, of course.

But I have to do something to protect her. Any suggestions?"
He looked at Lizzie and then at Andie, who sat in the back.

"I think you've got to out him when he's doing something illegal, like buying drugs. That should do it. That is, if Darla doesn't already know about it," Andie offered.

"Oh, I don't think she'd be involved in any way," Bob was quick to say.

Lizzie said, "You don't really know that, do you?"

Bob sighed. "You're right. It's what I want to believe and until I learn otherwise, that's what I'll go by. I have to, Lizzie. She's my kin."

"I know. So tell me what our next step should be."

"I just think I'll track down this punk who's dealing and have a little talk with him, see if he's willing to answer some questions, since they won't be official ones. Riser may remember me from his younger days. I'm hoping so, anyway."

"Uh-oh. I know a police chief who's going to hit the ceiling when he hears about that."

"But he won't, will he?"

"Not if you take me along with you."

"Me, too," Andie piped in.

"No," Bob and Lizzie said in unison.

"I appreciate your help today, Andie, but it really could get too dangerous. And if anything ever happened to you. . . ." She let it taper off. "Besides, could you imagine what your mama would do to me?"

"That would get her attention, for sure."

"Why don't you come and help out tomorrow at the community center, Bob? We're sorting more books and that would give you a good reason to just hang out around there and see if this guy shows up. He's obviously not worried about the trespass notice and if he's doing good business there, he may turn up again. It's a start anyway."

"Good idea. I'll be there."

"So will I," Andie said.

Lizzie checked the clock in her car as she pulled up out front of Teensy's rental house on Lee Street. Three o'clock on the nose. Teensy would be pleased.

Her knock on the door was answered by a surprised-looking Teensy. For a second, Lizzie wondered if she'd gotten it all wrong but Teensy gave her a wink before she turned around and announced her arrival.

"What a surprise, Lizzie. I'm so glad you dropped in, though. Just passing by? Anyway, I want you to meet a student of mine." She grabbed Lizzie's arm and ushered her into the living room to the right of the entry. "This is Fannie Hewitt and this is Lizzie Turner. She's a dear friend and also, a reading specialist with the school board. Hmm, while you're here, maybe you can have a quick read of Fannie's manuscript and give her a brief evaluation. Would you mind doing that?"

She focused on Fannie. "Wouldn't that be fun? Do you mind if she reads it, Fannie?"

Fannie obviously did mind a bit or else she was so taken aback that she didn't know what to say, Lizzie thought. She would wait her out.

"Uh, sure. I guess. I mean, it's not really ready for anyone to read it, except for Teensy. But that's because she's the teacher."

"Yes," Teensy jumped in, "and so is Lizzie so that's what makes her stopping by so opportune. She won't be real critical, will you, sugar?"

"I would be interested in reading it, Fannie, but only if it doesn't make you too uncomfortable."

Fannie shrugged. "I guess not. It's always better to have extra input and I'm sure not showing it to my husband." She laughed but Lizzie didn't hear any joy in it.

Fannie passed the sheets of paper she'd been holding over to Lizzie.

"Would you like some lemonade, Lizzie? Or maybe something stronger?"

Lizzie noted what looked to be Jack Daniel's in the glass beside one of the chairs, obviously where Teensy had been sitting. "Lemonade would be just fine, thanks."

"Fannie's one of my top students," Teensy said as she poured from the pitcher on the side table. "I'm sure you'll see what I mean when you read it." The sleeve of her multicolored caftan brushed Lizzie's arm as she swept back to her chair.

Lizzie took a sip, aware that they were both watching her. She glanced up at Teensy, who got the point.

"Now, Fannie, you were telling me about your garden. Why don't you continue while Lizzie takes a few minutes to read?"

Lizzie tuned out the talk about gardening while she quickly scanned the papers, trying to appear that it was the first time she'd seen them and trying to come up with something useful to say. She hadn't been prepared for this. She thought Teensy just wanted her to meet Fannie and get a feel for her, maybe do some amateur psychology and try to decide if she was the type to actually commit murder.

She finished after what she felt was the appropriate amount of time and waited until the others turned their attention back to her.

Teensy raised her eyebrows and Fannie fidgeted with the napkin in her lap.

"I agree with Teensy; you do have writing talent. It seems like it will be a fascinating story. The intrigue is certainly there and your main character is someone I'd like to get to know better." *So true.*

She paused for effect, trying to look deep in thought. "You know, it feels somehow very real. You manage to get into the protagonist's head very well."

She glanced at Teensy, who gave her a small nod.

Fannie broke out into a huge smile. "Why thank you, Lizzie. That's so wonderful to hear. I'm trying real hard for authenticity."

What to ask next? *Is that because it's really you? To what lengths will you go to make it real?*

"Is that hard to do? I mean, put yourself in your character's head?"

Fannie looked like she was giving the question a lot of thought. "No, not really. It's like I go into this zone, you know? When I'm having a good writing patch, it sometimes takes me a few minutes to get out of her head. You know what I mean?"

"Not really, I'm not a writer. But I have heard others say that very thing. I guess that makes all the difference."

"Do you really think so?" Fannie seemed to relax. "I can't tell you how much it means to hear you say all these nice things. And to think I was hesitant about letting you read it." She giggled. "How silly of me."

Lizzie couldn't think of anything else to say that might elicit information. "Well, I really have to be going. It was nice meeting you, Fannie."

"And you."

Teensy stood, ready to walk Lizzie to the door.

"What did you come to see Teensy about?" Fannie asked. "I took up all your time. I'm sorry."

Uh-oh.

"Lizzie was probably wondering if I'd like to go shopping with her, weren't you, sugar? We often do that, you know."

Lizzie nodded.

"Well, don't let me stop you. I should be getting home anyway." Fannie gathered up her things and stood.

Teensy looked surprised. "Well, all right then. I think we were finished anyway. And I'm sure Lizzie would be more than happy to give you some pointers anytime, too. Wouldn't you Lizzie?"

"Uh, sure." *Stop talking, Teensy.*

"Thanks, Lizzie. I do appreciate it. Bye now."

They watched Fannie get in her car and drive off. Then Lizzie spoke. "Thanks a lot, Teensy."

"Oh, don't you worry, sugar. She won't take you up on that, I'm sure. Not when I'm giving her all this extra time and attention. Now, maybe you should sit back down and have another glass of lemonade and just give her time to get out of the neighborhood before you leave. Alone."

Chapter Seventeen

◇◇◇

And there the case seemed to come to a halt.

AND THEN YOU DYE—MONICA FERRIS

Lizzie showed Bob around, introducing him to the others sorting books the next morning, and then left him to his own devices while she checked over the boxes that still needed to be dealt with. She'd already sent Wade, Darla and Andie out on another pickup route. This would probably be the last time. Donations by phone had dwindled away and she was pretty certain they'd reached saturation. Whatever else might be donated could probably be picked up by car. Besides, they were running out of space to store everything until the event, still two weeks off.

She was thrilled with the response. But she hadn't realized the amount of work involved. It was pure luck that the sale had been scheduled so soon after Easter break. If she hadn't had the time off, who knows how the work would have gotten done. Volunteers. She knew she'd have to round up more for the day of the sale, but with the help of Olivia at the Readers Are Us book club that should be easy. Anyway, it was all working out and she felt pretty certain the payoff would be a nice sum for the literacy program and well worth all the effort.

Bob wandered back into the sorting room and spoke in a low voice. "It's all quiet out back. What time are Wade and Darla due back? It might be a better time to be staking out the back at that point."

Lizzie looked at the clock mounted on the wall above the door. "Oh, anytime now, I'd think. What are you going to do if you catch Wade talking to Eddie Riser? Won't that sort of give away the fact that you suspect Wade of something?"

"I'll just keep watch and if Riser does show up, I'll follow him when he leaves. Don't look like that. I'm darned good at tailing bad guys. I've done a lot of that over the years."

"I bet you have," Lizzie was quick to answer. "Do you have your cell phone? Shouldn't we be in contact in case you need some backup or something?"

Bob pulled his phone out of his pocket. "I'm way ahead of you, girl. I've got you programmed in. Better check to see if you have my number."

Lizzie did that and added his number to her contacts. "If you'd like something to do while you're waiting, I could use a hand shifting those boxes over there," she said with a grin.

"Sure thing." He followed her over to a row of boxes piled two high and moved a couple of them over to the sorting table. "You sure that's it?"

Lizzie nodded.

"Okay, I think I'll hang around out back again."

Lizzie watched him leave. It wasn't the first time she'd noticed how little patience he had. He just didn't seem to be able to sit around and waste time, unless there was a fishing pole involved, she amended.

Lizzie got busy sorting the new box of books and had been at it for about fifteen minutes when a young woman rushed into the room. Lizzie recognized her as one of the center staff members.

"I'm sorry to burst in on y'all but we're in need of some help. A little girl attending one of our programs has gone missing. She's only six years old and we're just not sure what's happened." She sounded like she would start crying any minute.

"Of course, we'll help," Lizzie said, trying not to panic and looking at the three other people in the room. They all nodded and left their tasks, following the staff member out into the main entrance where another staff person, this one wearing a shirt that read "Leader" on the pocket, waited to speak to everyone. They'd managed to gather up around ten people from around the center.

"Thank you all for helping. We want to do a thorough search of the building and grounds before we call in the police. You three," she said, pointing to Lizzie and two young staffers standing beside her, "would you mind going out to the front yard and work your way around? I think if you divide up, and work toward each other, that would help."

"I'll go with them," Bob said, upon entering the room.

"Great. Now if the rest of you could divide up by twos and search the rooms, that should cover the center. We'll start at the west side."

Lizzie didn't hear the rest of the instructions. Her team members were already on their way outside. Bob grabbed her arm. "We'll work around that way," he said to the other two women. They nodded and went their way.

"Be sure to check behind shrubs," Bob said. "Sometimes it becomes a game of hide-and-seek with youngsters. They don't realize what the grown-ups are going through."

"Oh boy, I hope that's all this is," Lizzie said, her heart thumping. The center was such a busy place these days, almost anything or anyone could make something happen. She gave her head a shake, trying to toss away those thoughts. This was Ashton Corners. She would be found safe and unharmed.

They did a thorough search and made it around back, when Bob signaled Lizzie to hide behind him. He glanced back around the building toward the parking lot.

"What is it? What do you see?"

Bob waved her to be quiet. She tapped her toe, trying to be patient but dying to see what was going on. Finally, Bob started walking forward and she followed.

"What was that all about?"

"Wade showed up and he was talking to a guy who looked pretty much like your description of Riser." Bob scanned the rows of cars and over to the opposite corner of the building.

He shook his head. "Guess I'll have to track him down another time. There are never enough searchers when there's a young child involved. I will have a talk with Wade after, though."

Bob took another quick scan around to make sure both men had left. Then they split up and did a thorough search between the rows of cars, finally meeting up with the other team.

"Nothing," said one of the women.

Lizzie was starting to get a bit discouraged. How could a young child just disappear? Of course, the place was filled with people these days, either part of the day camp or helping sort books. *Try not to go there.*

"We'd better head back and check in," Bob suggested. They went inside and joined the search coordinator in the hall, reporting their findings, or rather, lack of.

"Okay. Thank you. How about taking the gym?" She pointed to the closed doors across from the main doors.

Bob nodded and the three others followed him in.

Lizzie and Bob did a thorough search of the equipment room while the others checked behind the stack of mats and chairs at one end of the gym. They'd just rejoined the leader in the hall when a cry went up from the office. They all ran over to it and crowded around as one of the office staff came walking through the door, carrying the little girl.

"I found her hiding under my desk. She thought this was fun." The relief was evident in her voice. "I was certain I looked there," the staffer said, shaking her head. The little girl flashed a wide grin all around.

"Thank heavens," Lizzie said softly, taking a minute to shake off the tension that had been building in her body, then headed back to the book room, Bob following.

Lizzie left the community center, wondering if she should have suggested to Bob that they both go searching for Eddie Riser. He was probably right, though. He was the ex-cop and knew how to handle such situations. Her tagging along might give Riser the edge, thinking it wasn't such a serious thing to be questioned by someone who was now mainly a book club member. That they'd had interactions while Bob was still police chief made it that much better.

She pulled up in front of A Novel Plot, planning to pick up a box of donated books to take in the next day. She found Stephanie, phone to her ear, behind the front desk. Lizzie gave her a wave and went directly to the back room, found the box and brought it out front. Stephanie was still on the phone, talking in hushed tones, so Lizzie wandered over to the shelves where the newly released titles were filed. She found the latest from Eva Gates in the Lighthouse Library Mystery series, something she'd been waiting for but had lost track of when it was supposed to arrive.

She heard Stephanie hang up the phone and sigh deeply.

"What's the problem? Or is it none of my business?"

Stephanie leaned against the back of her chair and looked to be in thought. "I don't really know if I should be telling you, Lizzie, but I'm just so concerned about her that I think I probably should."

"Who are we talking, or not talking, about?"

"Darla."

"Uh-huh. That was her on the phone?"

Stephanie nodded. "She just called me out of the blue. I don't think there's anyone else around here she feels she can talk to. And you know, she's lonely."

"She's got Molly and Bob."

"That's just it. She doesn't feel she can really talk to either of them."

"Well what about Wade? He seems to be around her all the time. Don't they talk?" Lizzie knew she was sounding a tad impatient and should dial it back. She had never considered that Darla might be lonely. So, it was a good thing she'd bonded with Stephanie, who was close in age.

"He's the problem. He doesn't really talk, he tells. And I know what that's like. That's why she felt she could tell me, I guess."

"Does he push her around?"

"She says not but I don't really believe her. It's all that code you talk in when someone's got power over you."

"Like what?"

"Oh, things like making excuses for his behavior. I've heard him belittle her and tell her how dumb she is, and when I mentioned it, she said he's not usually like that. It's only because he's lost his job and is in need of money."

"Did she say what he did for a living?"

"No and I didn't think to ask."

"What else?"

"Well, I thought he'd slapped her. She had a big red mark on her cheek. She admitted he had but said it was her fault because she'd gotten hysterical at the thought that they might be kicked out of the motel."

"Did you believe her?"

"Nope. I don't think Darla's the type to get hysterical."

Lizzie's thoughts exactly. She wondered how Stephanie knew so much about abuse. It wasn't something she'd mentioned when talking about her past. But maybe that's because she wasn't ready to talk about it. Lizzie wasn't about to push her on it now.

"Do you think one of us should step in?" Lizzie asked. "Maybe confront her or him?"

"I don't think so. She'd clam up for good then. If it's happening, she has to be the one to ask for help. Although, I think that sometimes you have to do an intervention or something. I guess I just wanted you to know about it at this point."

"Well, if it escalates in any way, you be sure to call me right away. Okay?"

Stephanie smiled. "Thanks, Lizzie. I knew I could count on you. Now, did you find the books all right?"

Lizzie pointed to the box at her feet.. "All set. Do you have plans for your afternoon off on Friday?"

Stephanie's smile grew even wider. "Yes I do. Roger is

taking the time off, too, and we're planning on taking Wendy to the petting zoo in Stoney Mills and then having a picnic along the way. Roger suggested it."

Lizzie felt a slight chill as the memory of her car being forced off the road on the way home from Stoney Mills, a year and a half ago. She and Sally-Jo had been looking for leads into the murder that took place in front of Molly's house the first night the book club had met. Neither of them were hurt but Lizzie now had a new car because of it. Not the outcome she'd wanted.

"He sounds real thoughtful," she said, rousing herself from the past.

"Oh, he is. Believe me." The phone rang before Stephanie could continue. Lizzie gave her a small wave, retrieved the box and left. She was happy that Stephanie had found someone who made her feel special. She'd been through a lot over the past few years and there hadn't been many positive things involved. The book club had been delighted to take her under their wing but she also needed to build a life for herself and her baby, and now it seemed like that's just what she was doing. She smiled to herself as she got into her car.

Lizzie stopped for a red light and noticed Darla walking along the opposite sidewalk, away from her. And alone. Lizzie glanced around for any sign of Wade but couldn't see him. This was as good a time as any for a little chat. She had some new questions to ask, these ones about why Darla had held on to the room. If that wasn't devious, she didn't know what was.

Chapter Eighteen

◇◇◇

I stopped, frozen, my hand still flat on the table.
There was something that would work even better.

THE ROAR OF THE CROWD—JANICE MACDONALD

Lizzie pulled over into the first vacant parking space and hurried across the street to catch up to Darla. She wanted it to seem that this was an accidental meeting.

"Hey, Darla. Out doing some shopping?"

Darla turned and when she saw that it was Lizzie, glanced nervously up and down the street. "Uh, something like that."

"How about if I walk with you?"

A look of panic flittered across Darla's face but she said, "Okay."

"How are you finding things here these days?"

"I dunno. Okay, I guess. But, like, I don't plan to stick around too much longer, though. I can't without any money." There was that whine in her voice again.

"What about if you could get a full-time job? What would

you like to do, Darla? If you had the choice of any job, what would it be?"

Darla glanced at Lizzie. "I dunno. I didn't take any schooling after high school, you know."

"Why is that? Couldn't you find something to study that interested you or were you more interested in going straight into a job?"

"I guess a bit of both."

Not much there. They walked in silence to the end of the block and then Darla said, "You know my granddaddy Cooper used to spoil me something rotten. I admit it. He gave me an allowance and I never had to look for a job after school. Anything I wanted was mine. But then he got sick and died and my grandmamma wasn't so nice to me. In fact, she told me I'd have to get a job if I decided not to go to college. So what was I supposed to do? I didn't take any of the courses I needed to get into some of the places she suggested, so I got a job training at a hair salon."

"Don't you need a course for that, too?"

"Oh, yeah, but they help pay for it if you work out real good washing hair and cleaning up the place. I didn't do so well, though. I'm not really handy with a broom and I hated touching other people's hair."

Lizzie managed to suppress a smile. She could see where that was a dead end. They stopped and looked at the display in the window of Pampered Pets. "You've had other jobs, though?"

"Uh-huh. I tried waitressing but I kept dropping the plates. That really got some of the customers upset. Especially the woman who'd just finished telling me she'd asked for dressing on the side, not on her salad, and sent it all back to the kitchen. I really didn't see her purse sticking out on the floor. I tripped and she got the whole mess down the back of her dress." Darla chortled. "I was fired on the spot."

She looked at Lizzie and burst out into full laughter. It took but a few seconds for Lizzie to join in. When they'd both settled down, Lizzie said, "So back to my question, can you see yourself happy doing some specific job?"

Darla actually smiled. "I'd like to help out at a veterinary office. I'm really good with animals. I always had a dog when I was growing up, and seeing them in pain or bloody doesn't bother me."

Lizzie almost gagged. Maybe that wasn't such a good thing.

"I mean, I feel sorry for them for sure, but I can deal with it and take care of them. I think that's a good thing, don't you?"

Lizzie nodded. "A very good thing. Have you looked into what training you'd need?"

They started walking again and rounded the corner, heading toward the large Target at the end of the street.

"Not really. I've been too busy selling magazine subscriptions, dishing out popcorn at the cinema and working at a call center to do anything more about it." She said in a whisper, "I need money, Lizzie. I have to keep working not take time out to train for something."

Lizzie wondered at the change of tone, then noticed Wade striding toward them.

"There you are. I've been looking for you, Darla. We got to be getting back."

He didn't even greet Lizzie but she said, "Nice to see you, Wade."

Wade looked at Lizzie and then grabbed Darla's arm. "Hurry up."

Lizzie was left to follow at a slower pace, which gave her time to think things through. Darla admitted to needing money so the theory about her hitting up Molly for it could still float. On the other hand, Lizzie had seen another side of Darla, basically a young kid floundering at finding a path in life. She actually felt sorry for the new Darla and wondered if she could help. Maybe help get rid of Wade for starters.

It didn't take long for Lizzie to realize she'd flubbed her chance to ask Darla some more questions about Rafe Shannon. That had been one of her objectives for today's visit, but she realized she was more focused on Darla's relationship with Molly and Bob. Too focused, perhaps. Maybe she should ask Sally-Jo to do the deed and question Darla, if she could get the girl alone. Her plane should have gotten in at noon and although she regretted not giving Sally-Jo a chance to catch her breath, a quick phone call couldn't hurt.

She went straight to the phone when she arrived home, but heard the message beep when she picked it up. Teensy telling her that she'd left for Atlanta and would be back in a couple of days. Lizzie shook her head. *That woman.* Stubborn might cover it. She was partly worried that Molly would find out and partly worried that Teensy might get into some kind of trouble. It had happened before. There was nothing she could do about it, though. Just wait for Teensy to call tonight, as she promised in her message.

Lizzie dialed Sally-Jo's number and resorted to leaving her own message when no one answered.

She was just about to dial Molly next when the phone rang. She was surprised to find it was Fannie Hewitt. It took several minutes of small talk before Fannie got to the point.

"I hope you don't mind my calling you but Teensy suggested it."

"You spoke to her today?"

"Yes. She called to say she had to go out of town for a couple of days but she wanted me to continue with my writing and thought that talking the plot through with you would be a help. I hope you don't mind?"

Uh-oh. "No, that's quite all right, Fannie. How is the book coming along?"

Lizzie heard her sigh. "Well, not as quickly as I'd hoped. I'm getting all tangled up in the details. I was going to have my heroine murder her husband and get away with it, but you know, there are so many ways to kill a person but not that many that are foolproof, I'm finding."

Good. "Maybe there's a solution other than murder?"

"I wondered that, too, so I thought about having her fake her own death and run away for a fresh start. Of course, she'd pin her murder on her husband."

"That might be preferable to murder. But have you thought of how she'd start all over? That's pretty hard to do, I'd think."

"Details, again. There are some books on how to disappear in the library. I checked online so maybe I'll take them out tomorrow."

"Well, how would she make it look like he'd done it?"

"Easy. She'd suggest they go for a picnic one Sunday and take the canoe, somewhere up river from here, or rather where I've set the book. She'll make sure he gets good and drunk, which will be easy, and then she'll take the canoe out by herself, tip it over, and swim off to where she's hidden a change of clothes and some money."

"Hmm. I'd think that just looks like an accident."

"Oh, but she'll be sure to set him up. Tell all her friends, albeit hesitantly, that he's becoming abusive and drinking a lot and beating on her. He's even said he'd kill her if she left him. Then, the police will think that's what he's done. What do you think?"

Oh boy. What to say? Tough call. Murder or framing him? "I'm leaning to the framing him but I still think you should look at other possibilities. What's her goal? To get away from him? How about blackmailing him into leaving her be?"

Fannie was silent for so long, Lizzie thought she'd lost her. "Are you still there?"

"Huh? Oh, yeah. I was just thinking about everything. You know, I think I'm leaning toward the original plot and killing him. Thanks, Lizzie. You've been a big help. We'll talk again. Bye."

Lizzie was left holding the phone, mouth agape. *Wait till I get my hands on Teensy. First, going to Atlanta, then siccing this obviously disturbed woman on me.*

She hoped Teensy would be back soon to take charge of this mess. Lizzie worried that she just might have to step in and do something, and she didn't have a clue as to what that should be.

Chapter Nineteen

◇◇◇

"If that's the case," I said barely above a whisper,
"then you have given me no choice but to meddle."

MURDER, PLAIN AND SIMPLE—ISABELLA ALAN

Darla was back on Lizzie's mind. She'd appeared during
the morning run and wouldn't leave. Lizzie's plan now
was to ask Molly to send Darla over to help out with the
book sorting in the afternoon, since it was the final day
they'd be at it. The books were just trickling in at this point,
so that should give Lizzie and Darla a chance to talk while
helping out. Lizzie had been assured by the Readers Are Us
book club that their members could take care of anything
after this point. The next involvement for the Ashton Corners Mystery Readers and Cheese Straws Society would be
at the actual sale, two weeks off.

She took a few minutes to check her email and was pleased
she had, as Sally-Jo had sent her one saying she'd be staying
a bit longer. No word on how things were going, though.
Lizzie hoped that was a good sign. Next, a call to Molly who

readily agreed to contact Darla. Lizzie felt a bit devious not telling Molly the real reason she wanted Darla on site, but she managed to overcome the feeling quite quickly. It was all for Molly's own good. *Oops, that's what Teensy had said.*

The cats lay in wait when Lizzie finished dressing and made her way back to the kitchen in search of a second espresso. Brie dashed out at her feet as the catnip-filled cotton mouse slid in front of her. She caught herself midstep, avoiding stepping on Brie's tail. The yowl would have brought Edam at a run, which would have ended up in a tussle, much to Brie's annoyance. She reached down, grabbed the mouse as it was batted past her again and threw it into the hallway. Brie was on it in a flash. Time for that espresso.

She hadn't heard from Bob at all and was dying to know if he'd actually talked to Eddie Riser. She eyed the phone and thought better of it. She'd pay him a visit instead since she had an entire morning with nothing planned. After downing the espresso in three quick gulps, she grabbed her handbag, stuck her iPhone in it and headed to her car.

Halfway to Bob's house, she pulled into a Starbucks parking lot, ducked in, and emerged with two coffees and an oat chocolate brownie in a bag. Bribery would work.

Bob's pickup and a small open trailer he sometimes used for various outdoor projects took up the driveway, so Lizzie parked on the verge in front of his house, overlooking the Tallapoosa River. She followed the sound of hammering and found Bob on his knees at the bottom step to his deck, about to drive another nail in the side.

"Do you have time for a coffee break?" She held out the goodies toward him.

Bob looked at her and removed three nails from his mouth. "Just what the doctor ordered."

He pushed himself up with a slight groan and Lizzie

realized once again that he was indeed aging. She had to stop and remind herself every now and then that both Bob and Molly were no longer as young and spry as they had been when she was growing up. Although neither would admit to slowing down, the signs were there, and it was sometimes a fine line in between volunteering to help and keeping the involvement minimal. Depending on the day, Bob could be prickly if he thought others believed he needed help.

She followed him up to the Adirondack chairs, set the coffees and bag on the table, and took a seat. She enjoyed looking out at the river, moving slowly around the bend. She could relate to the pull that kept Bob living in the two-bedroom house, despite its age and frequent need of repairs. He also loved the fact that he could just toss out a fishing line from the end of his property and sometimes, if luck was on his side, hook dinner.

"So, what brings you here this morning with these mouth-watering treats? If I were a betting man I'd say it has something to do with Eddie Riser." He grinned and demolished half the brownie in one bite.

"You got me. We didn't get a chance to talk yesterday and I was wondering if you'd had any luck. Or news."

Bob finished off the brownie and took a long drink from his cup before talking. "I did and I do." He leaned back in his chair, stretching out his legs in front of him, and stretching out the story, too, Lizzie noted.

"I tracked him down right away and then spent a good part of the day tailing him. That young lad is quite the businessman and he has more luck on his side than a leprechaun. He should by rights be behind bars, but his radar lets him know whenever the law gets close, and he closes up shop."

Lizzie looked at Bob, waiting for more.

"He's dealing drugs, Lizzie. And he's doing a good

business, too, from the looks of it. And I've written it all down, along with names of his customers, and I'm going to hand it over to the police just as soon as I've figured out what Wade Morris has to do with all this."

"Was he a customer?"

"They had a meeting of some sort but I didn't see anything exchange hands."

"That was taking a chance. You sure Wade didn't make you?"

"Make me? There you go with your TV cop show chatter again. But no, he didn't. I've had a lot of practice at this over the years and now that I'm getting on, I just sort of blend even more naturally into the background. You'd be surprised how many old folks go unnoticed out on the street in day-to-day living."

Lizzie hadn't thought about it. "That's sad."

"That's life, young lady. And for now, it's an advantage."

"What are you going to do next?"

"I'm thinking on it. I find nothing gets the brain working better than some good old physical labor. Of course, the step did need some reinforcing, too," he added with a chuckle.

"What can I do?"

"How are you with a hammer?"

Lizzie leaned across and chucked him on the arm. "I'm better at sleuthing."

"You *think* you are. I'd say it's getting real dangerous if drugs are involved in any way, shape or form."

"Do you think Rafe Shannon might have been part of it?"

"We don't know that he ever met up with Riser, do we?"

Lizzie shook her head.

"Well then, that's something we've got to find out."

"But how?"

"Aside from breaking into Riser's house and checking his records, if he even keeps any . . ." Bob's brow furrowed. "Just wipe that look of anticipation off your face, young lady. That's not even an option. Now, as I was saying, the only thing to do is ask the police to bring him in for questioning. I'm sure they have plenty of things they can legitimately detain him for. But whether they want to tip their hands, that's the question."

"Do you think he'll talk?"

"It depends on what's in it for him. He's not going to admit anything since he'll actually be incriminating himself if he says he's dealing. But if they have a pending charge or something already in the works against him, he might be persuaded to talk if they offer to make it disappear."

"Do you think Mark will go for that?"

Bob shrugged. "It's happened on many occasions. I'll stop by his office this afternoon." Bob finished off his coffee and picked up his hammer. "On second thought, although I know he doesn't like you poking your nose into police business, I'd bet he's more likely to do it if you ask him." Bob winked at her. "And he just might believe it's as good a way as any to deflect your investigative ways."

She smiled back. "You may be right. I'll talk to you later, Bob."

Lizzie pulled into the parking lot at the police station just as Mark was getting into his Jeep.

He shut the door and walked over to her car.

"To what do I owe the pleasure? It is pleasure, right. Not business?" He pushed his ball cap back further on his head.

Lizzie got out of her car and stood close to him. "I need to talk to you about business, first."

"Let me guess in two words. Rafe Shannon. Or Wade Morris. Or Darla Lyman."

"How about Eddie Riser." She put up her hand before he

could answer. "Who could be the one who knew Rafe Shannon and therefore could get Darla Lyman off the hook."

Mark sighed and leaned back against Lizzie's car. "What, no Wade Morris?"

"We know, or rather think, that Wade may have tried to buy drugs from Eddie Riser. That just makes him a jerk and someone Bob won't want involved with his granddaughter. We think that Eddie Riser might be the link here."

"We? Is the entire book club involved again?"

"Just trying to sort things out. Help out Bob."

Mark glanced at his watch. "I have time for a quick coffee, which is just enough time for you to tell me what it is that you've been up to that leads you to a Shannon-Riser connection." He pointed down the street and she nodded.

They walked across the street and down a few doors to the Cup'n Choc. There were a few empty tables and after they'd ordered, Mark steered her to the one in the far corner with few people close by. He took off his sunglasses, removed his cap, leaned back in his chair and crossed his arms.

"Talk."

Lizzie waited until their cappuccinos had been served before answering. "We're just trying to figure out who knew Rafe Shannon and why he'd be in town. We have one out-of-towner, Wade Morris, hooking up with Eddie. So, what if Rafe Shannon did so also?"

"You think Riser was dealing to him?"

"It's possible, isn't it?"

"Sure, it's possible. We know that's his business and if we had strong enough proof, Riser would be behind bars. How do you think we'll be able to tie Rafe Shannon into him? And, what does that have to do with the murder?"

"Eddie Riser could be the murderer."

Mark thought about it a moment. "Not likely, though. He's never resorted to violence in the past."

"But what if Rafe threatened him in some way? It could have been self-defense. What if Rafe was in town to shake up Eddie who might have sold some bad drugs to someone from Atlanta or been selling for someone from there? What if he was, and he absconded with the drugs and the money?"

"That's a lot of what-ifs, and I'd think Riser would be our dead body in that case. I also think you've been reading too many mysteries, which I may have mentioned in the past. These are all suppositions, Lizzie."

"But what if you bring him in and offer him some kind of immunity or something in exchange for information?"

"I need something definite before I can bring Riser in. We have no proof of any of this."

"What if you pretend you do?"

"What if you stop coming up with more suggestions?"

Lizzie knew Mark wouldn't budge. "What do you suggest, then?"

"I'll continue to do the police work and track down the killer while you and your merry band of readers, and I say that in the kindest way, go back to your meetings."

She knew when she'd been defeated, but she also knew that one closed door usually meant at least an open window in some other location.

Chapter Twenty

◇◇◇

"I'll be there as soon as I can."

THERE WAS AN OLD WOMAN—HALLIE EPHRON

Lizzie could hear her phone ringing as she got out of her car in her driveway. She'd decided to go home for a quick bite to eat before heading to the community center for sorting duties. She also wanted to check with Molly if Darla had said yes to helping out. She made a mad dash into her house and picked it up just before it went to message. She was glad, because Stephanie sounded upset.

"What's wrong?"

"Oh boy. I don't really think I should be calling you about this. I think Darla's going to be really mad at me but I'm so upset by it all and something has to be done."

"Stephanie, take a deep breath and then tell me what's happened."

"Darla just called me, all upset and crying. Wade got mad

about something or other and beat her up then drove off. He didn't tell her where he was going or anything."

"How badly hurt is she? Does she need to go to the hospital?"

"She said no but I think she'd say that regardless of how bad she was. He's got her scared and she's not going to admit to anyone what he does to her."

"I'll go over and see how she is."

"Would you, Lizzie? I know she'll be real mad. She might not even let you in. But something's got to be done and if she's really badly hurt and not doing anything about it . . . I can't bear to think about that."

"You calm down now, Stephanie. I'll leave right away and call you as soon as I know something. Don't you worry about it. You did the right thing phoning me."

"Okay. Just hurry before he gets back there. And you be careful, you hear?"

Lizzie smiled. "I will."

She grabbed her car keys then paused, wondering if she should ask Molly to go along. That would really make Darla mad, but it might be the only way to get in and see her. She gave Molly a quick call and explained the situation as she headed for her car.

Molly was ready and waiting when Lizzie pulled into her driveway. She got into the passenger seat and reached out to touch Lizzie's arm. "Do you think it's serious?"

Lizzie could see the worry in Molly's face.

"I don't know but I'm pretty sure it's happened before. I stopped by to see her a couple of days ago and she seemed really cowed by Wade when he appeared."

"Well, let's hope we can talk some sense into her then and get her to move back to my place."

Lizzie nodded and steered toward the motel. She didn't see Wade's pickup in the parking lot, much to her relief. She parked in front of the unit and led the way to the door.

After knocking and identifying herself, they waited a couple of minutes. When nothing happened, Molly tried. "Honey, it's Molly and I know you're in there. And I also know what happened. Now, I want you to stop this foolishness and open this door. We're here to help you."

It took several seconds before they heard the chain being removed and slowly, the door opened.

Lizzie gasped when she saw Darla in tears. Molly reached out and pulled Darla into her arms.

"Oh, honey. This is not right. Not right, at all." She held her back at arm's length and took a close look. Red welts peeked out from under the short sleeves of her T-shirt. On her left arm it looked like the outline of a hand had wrapped around and squeezed tightly until bruising occurred. A discolored patch peeked out from the neckline, at the base of her throat.

"That man is a brute and his behavior will not be tolerated. Now, you'll be safe with me. You just quickly pack up your things. Lizzie will help you. And we'll get out of here before he comes back."

"I can't leave him."

"Don't be silly. You can and you will. You are not something to be batted around. Now, hurry and we'll discuss it all later." She gave Darla a small shove toward the suitcase on the floor under the window.

Lizzie opened the closet door and pulled out what were obviously Darla's clothes. She didn't bother to fold them but rather stuffed some into the duffel bag she'd seen Darla using at Molly's. When Darla had finished packing her small suitcase, she took a quick look around, nodded to Molly, and they left the room.

Outside, Lizzie scanned the parking lot. No sign of Wade. They piled into her car and Lizzie tore out of there.

No one spoke on the ride back to Molly's. When they were inside, Molly told Darla to take her things upstairs while she made some hot tea. Lizzie followed her out to the kitchen.

"What about Bob? Will you tell him?"

"Oh my, yes. He needs to know this for sure. In fact, I'm going to call him to come over right now. If that Wade shows up here, and I'm certain he'll think this is where she'd come, I want a man present."

"Why don't I call Mark, also?"

"Hmm. Actually that might be a good idea, honey. But maybe he could just hover outside at first, at least until we get her feeling comfortable and maybe starting to talk about it all. Mark could be a deterrent to Wade, if he appears."

"Gotcha." Lizzie went outside to make the call to Mark, not wanting Darla to wander down and hear. Once she'd explained the situation to him, he agreed to come over as soon as he could get away. That done, she went back into the kitchen and caught the tail end of Molly's call to Bob.

"See you shortly, Bob. And don't drive like a maniac. We'll take good care of her."

Molly put the receiver down and turned to face Lizzie. "Oh my goodness, what situations we get ourselves into. That dear child has had a really rough time of late."

"I know you're worried about her, Molly, but I think she's pretty resilient. I'm just hoping she'll talk to us."

They heard some noise on the stairs and got busy getting the tea ready. Molly pointed to the pecan squares she'd taken out of the fridge and Lizzie was slicing them as Darla appeared.

"Now, you just sit down at the banquette, Darla, and we'll have this all ready in just a second. I think we'll stay indoors to have our tea." She glanced meaningfully at Lizzie as she put the teacups and pot on a tray.

Lizzie carried the plate of squares to the table and sat down across from Darla. "We want to help you, Darla."

Darla grabbed a piece and bit off half and chewed it quickly, but seemed to have trouble swallowing. Molly joined them and poured them each a cup of tea before talking.

"Lizzie is right. We're concerned about you, honey. No one should be treated in this way."

"He loves me." Darla's voice was devoid of emotion. She finished off the sweet in her hand.

"That's not love and if you think it is, we need to convince you otherwise."

They heard a car door slam. Lizzie held her breath, wondering which of the men had reached them first. They waited for the doorbell to ring but Bob came rushing around the side of the house, up to the back door. Lizzie jumped up and unlocked it to let him in. He took one look at Darla and his face looked like a thundercloud. Darla actually whimpered. He went to her.

"I'm not mad at you, Darla. I do want to throttle that Wade Morris, though." He bent over and gave her a hug. "I'm your granddaddy and it's my duty to protect you from such things."

Darla glanced at Molly, a stricken look on her face.

Molly stood. "Sit down, Bob, and I'll get you some tea. We were just having a talk and you should join in. But calmly." She put a hand on his arm and he roused himself and sat down next to Darla.

No one said anything until Molly had rejoined them. Bob shot her a look of thanks.

Molly said quietly, "Tell us what happened, honey."

Darla looked from one to the other but didn't speak. Bob

reached out to touch her hand and she flinched. Lizzie noticed the forlorn look on his face.

After a few minutes, Darla said, her voice soft, "He was mad when he came home. He'd gone out early to meet someone in town, and I guess it went wrong because when I asked, he told me to keep quiet. I should have. I know he has a bad temper but I'd been cooped up all morning. He'd told me not to go anywhere, so I demanded to know what was going on. That's when he started punching me." She started crying. "But he loves me. I know he does. He's just got a bad temper."

Bob stood abruptly and started pacing. Molly glanced quickly at him, then back at Darla. "It doesn't matter why someone does something like this, Darla. It's not allowed. And, I'm sorry to say, but if he did love you, he'd find some other way to deal with his temper."

"It's criminal action, that's what it is," Bob spat out.

"No," Darla almost shouted. "Don't tell the cops. I won't tell them what I told you. You can't make me. I don't want him to go to jail."

"Shh, shh. It's all right, Darla. That's not going to happen." Molly took hold of both her hands and waited until Darla looked at her. "But if you want us to not report him you have to do something for me."

"What?"

"You have to stay here and keep away from Wade while you're living under my roof. Is that understood?"

"Wade won't like it. I'll have to explain it to him."

"No, you won't," Bob said. "I'll tell him. And Molly's right. You are not to be alone with him while you're here in town. I'd love to be able to say you have to stay away from him in Atlanta, too, but I guess I don't have any right. I'll bet your mama knew though, didn't she? You said she didn't like him."

Darla nodded and sniffed. "She told me not to see him again. So I left town. That's when I came here."

Someone started pounding on the front door. "I'll bet I know who that is," Bob said, and headed toward it. Darla was right behind him. "You better stay in the kitchen," he told her.

"No. It's Wade. I gotta see him."

Lizzie and Molly followed close behind. Lizzie looked through the side window, searching for Mark's Jeep, as Bob opened the door.

"I know Darla's in there and I want her to come with me. Now," Wade bellowed.

Bob blocked the door. "Darla is indeed here and she's not going nowhere with you, young man. Do you know how badly you beat her? You're lucky you're not locked up behind bars right now."

Darla whimpered.

"I hear you, baby," Wade said, his voice a bit softer. He tried to peer around Bob. "Look, I never meant to hurt you. I love you and I want you to come with me."

"No," Bob spoke before Darla could say anything. "It doesn't matter what you say now. You beat her and there aren't any more chances where I come from."

"Look, old man, you're nothing in her life. You've never been there for her. You've got no right to stop me from see-ing her."

Bob bristled. "I am her granddaddy even if I've not been around when she was growing up. And you, punk, better leave right now before I throw you off the property."

"Oh yeah? You and who else. A house full of women? Nobody takes care of Darla like me. Not that grandmamma of hers, not since her old man died. She didn't even give Darla the money she's needing. And her mama don't care. So it's just me and her. Now, get out of my way."

Bob didn't notice the arm that shot out and pushed him backward, until he stumbled and almost went down. Wade leaned in and grabbed Darla's arm.

"Hold it right there!" Molly stepped out from behind the door, holding one of her dead husband's antique revolvers in her hands. She had it pointed straight at Wade, although Lizzie noticed her hands shaking a little.

"Molly's a crack shot so I would do as she says," Lizzie said, stepping in front of Bob before he could rush out at Wade.

Wade hesitated a moment. "That's just an old thing. Bet it won't even fire."

"That could be a dangerous bet," Molly said evenly.

Wade looked from Molly to Darla. "I'm leaving now but you'd better give it a lot of thought, Darla. I came here to help you and I'm not leaving town without you."

"Go," Molly said, her voice low and threatening.

Wade backed away and then turned and stomped back to his pickup. He glared at them as he backed up and drove off.

Molly's hands were shaking so badly at this point that Bob eased the gun out of her hand. "What in tarnation were you doing, woman?"

"I was using persuasion."

Bob checked the gun. "It's not even loaded."

"Of course not. But it had been the weapon of choice before when Frank Telford was killed outside here, so I thought it might do the trick."

Darla burst into tears and ran up the stairs to her room. They heard the door slam.

"Oh boy," Bob said.

"Amen."

Lizzie peered out the door, wondering where Mark could be.

* * *

He arrived twenty minutes later. The three of them were sitting out on the back patio. Molly and Lizzie sipped red wine while Bob was on his second beer.

"I'm real sorry I couldn't get here any sooner. Fill me in on what's happened."

Lizzie looked at Bob, who gave a slight nod. "It started with Darla calling Stephanie at the bookstore and then Stephanie called me," Lizzie started. "Darla had been beaten up by Wade so I picked up Molly"— she looked at Molly, who nodded—"because I thought she'd have a better chance of getting Darla to open the door. When we saw her, Molly insisted she pack her things and come here. She was really reluctant but eventually did. When we got here, Molly called Bob, who came over, and I called you. Then Wade showed up and demanded Darla go with him. Bob told him to leave or he'd call the police. He left but threatened Bob. And here we are." She thought it best to leave out the part about Molly and her gun.

Mark shook his head. "I'll go pick him up."

Bob leaned forward in his chair. "I've been thinking this through and although that's what I really want you to do, I'm thinking as soon as he gets out on bail he'll be right back at it and ornerier than ever, although I've no idea how he'd post it. But just to be on the safe side, let's assume he might have some connections. Why not let things simmer for a while? Darla stays here and I'm hoping we can talk some real sense into her so she'll dump the guy rather than be willing to follow him whenever he snaps his fingers. We'll keep an eye on her and maybe you'd have a patrol car pass by frequently."

"I can do that but I'd be happier putting him behind bars right away."

"Believe me, so would I." Bob leaned back and took a long drink from his bottle before continuing. "But maybe we can go about it in a different way. We know he connected with Eddie Riser behind the community center, and my bet is that he was buying drugs. They met up a second time, too. So, I followed Riser yesterday hoping to watch a deal going down between the two. Although nothing happened, he's sure to try again. It's been a couple of days now and he must be running low on whatever he's using. We watch and scoop them both up."

Mark considered it. "I like the idea but I don't think I can spare enough officers to do a proper surveillance right now. Got a couple out on sick leave and Officer Craig is still in Atlanta."

"I can help. I'm not too old to be sitting in a car watching, you know."

Mark stood and walked around the patio, snatching a cheese straw on his way back to his chair. "All right. I'll go along with it on two conditions. Only for a couple of days and no book club members are involved." He stared at Lizzie as he said the last part.

"Done."

Lizzie opened her mouth but quickly shut it, remembering that sometimes it was better to ask for forgiveness than permission.

Mark stood. "I'd like to talk to Darla before I leave."

Molly stood, too. "Oh, Mark. She's been through so much. Can't it wait until maybe tomorrow?"

"I gather she doesn't want to go to the hospital?"

They all shook their heads.

"All right. I'll call before coming over tomorrow morning, but I want someone to document her injuries. Molly, do you have a good-quality camera handy so you can take some pictures of her?"

"Yes, I do and we will."

"Okay. I've got to get back to the station. Keep me posted, and Bob, drop by the station later and we'll set up a surveillance schedule."

Bob nodded.

Lizzie waited until Mark would be in his car, then said, "I'm going to help with that surveillance."

"You could. But it's time consuming and boring. I think your talents are better used doing other things, don't you?"

Lizzie thought about it a moment. "Good idea."

Her iPhone rang and she answered. "Oh, hi. Yes, that's good for sure but look, I can't talk right now." She willed herself not to look at Molly, not wanting to take the chance that Molly would figure out it was Teensy calling. "Can I call you back later? Oh, okay. See you then."

She hung up and tried not to look guilty. Molly looked like she'd like nothing better than knowing who had been on the other end of the line, but Lizzie said instead, "I guess there's nothing else I can do here. I'll talk to you later, Molly."

Molly gave Lizzie a big hug. "Thanks for your help and for being concerned, honey. Now, if there's anything I can help you with"—she glanced at the phone still in Lizzie's hand—"be sure to let me know."

Chapter Twenty-one

◇◇◇

We'd found our mystery man, but he didn't solve
our mystery.

PAWS FOR MURDER—ANNIE KNOX

Lizzie drove straight home, hoping to connect again with
Teensy and find out just what information she'd been so
excited to share. The last thing Lizzie had wanted was for
Molly to find out about Teensy's trip to Atlanta, but if it
turned out to be relevant, they'd have to tell all. Just what
Molly's reaction would be, she had no idea.

She let herself into her house and dialed Teensy's cell
phone first thing. She answered on the third ring.

"Oh, I can't talk now, sweetie. I'm still in Atlanta and I'm
about to go out on a hot date. I met this rich and single fella
at the casino last night and he's taking me out to dinner."

"Can't you tell me what you found out?"

"It can wait until I get home. I'll leave straight after breakfast tomorrow. Be home in time for late lunch. Ta-ta for now."

Lizzie hung up, disappointed. Maybe it wasn't that

important after all, otherwise surely Teensy would be wanting to dish all. That was it; however, Lizzie was properly vexed. She never had been good at waiting. Especially at holiday times. She poured herself a glass of water from the Brita sitting on her counter top and sat down at the kitchen table, her mind traveling back to memories of waiting for her daddy to get home from a trip on her birthday, wanting him home and also wanting her gift.

When she was seven, she'd had an afternoon birthday party with five of her best pals attending. The living room at the Cavendish Street house had been small and the day had turned out rainy, unusual for a day in June. After everyone had left, Lizzie ignored the gifts strewn on the floor, and kept walking over to the window, checking to see if her daddy's old blue Chevy was pulling into the driveway. Her mama had to keep telling her to just be patient, that a watched pot never boiled, and other useful advice. Finally, with supper on the table, her daddy burst through the door, a golden Labrador puppy cradled in his arms.

Lizzie had been too excited to sleep that night. She'd kept getting up and sneaking down to the kitchen to sit with her new puppy, Lifer. The puppy Daddy's paycheck from *LIFE* magazine had bought, he loved to say.

She sighed. Less than a year later, they'd had to find a new home for the puppy because of her mama's allergies. There were no more pets in the Turner household, until now. Lizzie tucked the memory away and reached out to pat Edam, who'd jumped on her lap and was butting her chin with his head.

L izzie was one of the first to arrive at choir that evening. She liked to get there early, which didn't often happen, and just mellow out while listening to Tommy McCann, the accompanist, warm up on the piano. Tommy had been with the choir since it was started ten years ago. He was originally from New York City, and his resume listed several gigs with local choirs and his own performances as a soloist. Lizzie knew they were lucky he'd fallen in love with an Ashton Corners gal and decided to marry her and stay put.

By the time Stanton Giles arrived, almost everyone was in place and ready to go. He apologized for keeping them waiting, although by Lizzie's reckoning, he hadn't. Then he went right into rehearsals without the usual joking around. She wondered what was bothering him but realized it was none of her business. But what if he'd had a lover's tiff with Teensy? If they were still dating, that was. She'd have to look into that.

After an hour spent on the *Celtic Mass*, the main piece for the concert, Giles called for a break. Lizzie grabbed her bottle of water and wandered into the kitchen, hoping to find that someone had brought a box of chocolates, and wishing she'd thought of it earlier when there was none. She glanced out the window while listening to one of the altos in a group of four women, expounding on the virtues of a homeopathic remedy for sore throats with a name Lizzie couldn't even hope to spell, and almost dropped her bottle in surprise. She leaned forward to see out the window more clearly, trying to be sure of what she'd just seen. Or rather, who.

"Excuse me. I think I forgot to lock my car," she said, feeling rude but desperate to get out the back door.

By the time she made it down the hall and out the door into the parking lot, it was empty of people. But she was certain she'd seen Eddie Riser. What had he been doing skulking around the lot? Meeting up to make another sale? She wondered if she should give Mark a call but Eddie looked to be long gone.

She took another look around, just to be sure, and then went back inside just as Tommy's famous fanfare signaled it was time to get back down to singing. The last half of the evening was spent fine-tuning two pieces that comprised the remainder of the program. By the end of the rehearsal, Lizzie felt exhausted. The combination of missing out on a good night's sleep the evening before, and all the energy needed to go over and over the music, had her longing for home and bed.

The next morning was all about housework. Lizzie took a page from Bob's book and attacked her cupboards with vigor, hoping to trigger some activity in her brain cells. She felt she was floundering in too many details, too many paths with none of them leading directly to Rafe Shannon.

What with all that had been going on lately, starting with the arrival of Darla, then the murder, the arrival of Wade and his beating up of Darla, and throwing in Teensy's task to deal with Fannie Hewitt, there was far too much to keep proper track of. And she'd been hoping for a quiet Easter break during which she'd get caught up on some other tasks.

The key to finding the murderer, she felt certain, lay in the reason Rafe had come to Ashton Corners. She was pretty certain Darla wasn't the killer, but believed she had to be involved in some way. The fact that Darla clammed up every time Lizzie tried asking her about the guy certainly raised her suspicions.

But why would someone like Rafe come to this town? The reason probably wasn't a good one, given his background. She wondered briefly if Amber Craig had discovered anything relevant about her errant cousin and also, when would she be back home so that Lizzie could talk to her?

And what was Wade doing talking to Eddie Riser? Was

he buying drugs? Or was he selling them? Lizzie stopped in the middle of putting some plates back in the cupboard. That didn't make any sense whatsoever. Eddie must already have a supplier; he'd been in the business for a while now, according to Bob.

Had Eddie met with Rafe for something involving drugs? The only way to find out seemed to be asking Eddie flat out. Not the safest, though. But what would he do? Kill her? Not likely. Deny it? Probably. Maybe he'd give himself away by his reaction to the question or in some other manner. Could she chance it? Not alone, she realized. But she couldn't take Bob with her. His presence would ensure no cooperation at all. Molly was out of the question. She didn't want her to hear if Darla's name came up. And, certainly no Andie nor Stephanie. She didn't want either of them even remotely involved with the likes of Eddie Riser.

Teensy should be back by noon, if she'd left Atlanta at a reasonable hour. That was her backup, for better or worse. She'd just leave Teensy a message on her home phone to call, and then finish off the housework. A good way to plot how to approach the drug-dealing Eddie Riser. Not known to get violent, she kept saying to reassure herself.

Teensy called at noon. "I got your message, sugar, but you didn't have to worry. You're the first person I'd planned to talk to. Can I come on over?"

"That would be great, Teensy. And I have a plan that I need your help with."

"Oh, goody. Some action, I hope. I'll be there in, say, a half hour."

Lizzie had just finished dusting when the front doorbell rang. Teensy gave her a big hug and grabbed her hand, leading Lizzie to the kitchen. "I'm just dying for an iced tea, sugar." She sat at the table and waited to be served.

Lizzie smiled and filled two glasses. "Here you go, now tell all."

"You first."

"All right. I want to talk to Eddie Riser and ask if he had any dealings with Rafe Shannon. Are you in?"

Teensy wiggled in her seat. "Like a duck on a june bug. But it may not be important. Wait till you hear what I learned."

Lizzie cocked an eyebrow at Teensy, wishing she'd get on with it.

"Okay. Now, I talked to Lily Lyman, Darla's mama, and at first she didn't even want me to mention Darla's name in her presence. That woman had no nurturing skills at all, I thought, and all I wanted to do was slap her silly. But I filled her in on all that had happened and she did a turnaround and got all concerned. She loves her baby and is worried about what's been going on in her life is all. Lily had a bad feeling about the amount of control Wade Morris seemed to have on Darla so she told her to break it off. Probably not the best way to handle the situation, and she certainly realizes that now. Seems that jerk was only part of the problem.

"Anyway"—Teensy leaned forward, her elbows on the table—"Darla has a bit of a gambling problem. She'd been borrowing large sums of money from her granddaddy, not Bob of course, the other one, to pay off her debts 'cause she's terrible at earning money. But then he up and died and her grandmamma, that would be Sue-Ann, told her to stop wasting money and to get a job. But then of course, Sue-Ann passed but that still didn't solve her money problems. So it all came tumbling down on the child. She turned tail and ran, owing money and leaving an upset mama behind."

Lizzie sank against the back of her chair. "Oh boy. That poor kid. She's got a lot of trouble coming at her from all sides." Lizzie sipped some tea. "Do you think Rafe Shannon came looking for her? He worked for some casinos at times. Maybe he was an enforcer or a debt collector. Or whatever they're called."

"Could be. But Lily didn't have any information about that. No one came looking for Darla at home or anything, so no direct tie-in to our dead guy."

"Which is good for Darla. But seems like an awfully big coincidence, them both turning up here in town."

Teensy nodded. "Well, I say it's time we talk to the drug dealer, then. We can try asking Darla, too, for all the good it will do us. By the way, did Molly happen to ask where I was?"

"No. She's been pretty wrapped up in events here." Lizzie filled her in on what had happened to Darla.

"Oh, landsakes, that poor child. It must feel like the world is collapsing on her. Mind you, she should have been up-front about the real reason she's here." Teensy sat silent for a few moments, then straightened the neckline of her low-cut, short-sleeved orange blouse. "Well, I guess the best thing we can do to help is go track down that Eddie Riser and have a little heart-to-heart with him." She finished off her tea, grabbed her large purple handbag as she stood, and folded her arms across her waist. "Let's get going, sugar. Time's a-wastin'."

Lizzie quickly stashed the empty glasses in the sink and grabbed her own handbag as they left by the back door.

"I'm blocking you but that's okay, we'll take my car," Teensy said, climbing into the driver's seat of her Cadillac. Lizzie slid into the passenger seat and had barely buckled her seat belt when Teensy backed out.

"Where to?"

"That could be the biggest flaw with this plan. I'm not really sure. Let's try the community center for starters. It's easiest and we might just get lucky. If he's not hanging out behind the center, I'm pretty sure Bob said he followed him over to Dexter Street, where Eddie hung out in front of a bar."

"You've got it."

"Oops, that reminds me, Bob may be conducting surveillance once again. He probably won't like seeing us appear."

"Tosh. What's the worst he could do to us? Ground us? I don't think so."

Lizzie smiled and hoped that some of Teensy's confidence would wash over her.

"What did Bob say when he heard about Wade beating on Darla?" Teensy asked after a couple of minutes.

"Just what you'd imagine but he did manage to restrain himself. I think he's hoping that Darla will now come to her senses and leave the guy without any pressure from him."

"That would be best. It certainly can't help Bob's relationship with her if he's already on her back about her boyfriend."

Lizzie adjusted her position slightly so she could look at Teensy. "What is your sense about this gambling thing? Do you think Rafe Shannon tracked Darla down here, even if her mama said he didn't come by the house? But how would he know where she'd gone, or even that she'd left, unless he was keeping an eye on her? I wonder just how much she owes."

"Lily either didn't know or chose not to tell me."

"It doesn't make any sense otherwise, not with his car being found next door to Molly's. It was like he felt bold enough to let Darla know he was around but sly enough to want to surprise her. If he hadn't been killed, I wonder what he would have done to Darla."

"He had his chance to break some bones back in town the other day, didn't he?"

"Uh-huh. But it was daylight and maybe that was meant to be her last warning. Do you think he had been watching Darla and realized that her staying at Molly's might mean he'd get his money after all? Like in, from Molly?"

"There is that. I'm sure Molly is just crazy enough to have given it to Darla, if she'd asked."

"Maybe not crazy, just concerned. Darla is Bob's granddaughter, after all."

"Humpf. I don't know why the two of them, Mopsy and Bob that is, just don't up and move in to together or get married or something."

"Teensy!" Lizzie couldn't keep the surprise out of her voice but it quickly turned to amusement. "I can't think of a single thing to say to that."

"No need, sugar. We can all see with our own eyes that those two are tipsy-toeing around that spark that's there between them. Always was, as I recall, even though Molly's mama, as nice a lady as she was, would probably not have approved if they'd started dating back in our youthhood. They traveled in different social classes but Bob was always there, at the periphery, willing to help out Molly if need be."

"Help out, in what way?" Lizzie had never heard any of this before and she was intrigued.

"Well, there was that time Billy Broder stole Molly's pencil case. That was back in the second grade. Bob got into a little scuffle with Billy and soon that case was returned. Things like that over the years. And then in high school, I think it was sophomore year, before Molly's coming out anyway, she was asked out on a date by Walter Buford, who then bragged about what he planned to do but instead ended up with a black eye, courtesy of Bob." Teensy chuckled. "Her white knight, even if she didn't know it."

"Wow. I never realized. I knew they'd known each other since childhood. I just never thought about what that meant. It is rather obvious there's affection there, although who knows where that will lead. If anywhere."

"Nowhere unless one of them gets off his or her duff and

does something about it. Or, unless they get a little help in that corner."

"What are you thinking? No, maybe I shouldn't know. Anyway, as charming as that may be we need to focus on what to do next. If you just park over there toward the back, I'll check to see if Eddie is hanging out and trying to keep out of sight."

"I'm coming with you, young lady." Teensy shut off the engine and shot out of the car, following Lizzie.

"We'll just pretend we're out for a stroll," Lizzie said, picking up the pace.

"And when we stroll into him, out back of the community center I might add, which will look sort of strange don't you think? What do we say? Do you have a good plan?"

"I plan to be very honest and up-front with him. Maybe that will impress him or at least surprise him so he answers my questions."

"Well, it's a plan."

Lizzie felt all her anticipation evaporate when the back lot turned out to be empty. "Maybe we'll just hang around awhile and see if he appears."

Teensy looked around the sparse lot. "What was that backup plan?"

"Okay. You're right. There's no place comfortable and we'd be totally in view, so that would probably scare him off if he did come along to conduct some business. Let's cruise on by the Road Rack bar on Dexter Street and see if he's there."

They bustled back to the car and Teensy shot down the street.

"I think it's best to avoid sudden appearances and speeding tickets when undertaking an action like this," Lizzie said after a few moments.

"Huh. Oh, yeah. Right." She slowed to the speed limit and turned onto Dexter. As they passed the bar, Lizzie had a good look at the front and down the side alley.

"I don't see him. But let's park, check inside, and then do a walk around the block."

"Um, check inside?"

"You're backing out now?"

Teensy shook her head. "No sirree but I just wanted to make sure you'd thought through this plan. It's midafternoon and we're going into a somewhat sleazy bar that probably has a ton of drunks even at this hour of day, without getting hit upon, thrown up on, or tossed out?"

Lizzie smiled. "It will be a cinch." She stuck her left hand down beside the seat and crossed her fingers. Maybe not her best plan but she needed to find the guy.

"This is what Ashton Corners touts as a sleazy bar?" Teensy whispered as they stood just inside the door.

Lizzie breathed a sigh of relief. It wasn't near as bad as she'd imagined. The lighting was dim but it didn't give her the creeps. They strolled over to the bar, trying to look nonchalant while Lizzie scoured the room for Eddie Riser. Fortunately, it wasn't as busy as Teensy had predicted and it took less than a minute to determine he wasn't around. She tossed around the idea of asking the bartender but didn't want him to alert Eddie that someone was looking for him. After another minute, she tilted her head toward the door, Teensy nodded, and they left.

"So what now?" Teensy asked when they were back outside, each one looking in the opposite direction, scoping out the street.

Lizzie nodded. "How about we take a quick walk down

the alley? He could be hanging around there, waiting for a buyer."

"He won't be too happy to see us, in that case."

"Well, it's either that, wait in the bar a bit, or try again another day."

Teensy peered around the corner. "Okay. Let's get it over with."

Lizzie gave her own quick look around, wondering if Bob was somewhere out there watching. And gritting his teeth. If so, she couldn't spot him. He was either very good, as he claimed, or very much not there.

They linked arms and walked briskly to the other end of the alley, easing around overturned garbage cans, avoiding splotches of disgusting things, and trying not to make too much noise.

"Well, another dead end, so to speak," Teensy said. "That was certainly worse than the bar. I'd say this shorter alley should lead us back onto Dexter, sugar. What say we take it?"

They were back in the car, doors locked, eyeing the lane within a minute.

"I think it's a bust. What say we try it another day?" Teensy asked.

Lizzie was just about to agree when she saw a figure approaching the bar, slouched down, and talking into a cell phone. Even with his ball cap pulled down low over his forehead, she was certain it was Eddie Riser.

"That's him. I think it's him. Yes, it is. Let's go confront him before he heads inside." She leapt out of the car and tried to walk casually across the street, not wanting to spook Eddie. By the time he looked up, she was next to him. Teensy stood behind her.

"Hi, Eddie. We haven't formally met but I'm Lizzie and

I do some work out of the community center." She hurried on, not wanting to give him a chance to duck away. "I really need to ask you a question. I hope you don't mind. It won't take but a minute. And it's very important."

"Yeah? To who?" Eddie asked, sounding more curious than anything.

Up close, he didn't look too scary to Lizzie. His dark hair was clean and pushed back behind his ears, skimming the top of his collar. A nose ring in his left nostril balanced the earring in his right lobe.

His blue eyes were wary and his thick lips looked like they might be in a perpetual pout.

"Well, to me and some of my friends."

"Are you buying?"

"Information? I hadn't . . . no."

"No, I mean, are you *buying*?"

"Oh, right. No but that leads right into my question." He hadn't said no so she took that as a good sign. "Did you know Rafe Shannon?"

Eddie blanched and shoved his cell into his jean pocket. "No."

Lizzie crossed her arms and assumed her most commanding teacher tone. "That's not the message I'm getting from you?"

"Message? What message? What the f—"

Lizzie held up her hand. "Oh, cut the crap, Eddie. I know you sell drugs but I don't care about that. Well, I do but not at the moment. What I want to know is if Rafe Shannon had any dealings with you and if that's why he came to Ashton Corners."

"What's it worth to you?"

"Oh, probably not going to the police with all the information I've accumulated about your drug dealings over the past while. Do you even know how often you turn up at the community center parking lot?" Lizzie was taking a stab in the dark here.

Eddie shifted from one foot to the other. He eyed her speculatively. *Sizing me up.* "Okay. Let's talk a little. Why do you want to know? Is this going to get me into trouble?"

"It shouldn't if you're truthful. I just am trying to help clear a friend of his murder but I need to know why he came to town."

"Who's this friend?"

Lizzie wondered if she should be mentioning Darla's name but she'd opted for honestly. Well, mostly. "Darla Lyman."

"The chick from Atlanta? We've got a lot of those folks in town these days." Eddie stuck out his chin, looking defiant, not a look Lizzie had hoped for. "Yeah, he was here to meet me but I'm not going to tell you why. That's called entrapment or something and how do I know the cops don't have you wired? In fact, maybe I should just frisk you to be sure." He flashed Lizzie a grin that bordered on a leer and she backed away. Then he laughed and continued talking.

"He saw that Darla. That's her name isn't it? Said he had to have a little chat with her about some money she owed some people back home. That's the last I saw him. We'd set up a meet the next day but he didn't turn up, then I heard the next day that he'd been found dead. Now, that's all I know. And I'm telling you now, if you do go to the police I'm denying everything. Even with your backup there. They won't believe you because I have some very powerful friends who will get very antsy about not being able to make any purchases. Just so's you know." He folded his arms across his chest.

"Okay," Lizzie said hesitantly. Could it be true? "Did he tell you about anyone else in town he knew or might be talking to?"

"Give me a break. Why would he tell me anything? That's all I know. Now I'd suggest we end this little meeting because you, ladies, are bad for business."

Lizzie glanced around and realized a man, his ball cap pulled way down on his forehead to eyebrow level, was leaning against the wall in the alley. "Okay. Thanks, Eddie."

"Don't mention it, and I mean that."

Chapter Twenty-two

◇◇◇

Even as I struggled with the emotional aftermath of my decision, that seemed to have quite a bit to recommend it.

HERBIE'S GAME—TIMOTHY HALLINAN

After Lizzie had been dropped off back home by Teensy, she grabbed her own car and drove to the Winn-Dixie to pick up some groceries, all the while thinking about what they'd learned. She felt pretty sure that Eddie wasn't the killer, because what would it get him? Maybe Rafe wanted to work with him, not compete with him. Maybe as a supplier? Why hadn't she asked? If that were true, Rafe would be competing with someone. Eddie's current supplier. That could be enough to get Rafe killed. She realized this was way out of her league and even if she asked Eddie about his supplier, it was unlikely she'd get anywhere, except maybe a bed in the hospital or even the morgue.

She shuddered and quickly paid for her items, then headed for the police station. Luck would have it that Mark's Jeep was in the parking lot. She hurried inside and impatiently waited for Mark to finish a phone call before coming out front to get her.

Inside his office, she told him all about Teensy and her meeting with Eddie Riser and then held her breath, waiting for the explosion. It didn't take long.

"You what?"

Lizzie was certain the entire station heard him yelling at her. She tried for a meek smile and reached out to touch his arm.

"Now it's not as bad as it seems, and I'm telling you because I know it's time to back off. That's good, isn't it?"

Mark started pacing, hard to do in his small office. "It's about time but meanwhile, I could be visiting you in the hospital tonight instead of at your place. You do realize that?"

"Yes, but I had Teensy with me."

"You think one extra woman would make a difference if the bad guys wanted to get rid of you? Lizzie, this is really too much this time. You seem to think this is one of your mystery novels. Well, it's not. The violence is very real and can be very brutal. Eddie Riser isn't a misguided kid who deals drugs but has a heart of gold. He's cold-blooded and he's dealing in death. And I don't say that to be overdramatic. Drugs can lead to an early death for some of the kids that get caught in the trap."

He clenched his right hand in a fist and hit the open palm of his left hand. "Guys like him should be marked with a Grim Reaper on their foreheads to warn off the unsuspecting. You don't know how many high school kids I see end up in the hospital or even in jail, Lizzie. All hooked on drugs supplied by Riser and others like him. If there's one thing I'd like to accomplish as police chief it's to rid the town of all the scumbags like Eddie Riser. You know what, though, it's not going to happen. They're like weeds. Pull one out and another takes its place. It's never going to end."

He went back to his desk and sat down. Lizzie was glad, because she had worried he'd have a heart attack or something.

He took a deep breath and continued in a lower but uncompromising voice, "It's dangerous, Lizzie, and you have no place in it at all. It's a big business and they play rough. Besides, you may have jeopardized an ongoing investigation into Riser's drug dealings."

He still looked angry, Lizzie thought. She wasn't sure how much of that anger was directed at her, though. She tried to find a positive point. "Well, don't you think this narrows the field down on possible murder suspects? Eddie doesn't really have a motive but his supplier would, if he thought Rafe Shannon was butting into his territory. Couldn't you make Eddie tell you who it is?"

"We're pretty sure we know who it is."

"You do? And he's still out there supplying drugs?"

"It's a little matter of having enough evidence to arrest him and make it stick, something I already mentioned that you may now have jeopardized."

"I'm sorry if I did, Mark. Truly I am. I'm just trying to help Darla."

"And you may have thrown her back into the thick of it. Did you think of that?"

"What do you mean?"

"Well, we know about the gambling now and maybe Shannon did lean on her to get the money, and she cracked and killed him."

Lizzie sat down hard. "I hadn't thought of that. But women don't usually bludgeon to death their victims, do they? I'm sure I read that somewhere. They're more likely to use poison. Or a pillow."

Mark finally grinned. "And how do you think Darla would have gotten Shannon in the position to use either poison or a pillow?"

Lizzie dared to breathe easier. Mark looked more relaxed. The worst had passed. She shrugged, trying to relax her shoulders and reduce her tension. "My point exactly. Darla is not the killer."

Mark grimaced, then glanced at the phone. He let out a long sigh. "I have some more calls to make before a lunch meeting."

"My cue to exit." She sprang out of the chair, anxious to get out of the office and have this conversation put to rest.

"And Lizzie . . ."

She held off opening the door and turned back to him. "Yes?"

"The Eddie Riser I know would not tell the truth if his life depended on it. He's not your reliable source of information. Stay away from him."

"Got it." She hesitated before asking. "See you later?"

"You can bet on it. And just one more thing," Mark said.

Uh-oh.

"Your sleuthing days are over. Right?"

She nodded. "I'm totally staying away from all things drug related."

Mark sighed. "Somehow I think you're avoiding the point. But I'll settle for that right now." He got up and walked over, leaning behind her to open the door for her.

On the drive home, Lizzie pondered the fact that she'd managed to flip things over and point the finger once again at Darla.

Not good. She'd have to do something about that.

* * *

She was headed home when she suddenly decided to veer right and cross over to Highway 2, in the opposite direction from the Mountain View Motel, and take a drive. She tried to put her brain on hold as she made her way about eight miles out of town to a small, grassy clearing beside the river. There was room for about four cars to park and no one was there. She sighed in relief. She just wanted some time alone to think things through. What Mark had said had truly shaken her. Not only the part about being in real danger but also the fact that she'd never seen him quite so mad at her, and that had scared her.

She turned off the motor and got out, taking time to stretch and suck in a deep breath. Already she felt the knots in her shoulders loosening. She walked over to a wooden bench facing the river and tucked behind some bushes that gave it some privacy from the road and passing traffic.

She sat and stared for a few minutes, trying for a while longer without any turbulence in her mind but finally, she focused on the thought that every now and then burst onto the scene to plague her. What if Mark realized she was more trouble than the relationship was worth? She knew she was being childish, but she had this deep-down fear that someday it would be over, and he'd leave her and not look back.

She wasn't one given to analyzing any situation too closely, not a personal one anyway. What did it matter if she had an irrational fear of being left because her daddy died while she was at a formative age? That's something she had read once, had thought about, and then decided it didn't really matter. She had to deal with each situation as it came up and decide what was relevant. The past wasn't, in her opinion. However, she did have to admit that, over the years, she'd had trouble letting men get close to her. Of course, none of them had felt like Mr. Right.

And she had to admit, maybe that was why she'd never come right out and told Mark that she loved him. When she'd first realized it, she'd been overwhelmed and filled with joy. That would have been the time to tell him. But she hadn't been sure he felt the same way. In fact, it had taken him a long time to tell her just how he felt. And at that moment, she felt it lessened what she meant if she answered right back.

She gave herself a mental head slap. Now she felt she was just overanalyzing everything. Something she said she never did.

She threw up her hands and watched two ducks waddling, one behind the other, along the water's edge, oblivious to their frazzled neighbor. *Get a grip. Focus on the murder.*

Go back to the beginning of the story, just as if reading a novel. Darla arrives in town, obviously in need of a place to stay and also some money.

Lizzie notices Rafe Shannon accosting Darla in town. They argue and Darla breaks away.

Rafe Shannon's body is found in Molly's backyard. His car is parked on the street, so he obviously drove himself there. But why? To confront Darla again?

Darla is questioned about the murder and released.

Wade Morris turns up in town and convinces Darla to move back into the motel with him.

Lizzie notices Wade talking to drug dealer Eddie Riser behind the community center.

Wade beats on Darla, who then moves back in with Molly.

Teensy comes back from Atlanta with news about Darla's gambling debts. Rafe did some collections for casinos and bookies. Did he follow her to town?

Eddie Riser sort of admits Rafe Shannon wanted to do some business involving drugs with him.

Okay, that was it. The plot points. Now, to fill the rest in. Who were the possible suspects? Darla had to be on the list but not a serious contender, even with Mark's most recent conjecture. Eddie Riser was on it, since he'd had contact with Rafe, but also not a probable killer. Eddie's current supplier, very possible if Rafe had wanted to butt in but his identity was unknown, except to the police. So leave it with them. Yes. No.

The question about what Rafe had been doing at Molly's was in no way explained. And, the only other person in the story at this point was Wade Morris.

Could he be part of the plot? But how? He didn't arrive until after the murder. Or did he? Was that the reason Darla hadn't given up her room at the motel? But what would be his motive to kill Shannon?

Lizzie heard a car pull into the parking area and knew it was time to go. Her thinking time was over. Good decision as she was almost run down by three kids stampeding to the river's edge, followed by a haggard-looking mama. By the time she reached her house, she'd decided to concentrate on making sure she was ready for the start of school, still another week off, but she knew if she left it too long, it would then become a chore. She had a workshop for the teachers all ready to go but she still had a couple of assignments from her Tuesday evening literacy class to mark. A tall iced tea and a garden chair would make the perfect setting for that.

As she rounded the corner onto her street, she saw Sally-Jo getting back into her silver Kia Rio parked on the street in front of Lizzie's house. Lizzie honked the horn and pulled into the driveway. By the time she was out of the car, Sally-Jo had run over and gave her a big hug.

"Hey, Sally-Jo, you're back. It's so good to see you," Lizzie said.

"Yeah, well I changed my mind again and hopped on a

plane this morning. I stopped by on a whim and was disappointed when you were out. I'm just bursting to talk about the wedding plans, no surprise there."

"Come on. We'll grab something cold to drink and gab in the backyard. How did everything go overall? You were pretty silent the last couple of days."

"I was into some heavy-duty negotiations with my mama."

"And?"

"And, I'll show you a photo of my dress when we get all comfy."

Lizzie unlocked the back door and went inside to get the drinks while Sally-Jo pulled two wicker chairs close to each other.

"Now talk," Lizzie ordered, handing over a frosted glass of iced tea.

Sally-Jo pulled out her phone and flashed a photo of her wedding dress at Lizzie.

"Wow, that's the one you wanted. It's so perfect for you. Did you really talk your mama into it?"

"I sure did. Well, rather we bargained. I got my dress and mama gets to choose the menu."

"And you feel what about that?"

Sally-Jo shrugged. "I guess it's okay. I mean, I really, really wanted this dress and Mama's a good cook and really knows her food, so I think she'll probably choose something that works. I hope so anyway. Jacob, bless his soul, just smiles whenever I say anything about the wedding these days."

"Self-preservation."

Sally-Jo nodded. "Exactly. Now, if I can enjoy this last week before school starts in relative peace and quiet, I'll be a happy woman. Too much histrionics for one week."

Lizzie grinned. "Your mama can certainly put on a good show."

"Yeah. Lucky me. So tell me, what's been happening here? Is the murderer caught and behind bars?"

"No such luck. In fact, I really don't know how close Mark is to finding out who did it."

"Well, what about the gang? I know you haven't all been sitting on your hands. Any leads?"

"I thought we had a good one. In fact, Teensy and I had a talk with him this morning and then Mark read me the riot act."

"Ouch. Who is this guy?"

Lizzie filled her in on what they'd learned and who they had approached the past week. When she'd finished, Sally-Jo sat still, saying nothing.

"What do you think?" Lizzie finally asked.

"I'm processing."

Lizzie watched her with growing impatience and was just about to ask her again when Sally-Jo looked at her and said, "Well, have you asked Darla about all this?"

"I haven't had a chance, not with everything that's been happening."

"I think that's gotta be the next step, don't you?"

"You're right. I'm just not sure how to go about it. I feel like I'm staging every confrontation, deciding who gets to go where. I don't want Molly to hear me questioning Darla in case anything really negative or illegal comes out. And Teensy is so set against Darla and how she's manipulating Molly to get money out of her, that she doesn't qualify as an unbiased observer." Lizzie looked straight at Sally-Jo. "You do, though."

"Right on. I'm anxious to get into the fray now that things are settling down in my life. I hope." She held up her hand and crossed her fingers. "Where do you think we'll find Darla? At Molly's?"

"Probably. She's been lying low since the beating, afraid

she'll run into Wade, although I'd bet she'd go back to him in a heartbeat."

"Uh-oh. That's bad news."

They finished their drinks in silence. "Ready?" Lizzie asked.

Sally-Jo nodded. "Let me drive. Now how are we going to do this? Good cop, bad cop?"

Lizzie bit back a smile. Sally-Jo sounded so serious she didn't want to offend her. "I think we'll both be good cops and maybe that way she'll open up to us. One of the girls. Nice and sympathetic."

"Sounds good."

Sally-Jo kept up a flow of dialogue on all she'd done back home in Fort Myers, which turned out to be more than just shopping for a bridal gown. One of her sisters, Meg, had come home too, so they got caught up on each other's lives and revisited a lot of their childhood haunts. "Of course, it helped that Meg was on my side about the dress," Sally-Jo admitted as she pulled into Molly's driveway.

They tried knocking on the front door but didn't get a response, so they walked around to the backyard. No one answered when they banged on that door either.

Sally-Jo glanced at Lizzie. "You could use your key."

"Ugh, I feel odd doing that if Darla doesn't want to talk to us."

"She may not be here. Maybe she's out with Molly somewhere."

"In that case, I have no reason to go into the house."

"But you'll never know unless you go into the house."

They heard a car door slam out front. As they rounded the side of the house, Molly was just letting herself inside. She glanced over at them.

"Were you looking for me or Darla?"

"Well, both," said Lizzie, feeling a bit guilty.

"She should be here. I just went over to Blanchard's Deli to pick up some salads for supper tonight. Come on in, girls. Sally-Jo, it's nice to have you back. How are things with your mama?"

Sally-Jo went through her explanation as they entered the house. Lizzie glanced up the staircase, wondering if Darla would come down and join them.

Molly followed her glance and called out again. After waiting a minute with no answer, Molly said, "Why don't you girls just go and pour us all some tea. I'll just go upstairs and see what Darla is up to."

Lizzie led the way and was just pouring out three glasses when Molly came in. "There's no sign of her and what's worse, her clothes are gone."

"You don't think she's run away?" Sally-Jo asked.

Lizzie shook her head. "I'll bet she's back with Wade."

Molly let out a gasp. "I didn't see that coming but you're probably right. Isn't that what abused women do? Go back to their man when given the opportunity?"

"It may not have been voluntary. Wade may have waited for you to leave and then strong-armed her into going with him. I think I should call Mark."

Molly nodded. "That's probably a good idea. I don't want Bob going over there. No telling what he might do."

Lizzie picked up the phone and dialed the station. She was put right through. After explaining the situation, she listened awhile and then agreed. After she'd hung up, she explained to the others, "Mark will stop by but if Darla is okay, he can't force her to leave. He will warn Wade, though, that any new mark on her and he'll be in jail faster than a hot knife through butter, according to Mark." Lizzie smiled. She got a kick out of his reverting to some of the phrases she'd heard her daddy use.

"Oh, dear. I guess that will have to do. I'd like to try talking to her, though. She needs to have some sense drummed into that head of hers. I'm sure it's just a matter of time before he beats on her again," Molly said, wringing her hands.

Lizzie took hold of her arm and led her to a chair at the banquette. "Sit. Now, take a sip and try to relax. I'd say she's safe for now anyway. Wade won't try anything with Mark breathing down his back. Tomorrow, I think it's time for some action. I'll just park outside and wait until Wade leaves, then dash in and talk to Darla."

"I don't want you doing that alone, Lizzie. I'm going with you," Molly said, slamming her glass on the table.

"I don't think so, Molly. Sally-Jo, what about Jacob?" Lizzie looked over at her. "I think it might be good to have a man as deflection."

"I'm sure he would but he's driving to Birmingham tomorrow, something to do with work. But I'll go with you."

"That's great. But it will be in the afternoon. I'm having lunch with Mama so I'll give you a call when I'm ready."

When she got home she found Mark sitting in the backyard, nursing a bottle of Coors beer. Patchett was stretched out on the patio at Mark's feet. He raised his head and acknowledged her rubbing of his ears, and then resumed his sleeping pose.

"I hope you don't mind. I helped myself to a beer and then thought this would make a perfect spot to end the day. This is Patchett's favorite place, too."

"Sounds like a great idea to me. I'll grab something and join you. Both of you." She gave a silent cheer, grateful that Mark didn't seem to be mad at her any longer.

Lizzie gave Mark's head a small pat as she walked past him. She smiled, wondering if he realized how hot she thought he looked being bald. She'd not told him and she wasn't about to, not yet anyway. She'd always thought that about bald men for no reason other than it was what it was.

By the time she rejoined him, Mark had pulled a chair up close, right next to his. She sat down and he grabbed her hand, lightly caressing it.

"How did it go with Darla?" Lizzie asked.

"She's okay. For now. How was the rest of your day?"

Was this a trick question? She hadn't gotten into any more trouble, as far as she knew. "It was good but exhausting."

"I hope not too exhausting." He gave her hand a squeeze.

"Never." Lizzie sipped on her red wine and wondered if she dare ask anything about the investigation. *Probably not.* She shouldn't even think it.

Mark sighed. "Good. I've been thinking this afternoon that there may be only one way to get your mind off this murder."

"And that would be?" She had an inkling.

"Come with me and I'll show you." He stood and held out his hand to her. "Patchett will stay in the kitchen."

Chapter Twenty-three

◇◇◇

I ought never to have dared the thought.

JANE AND THE TWELVE DAYS OF CHRISTMAS—
STEPHANIE BARRON

Mark was already tying his running shoes by the time Lizzie made it downstairs the next morning. "What are you up to?"

"I thought I'd join you for a run this morning." He pointed at Patchett who lay across the back door opening. "He said he was in need of some exercise."

Lizzie let out an unladylike snort. "Some exercise running with him."

Mark knelt down and patted the dog. "Don't worry, son, she's not really picking on you. It only sounds that way and that's because she hasn't had her morning java yet." He stood and opened the back door. "Okay, Patchett can stand guard in the Jeep. You and I will do the exercise part."

Lizzie couldn't say no to that. They were about fifteen

minutes into the run, having headed toward the pathway along the river into town, when Mark finally spoke.

"I'm taking the day off since Amber Craig is back. She's in charge today."

"Oh, and what are you planning to do?"

"I thought I'd do a little unofficial surveillance with you."

Lizzie glanced at him. "What do you mean?"

"Come on now. I know you. That mind of yours just won't leave this case nor Darla's situation alone. I'll just bet you're planning to sit outside that motel until Wade Morris goes out and then you'll have a talk with Darla, try and convince her to go back to Molly's."

Lizzie gasped. "How did you know that?"

"Like I said, I know you, Lizzie Turner. I'll bet you talked Sally-Jo into going with you, too."

"Actually, you don't know everything. She offered."

Mark chuckled and slowed his pace. "I actually think it's a good idea to try and talk her out of that motel room, but there'll be hell to pay if he comes back while you're there. I'll just provide some backup."

Lizzie stopped and grabbed Mark's hand. "Thanks, Mark. We're all so worried about her being back there, and coming face-to-face with him is not something I want to do."

Mark gave her a quick kiss. "Just this once I'll take part in one of your schemes."

"I need to visit Mama first though. Do you want to come along and have lunch with us?"

"Why don't you have your visit and I'll take Patchett home. Give me a call as you're leaving your mama and I'll meet you at your place."

"Good idea. But before doing anything, I'd better call Sally-Jo about the change in plans." She glanced down at Patchett then took off at a run. "Try to keep up, boys."

* * *

Lizzie parked in the only available space out front at Magnolia Manor. She was surprised to see so many cars in the lot and then remembered that today was the twenty-fifth anniversary celebration for the residence. The still-stately mansion had been bought and renovated into the elegant assisted living place that Evelyn Turner now called home.

A large panorama showcasing photos from the days of renovation until the present greeted everyone entering through the front door. To the right of it, a bulletin board listed the many events scheduled for that day. Lizzie was pleased to note that a luncheon had been planned for the back lawn. She glanced out there and was awed by the huge tent that had been erected. Residents were already starting to filter in and find tables. Lizzie hurried down to her mama's room and gave a quick knock before entering.

Evelyn sat on the edge of her bed wearing her best dress, a flowing chiffon number in multi-shades of blue, with a drop waist and sleeves to her elbows. A wide-brimmed white straw hat lay next to her on the bed.

Lizzie gave her a hug and kissed her cheek. "Mama, you're looking so pretty today. I had totally forgotten about the anniversary party. I'm sorry I'm not all dressed up, too. Will it be all right for me to attend the luncheon wearing this?"

She watched closely to see if Evelyn would check her out. After a couple of minutes, Lizzie carried on. "Well, then. Let's go join the others, shall we? I'm sure you must be getting hungry. I know I am."

She took hold of her mama's hand and led her to the door. Just before Lizzie opened it, Evelyn pulled back and reached out for her hat. She turned to the mirror and placed it carefully on her head. When she looked back at Lizzie, there was a big smile on her face.

Lizzie let out a small gasp. Evelyn had done this herself. She had remembered her hat and put it on. It would be a good afternoon. "You look so beautiful, Mama."

They found their name tags on a table for four and joined Evelyn's old friend Queenie Duggan and her younger sister, Nola.

"It's so lovely to see you again, Elizabeth. I don't know if I would have recognized you if I'd run into you at the Winn-Dixie. In fact, I'll just bet I've walked past you dozens of times in town." Queenie let out a schoolgirl giggle. "And you, Evelyn, look very lovely today." She touched the brim of her own straw-colored hat festooned with dozens of artificial flowers. "I just threw on this old thing. Haven't worn it since the Founders Day Festival in May 1989."

"How do you remember that?" Nola asked sharply.

Queenie smiled. "I just do, my dear. You will too, if you give it some thought."

Nola reached for the menu and looked to be reading it intently. She let out a small cry that caused everyone at the table and those close by to look at her. "Queenie. That's the day that Gregory Kaiser moved to town!"

"Precisely."

Lizzie looked from one to the other, wondering if she should ask who that was.

Queenie reached out and touched Lizzie on her hand. "Gregory, my dear, was the love of our lives. Oh, yes, we both fell in love with him. He was well on his way to having a head full of gray hair by that point but he was still handsome. Much like the other Gregory who stole our hearts at a younger age. You know, Gregory Peck. And what a charmer." She sighed.

"What happened?" Lizzie asked.

"Happened? Oh, he was also very sly and started wooing both of us, without the other knowing it. Quite the charmer. But unfortunately, he passed on."

"He died?"

"No, child, he moved away with Ursula Farmer. You see, he had been also seeing her on the side and as everyone knows, Ursula had loads of money from the untimely death of her former husband. Number three it was. Now, what's on the menu, sister dear?" She looked at Nola, who also sighed before handing over her copy.

"Wow." Lizzie couldn't think of anything else to say.

"Hmm, yes," answered Queenie. "Now, I hear tell you're spending a lot of time with that sexy looking chief of police."

"Sister," Nola said, sounding shocked.

"Well, I did hear that and he certainly is. I knew his mama before she married Ken Dreyfus. She was a beauty. I think he has her big brown eyes. But the rest of him is all manly."

"You shush up now, sister. Who knows what Elizabeth is thinking about you? Such talk." Nola leaned toward Lizzie. "You have to excuse Queenie. She tends to get a bit carried away every now and then."

"Oh, I don't mind, ma'am. In fact, I have to agree with her."

Queenie winked and Lizzie flashed a smile back. She looked over at her mama, wondering what she thought about all this. Or if she'd been following. Their server came and took their orders, Lizzie choosing the green salad with chicken strips for herself and the same for Evelyn, while the sisters took the roast beef and mashed potatoes, the only other entrée.

"I was just thinking," said Nola, "I heard that Bob Miller's granddaughter is in town. Is that right?"

"Yes, it is. Her name's Darla Lyman and she arrived last week."

"Hmm. I can still remember Lily Miller, that would be her mama, picking tulips from my front yard one day in summer, cheery as can be, as if she owned the place. When I told Sue-Ann, that would be her mama, Bob's former wife, she told me to stop picking on her little girl. Harrumph. Can you imagine? That Sue-Ann never did have a lick of sense but she knew what she wanted. Went after young Bob Miller like a moth in a mitten, even though it was plain as the nose on your face how he felt about Molly Mathews."

Lizzie leaned forward. "How did he feel?"

"Oh, anyone could see that Bob was sweet on Molly but I think in her mind, they were just good friends. At least, that's how it seemed. I wasn't right in Molly's group, you understand, but it looked like she didn't have her heart set on anyone in those days. Not until Claydon Mathews set his sights on her. Of course, that was long after Sue-Ann had a wedding ring on her finger. Claydon was probably the better match anyway. For Molly, I'm saying. Both from well-off families and him so dashing and into the social set and all." She sighed. "How is Molly these days? I don't see much of her anymore."

"She's doing just fine and keeping very busy with all her projects." A basket of rolls was placed on the table and Lizzie grabbed it, passing it to Nola, hoping to forestall any more questions. While she loved hearing about Molly's younger days, she was reluctant to share information about her dear friend.

The meal appeared shortly after and they ate in silence. Lizzie wondered when Nola had last eaten, judging from the speed with which she cleaned her plate. Probably living on her own led to easy and spare meals, possibly even skipped ones. Maybe Nola should think about a room of her own in Magnolia Manor.

Lizzie thought about the luncheon on the drive home. She'd enjoyed the visit with Queenie and Nola Duggan, and her mama seemed to, also. She'd been ready for her nap, though, by the time Lizzie left. Even though she didn't participate in conversations, Lizzie was certain her mother took in everything, which could be exhausting when those around were as talkative as the Duggan sisters.

"I see we have company," Lizzie said as she hopped into Mark's Jeep.

He looked over his shoulder and grinned. "Patchett might come in handy. There's nothing less threatening than someone walking a dog."

"He's a prop." She turned to give him a pat. "Such an honor, Patchett."

He slobbered over her hand before she had a chance to pull it away. She wiped it on the towel Mark kept stuffed between the seats.

"How much do you know about the psychology of all this?" Lizzie asked.

"You mean, why a woman keeps going back to an abusive relationship?"

"Uh-huh."

"I worked with a social worker on my first case as chief. It was a situation just like this. We had a hard time convincing the wife to leave. She jumped back and forth between believing he'd change and being scared stiff that he'd find her and kill her."

"What happened?"

"We finally got her to a women's shelter. He eventually found where she was staying, my bet is that she got in touch with him, and he went there and shot himself on the front lawn."

"I remember that in the paper. Wow, what a pathetic story."

"He realized he couldn't get at her or maybe he realized there was no happy ending in any way."

"If she'd killed him, would it have been self-defense?"

"Whoa. Where is that coming from?"

"Oh, just wondering what other endings there could have been." She glanced out the side window so she wouldn't have to face him. She knew he couldn't read her thoughts and would know nothing about Fannie Hewitt, but she didn't want him to see any evasiveness in her eyes.

"No matter how much the guy may have deserved such an ending that would be a hard thing for his wife to have to live with. Fortunately, it didn't get to that point."

Lizzie nodded and continued to watch the houses pass by. As much as she wanted it to be Teensy's problem, she realized she'd have to figure out what do to about Fannie real soon.

Mark parked in an alley across the street from the motel. Although they couldn't see the unit, they could see if anyone entered or left the parking lot. "We wait. Welcome to the totally boring side of police work."

He settled back in his seat, and Patchett managed to wiggle his way through the opening between the seats and onto Mark's lap. Mark opened the window and Patchett sat with his head on the sill. Lizzie took a sip of the coffee they'd stopped to pick up at Starbucks, and tried to clear her head of all thoughts, wanting to concentrate on the scene in front of her.

After about ten minutes she asked, "Can we talk?"

"Do you mean, just talk about things in general or something specific?"

"Just talk. Or do we have to remain silent?"

Mark chuckled. "No we don't have to keep silent. Talk away."

Patchett turned to look at her, and then with difficulty

fumbled his way over to her lap. Mark turned the ignition on so she could open her window, too. Once Patchett had settled, Lizzie asked, "Do you think Rafe Shannon died because of drugs?"

Mark sighed. "I guess there's no way we can avoid that topic today. I still am without a definitive motive for his murder but his alleged involvement with Eddie Riser is raising all sorts of red flags. I will allow that you could be right about his supplier. From what we know about this guy, he would stop at nothing to prevent someone from horning in on his territory."

"So he, whoever he is, is the main suspect?"

"He's pretty close to the top of the list but like all things to do with this guy, there's no way to prove it. Amber Craig does believe that Shannon was into more than being the muscle for some shady guys. She thinks he's a mule, transporting drugs between supplier and dealers. She also has proof that he's been doing some small-time dealing himself."

"Wow. That's gotta be it then."

"It could be and we're looking at ways to prove it but so far, nada." He turned slightly to face her. "I'm telling you this in the hopes that you'll show some restraint in future. You know we're working on it so there's no need for you to go getting involved again. Got it?"

"Uh-huh. By the way, did anything come from Bob's surveillance gig?"

Mark shook his head.

She didn't know if that meant that nothing had happened or that he wasn't telling.

She glanced back outside. "Look. That's Wade. There he goes." Lizzie opened the door but turned back as Mark did the same. "I think I should go in alone. If she sees you, she'll think you're there to arrest Wade and you know how that went over last time."

Mark stared at her a moment. "All right. I'll keep an eye out for Wade in case he returns quickly."

"What should I do if he does?"

"I'll show up at the door right behind him. Believe me, he won't try anything."

Lizzie smiled her thanks and hopped out of the Jeep. She checked for traffic, then sprinted across the street. She paused before knocking on the door. What would she say? Just try to talk some sense into her, she guessed. It also wouldn't hurt to find out just how much she knew about Rafe's other career.

Darla answered on the fourth knock. Lizzie had been ready to start pounding on it in exasperation but quickly tacked a smile on her face. "Hi, Darla. We've all been worried about you. Can we talk?"

Darla started to close the door, shaking her head. "Wade will be really, really mad if he finds you here."

"Don't worry about that. I've got backup." She looked behind her at where Mark was parked.

Darla's eyes widened. "So, he might not get mad at you but he'll take it out on me when you leave."

Lizzie saw her opportunity. "Why do you stay with him then?" She put her arm around Darla's shoulder and eased her way through the door.

Darla looked bewildered. "Why? 'Cause he loves me. He just has a small problem with his temper sometimes."

"But do you love him?"

Darla shrugged. "Yeah, I guess. I mean, he's all that I've got."

"Not true. Your mama's worried about you."

Darla shot her a glance. "How do you know that?"

Uh-oh. "There's been contact with her. She's really

worried and I'll bet, if you went on home, things might be a bit different."

"Not likely. You don't know what's going on."

"You mean, your gambling debts?"

Darla looked like she'd been slapped. "How do you know? Did Mama tell you? How could she? I hate her."

"No you don't. She did talk about it because she loves you and is worried about you." Lizzie watched while Darla wandered around the room.

"How much do you owe?"

"Huh? Oh, I'm not really sure. About nine thousand, I think. Maybe a bit more."

Wow. "We know that Rafe Shannon has worked for various casinos and bookies over the years. Was he really here following you to try and collect the debt?"

Darla shook her head. "No. At least, he said he wasn't. He did try to get it, of course. Like I'd said before, I just happened to run into him downtown. He was as surprised to see me as I was him. But he said, since he'd found me, he'd take the money back with him. He gave me two days to find it or else."

"Why two days?"

"He said he'd be finished with his business by then and would head back to Atlanta."

"Did he say what the other business was?"

Darla shrugged. "Why would he tell me?" She sounded like she was beginning to lose patience.

Aha, you lied. You said you didn't know him. What else are you keeping from us?

"Well, the main reason I'm here, as you can probably guess, is we'd all like you to go back to Molly's. Why would you move back with Wade when you said yourself that he has a bad temper?"

Darla shrugged and flopped on the bed.

Lizzie wondered how to convince her. How could they get her out of Wade's grip? *Wade. I wonder . . .* "Darla, did Wade know Rafe Shannon?"

"He could have. I don't know all the dealings Wade has."

"Does he gamble also?"

"Naw. He's more into making money than losing it. Always working on a new scheme and they're usually fool-proof, or so he says."

Lizzie had an idea that was forming but she needed to focus on Darla at the moment. "Darla, get off that bed and come with me, right now." She hoped some tough love would work.

Darla sat up looking surprised. "I don't want to." She stared up at the ceiling. "I'm afraid to. He really would come after me."

"But you know we can protect you."

"No, you don't know that. You don't know what he's capable of. And, besides, he threatened to harm my grand-daddy and Molly if I don't cooperate."

Lizzie's jaw dropped. Oh boy, this guy was scarier than she'd imagined.

Darla was off the bed in a shot and grabbed Lizzie's arm, shoving her toward the door. "Look, I know you think you're trying to help but I do love Wade and I'm not leaving him. Now, you'd better get going before he comes back. If he finds you here, that means trouble for everyone."

She'd shoved Lizzie through the door before she could react. Lizzie glanced quickly up the street and then over to the Jeep. No Wade but no Mark, either. She rushed across the street and looked through the window. No one. She heard Patchett bark and turned to see Mark with Patchett on leash, heading toward her.

"No luck?" he asked when he reached her.

"No. Maybe we should get out of here before he gets back. I'll tell you all about it on the way over to Molly's."

Lizzie had just finished filling him in as he turned into Molly's driveway. Fortunately, Bob's pickup was parked there. They got out, Mark leaving Patchett in the Jeep with windows open, and went around back to find Bob and Molly working in the garden.

"You've got a new gardener, Molly," Lizzie called out.

Bob turned around at the same time as Molly and grinned. "Just working toward a meal here. What brings you two around?"

"Now, Bob," Molly said, brushing off the knees of her khaki pants, "that's a rather forward question."

"What? I'm just asking is all."

"It almost sounds as if they're not welcome, and that could not be further away from the truth. Can I get you something cold to drink?"

"Why don't I get that?" Lizzie asked. "You two look like it's time for a break."

Molly nodded and sank into a wicker chair. "Those gardenias seem to need a lot more care every year. There's a pitcher of lemonade freshly made in the fridge, honey."

When Lizzie returned with a tray of glasses and the pitcher, the others were talking gardens. Lizzie poured everyone their drinks and sat across from Mark.

Bob drank almost half of the glass at once and then asked, "Any news on our mutual friend Wade?"

Mark shook his head. "We were just over at the Mountain View Motel. We waited until he left and then Lizzie talked to Darla."

Bob stiffened. "Did you talk her into coming back?"

"She wouldn't budge but I think it's because she's not only scared for herself but also for you two," Lizzie added.

"What? What's that hooligan been saying?"

"He's threatened both of you if she leaves him."

Bob bolted out of his chair. "Just let me at that guy."

Mark stood, too, and put a hand on Bob's arm. "That's not the way to handle this and you know it. Just sit back down and let's figure out something that will work."

Bob took a few moments, then looked at Mark and nodded. When they'd both sat down again, Mark continued. "I'd say that Darla sharing that information with Lizzie tells us that she really doesn't want to be there even though part of her says she's staying because she loves him. So I think if we put him away behind bars and convince her that you two won't be harmed by him, then she'll come along."

"What can you charge him with?" Lizzie asked.

"That's just it. At the moment, all we have is suspicions that he beat on Darla." He held up his hand as Molly was about to protest. "Darla won't testify and no one saw him do it so there's nothing I can really do about it. And the only other thing is his meeting with Eddie Riser. If he has dealings with Riser, we may be able to get him there."

"But you don't know that for sure." Lizzie knew that if Mark had any evidence from their ongoing investigation into the drug business, he would have used it by now to arrest Wade.

"We're looking at it, Lizzie. I said that already. It takes time."

"But we don't have time if he starts beating on her again." Lizzie wasn't about to give up. "And what if they send someone else to deal with Darla and her debts?"

"I thought she said Rafe Shannon was surprised to see her here."

"But he may have told his bosses and they may be doing something about it."

"Hm. That may be the way to get her to move back in. If I tell Darla that I'll have someone keep an eye on the motel to protect her from the debt collectors, I'm sure that if Wade's up to no good he won't want the police hanging around at the motel. So he may be willing to let her move back here."

"That makes sense," Molly said. "I like that idea very much, although I wish you hadn't thought of the possibility that her life is back in danger."

Bob touched Molly's arm. "If they wanted to really harm her, they would have done it by now. Although nine grand seems a lot to us, to them it's peanuts. They know they'll wring it out of her at some point so I think it makes sense, economically, that they use their heavies to collect the larger debts."

Molly sighed and nodded.

"Now then," Bob continued, "I think you and I should go right over there, Mark. And I am going with you so don't try talking me out of it."

"I wasn't about to."

"And me," Lizzie threw in.

"Only if you stay in the Jeep and keep Patchett company. I think we'll impress Wade more if there's just the two of us, but it would be a good idea for you to settle Darla down once she's left with us."

It took just a few minutes to reach the motel and Lizzie did as told, waiting in the Jeep with Patchett. She watched as Wade opened the door and the two men entered. She realized she was holding her breath, ears attuned to any loud noises that might reach the open window. Just as she checked her iPhone clock the third time, the door opened and Bob stepped out, holding Darla by the arm. He carried a back-pack in his left hand.

Mark emerged a minute later, waiting by the closed door until Bob and Darla were safely in the Jeep, and then he joined them.

"Are you all right, Darla?" Lizzie asked as Darla pressed her forehead against the side window, staring at the motel.

"Sure, why wouldn't I be?" She sounded hostile once again.

"Look, we know this isn't what you want but it's for the best. You have to trust us on that."

Bob shifted in his seat to look back at Darla. "Lizzie's right. Once things have settled down a bit, we'll try to work all this out with Wade. All I ask is that you give our way a try. We really do have your best interests at heart."

Darla continued staring out the window even though the motel was far behind them. "What about the money?"

"What about it?"

She turned to glare at Bob. "The nine thousand I owe. Well, y'all are right. Now that they know where I am, they'll come again and try to get it off me and I don't have the money to pay them." She sniffled but Lizzie wasn't sure if it was more for effect than real.

"I thought you told Lizzie you bumped into Shannon unexpectedly."

"I did but it's just like you told Wade, they could be coming to get me. And I don't have their stupid money."

Lizzie could see Mark's eyes in the rearview mirror, shifting from Darla and over to Bob. This was something only those two could take part in.

Bob finally sighed. "We'll come up with it somehow. Don't you worry yourself about that. Even if I have to bor-row it, we'll make sure those goons are paid off, but you will have to give me your solemn promise that that's it for the gambling. And, you will have to pay me back. I'll help you find a job if you decide to stay here in Ashton Corners. And, if you decide to go back to Atlanta, I'll try to work something out for you with your mama."

Darla was silent for longer than Lizzie was comfortable with. Finally she answered in a soft voice, "Fine."

Chapter Twenty-four

◇◇◇

"No. She's cleared out."

FINGER LICKIN' FIFTEEN—JANET EVANOVICH

Lizzie slid an eye open and tried to focus on the clock. Three in the morning and who was on the phone. She bolted upright, knowing it couldn't be anything good. Her mama, Molly, Mark . . . all raced through her mind in seconds. It was Molly's voice that greeted her.

"I'm so sorry to call at this hour, honey."

"What's wrong, Molly? Are you ill?"

"No, I'm fine. It's just that Darla has gone sneaking out. Something awakened me and when I went to check the doors and everything, I noticed her jacket was missing from the hall where she'd left it. Then I checked her room and she wasn't there."

"You think she went back to Wade?"

"I don't know what to think but I'm worried sick. I don't

want to call Bob but I certainly don't want you going out looking for her either. That's not why I called. I just needed to talk it through. I hope you don't mind."

Lizzie rested back against the brass headboard of her bed. The cats returned to their sleeping spots, and ignored the conversation.

"I'm sure she went back to him and I don't think he's going to start in on her tonight anyway. He'll probably see it as reaffirmation that she loves him." *Or beat her up for leaving in the first place.* "I'm certain the guys put the fear of jail in him with that visit. Why don't you just try going back to sleep. She might even be back when you get up in the morning. If not, give me a call and we'll think of what to do next. Okay?"

"Umm, that sounds like the most reasonable approach. I'll try to sleep and I will call in the morning. Thanks for listening to me. I'm so sorry to have awoken you."

"Don't worry about it, Molly. We'll talk tomorrow."

Lizzie had a hard time getting back to sleep. She toyed with the idea of driving right over to the motel to check on Darla but realized it might cause the girl more trouble than help. If she couldn't physically help her then maybe she could work through to another solution. But first, she'd really have to get into Darla's head and try to figure out what really was going on with her.

She tried to picture Darla as she'd first seen her at Molly's door a couple of weeks earlier. Darla had come across as defiant and yet, Lizzie had sensed a vulnerability in her when Molly had appeared. Darla had seemed eager to meet Bob and readily came to the barbecue the next day.

So, I'm a young woman about to meet the granddad that everyone's been dissing all my life. How do I feel? Angry, unsure, afraid of rejection? Darla's reactions that afternoon had seemed in keeping with all those emotions. But Lizzie had sensed a cold, unemotional side, too. Like someone with a goal in mind, something other than being enveloped in warm, loving arms. *Or, am I projecting that on her?*

Lizzie's next impression had been that Darla wanted money from Bob or Molly, mainly because she'd admitted to being destitute. How valid was that impression? Had Darla wanted money to survive or, as it turned out, to pay her debts? Of course she hadn't mentioned the gambling to start with. She'd probably known that would not put her in a sympathetic light.

And then there was the Rafe Shannon thing. He'd obviously upped the pressure on her to pay up but had he followed up on it? Is that what he was doing at Molly's that night? It made sense. But it didn't make sense that Darla would kill him. If he'd put her on the spot right then and there she could have just appealed to Molly. Lizzie was certain Molly would have paid right on the spot. And Darla would have figured that all out by that point. So there was no real motive for Darla to kill Rafe.

Then who?

She realized she'd spend the rest of the night wandering around this mind maze unless she did something drastic. Without disturbing the cats, she slid out of bed and went downstairs, checked the cupboards and pulled out a box of chamomile tea. *Okay, not really drastic but it might do the trick.* By the time she was back in bed, her mind was focused on a new list, fifty places to travel before she retired.

A run was definitely in order that morning. Lizzie pushed herself hard and covered an extra mile by the time she had slowed to a walk for the final block home.

Lizzie started to open the back door and stopped in her tracks as strains of a heavy metal band assailed her ears.

Someone's in the house. She knew to get out immediately and call the police. But surely a burglar wouldn't play music to rob by.

She'd opened the door when Darla's voice rang out. "Is that you, Lizzie?"

Lizzie spun around and, bouncing between relief and anger, marched into the living room to find Darla reclining on the love seat.

"How did you get in here?"

"It's real easy picking your back door lock. Did you know that? You really should get a better one. I'm surprised your cop boyfriend hasn't told you."

Lizzie gritted her teeth. "This is a quiet community. *Till now.* Do you really think that was appropriate, your breaking in?"

Darla pouted. "I thought you'd want me to get out of sight in case Wade came looking for me."

Lizzie softened a bit. "Did you go back to him last night?"

"I did but he wasn't there and I didn't have a key to get into the room."

"What did you do?"

"I slept on a bench down by the river. Don't look so shocked. I've done that before and at least here you're not bothered by creepy street people trying to grab your spot." She shrugged. "I helped myself to some food. I was real hungry. Anyway, I went back to the motel this morning but still no show."

"Do you think he's left town?"

"Not without me. Believe me."

"Well then, do you think he's involved in drugs or something illegal?"

Darla shrugged again and the neckline of her T-shirt slid down her arm, revealing the ugly yellow and purple of a slow-healing bruise. "He always has to have an angle. That's how he survives. In fact"—Darla lowered her eyes, which Lizzie thought was pretty effective—"he told me to hit on Molly and my granddaddy for money. He thought they couldn't say no if I told them we needed it to survive."

Lizzie bristled. *And he was right.* "How long had he planned on mooching off them?"

"I'm not sure. He has something else in the works and maybe once that's done, we'll leave."

Lizzie watched her closely, trying to figure out just how sincere she was and why she was sharing this now. "You're saying you'll go with him?"

"He'll just come after me if I don't. Might as well skip all the in-between."

"Why not go home? It sounds like your mama really wants to make things up between you."

"She's saying that now but believe me, when Wade shows up, and he will, the door will slam on me again."

Lizzie wondered what she could say. She wasn't a social worker nor was she used to butting in, unless it was in pursuit of a murderer. That's where all this had started and they were still no closer to solving the case. By this point, she was pretty certain Darla didn't do the deed. Now Wade might be another matter. She'd seen his temper.

"Did Wade have any dealings with Rafe Shannon?"

"Not that I know."

"Hm. What about with someone called Eddie Riser?"

Darla's mouth twitched ever so slightly that Lizzie wasn't certain that's what she'd seen, but it did take Darla a few seconds to answer.

"Never heard him mention that name."

"So, let me ask you, what's your take on the murder?"

"The murder?" Darla sounded incredulous. "Why are you still bothering me about that? I'm not a killer. I'm the victim here. And I need help."

"You say that but you're the one who left Molly's voluntarily last night." Lizzie wasn't about to let her off the hook on that one.

"I told you, I love him."

Oh, boy. "Why don't we get you back to Molly's? She's been worrying about you."

Darla looked surprised and then shrugged. "That's like, nice of her and all, but I have to go back to the motel room first. There's something I have to do."

"Do you want me to come with you?"

"No way. I might, like, stay a while." She looked Lizzie in the eye. "Don't worry, I know what I'm doing."

Lizzie felt helpless watching Darla sauntering down the driveway. She felt in the pit of her stomach that this was a bad idea but she couldn't see how to prevent it. She phoned Molly to let her know that Darla was all right and quickly explained what had happened.

"Why didn't you keep her there?" Molly asked, rather sharply, Lizzie thought.

"How? Sit on her?" Lizzie regretted the words as soon as they'd left her mouth. She hadn't meant to sound so flippant. She was just so totally exasperated by both Darla and Molly, at this point.

"I'm sorry," she said. "I really couldn't force her to stay or go to your place even, although I did try that."

"I know you did and I'm the one who is sorry. I spoke too abruptly. It's not your fault she left and furthermore, she's not your responsibility. I'm just so worried about her."

"I know you are, Molly. But she did say she knows what

she's doing." Lizzie left out the part about Darla saying she had something to do. Even Lizzie didn't like the sound of that.

Lizzie tried reassuring Molly some more before hanging up. She thought about phoning Mark but he was due over in a couple of hours. It could wait.

She hoped.

Chapter Twenty-five

∞

"This is turning out to be a long day," Jane murmured and ran her hands through her hair. "There are way too many hours between now and cocktail time."

MURDER IN THE MYSTERY SUITE—ELLERY ADAMS

Lizzie loved her job. She really did. But she was so happy there was still another week of holidays before having to head back to work. Tuesday's literacy class had also been cancelled because the community center was doing extra programming for the kids, so even classes held off-site, like at Molly's, were included in the change. She mentally ticked off her 'To Do' list. Housework just wouldn't go away. Today must be the day.

She'd just finished vacuuming the main floor and was hauling the vacuum upstairs when the front doorbell rang.

"Lizzie, sugar, I'm just so pleased you are actually at home. I tried your back door first, of course, but your buzzer's probably not working. Not that it matters. Here you are and we must have a confab right this instant. I'm just in such a tizzy after my creative writing class this morning." Teensy waved a sheaf of papers in Lizzie's face.

Uh-oh. Must be something to do with Fannie Hewitt. Lizzie dreaded asking the question. "What's happened?"

"Just read this and you'll see what I mean." She thrust the papers into Lizzie's hands.

Lizzie raised an eyebrow. "Fannie's?"

"Oh, Lordy, yes."

Lizzie led her into the kitchen and poured them both a cup of coffee. Teensy paced while Lizzie quickly read the short chapter of five pages. She looked up at Teensy when she'd finished. "She poisons her husband."

"Yes, yes, she does. Do you think this means she's actually going to do it? We haven't had a chance to talk very much about this lately. And in fact, I'll admit I've been so drawn up in Molly's problem that I haven't given poor Fannie enough thought. What do you think?"

Lizzie sat back in her chair. "I really don't know, Teensy, but I do find it hard to believe she'll actually follow through in real life. The last time I spoke to Fannie, she seemed more intent on framing her husband, or rather, the husband in the novel, for the disappearance of the wife." Lizzie picked up the papers again. "Although she did say she'd probably go with murdering him after all. I was hoping she'd change her mind again."

"Well, she was wearing a large scarf draped around her neck and shoulders to class today. And you know how hot it gets in those classrooms." Teensy raised her eyebrows in a knowing look.

"That could be a bad sign. I don't know what to say. What do you want to do?"

Teensy sat across from Lizzie, crossed one leg over the other and started pumping away, concerning Lizzie that the blue sparkly sandal on Teensy's right foot might go flying across the room. Or straight at Lizzie. Finally, the leg stopped and Teensy leaned forward.

"An intervention. Right now. We both go over to Fannie's house and confront her."

"We did try something like that already and it didn't really clarify much," Lizzie pointed out.

"Hmm. You're right, of course. But we were probably too subtle or gentle the last time. This time we need to ask her right out. How about I just take some time to figure out how we'll finesse this and we head over there later on?"

Lizzie sighed, knowing there was no way out of it. On the one hand, she hated the thought of confronting Fannie with such an accusation, especially if it wasn't true. And it might not be. However, she'd feel worse if they did nothing and Fannie did follow through, as Teensy seemed to think. She nodded her agreement.

Teensy bounded up. "Good. I'll pick you up this afternoon at four sharp. I do have a spa appointment which will take a goodly part of the afternoon."

"What if Mr. Fannie is at home?"

"We'll just tell him we're taking her out for a coffee, which we'll do, and that we're so impressed with her writing, we wanted to talk about it, which we do." Teensy's face broke into a large smile. She was obviously pleased with her plan. "See you later. Ta-ta."

Teensy honked the horn of her yellow Cadillac out in Lizzie's driveway at four sharp. Lizzie, knowing Teensy was always on time, had one foot out the door before the honking stopped. She slid into the passenger seat and stopped to admire Teensy's outfit before talking. Her orange and yellow long top was layered and of a floating material. She wore white leggings with it and what appeared to be lime green stiletto sandals. Her thick, bottle-red hair had been captured in a lime green scarf.

"You look amazing," Lizzie said. "Now, what's the game plan?"

"Why, thank you, sugar. And, exactly as I said earlier today. Just ask her straight out."

"And have you thought of what to do with that answer? What if she admits she's planning to kill her husband? Or, what if she denies it and gets angry or upset that you've assumed that?"

"Humph. I guess I hadn't taken it that far." Teensy sat drumming her fingers on the steering wheel. "What would you do?"

"I probably wouldn't do this in the first place."

"Now that's not the right answer and you know it. We have a duty to help poor Fannie and divert her from the pathway to jail. I suppose I could start by confiding in her that I'm drawn to her work because I went through the exact same thing in my marriage. That I had many times plotted to do him in but when it came around to it, I just couldn't bring myself to commit such a heinous act. Plus, the thought of spending the rest of my life in jail was none too appealing. I could say I blackmailed him into letting me leave. Yes, that's what I'll say." Teensy looked pleased with herself.

Lizzie felt stunned but then thought about it. "None of that's true, is it?"

"Of course not, sugar. But I can be a good liar and it's known as a big white lie when someone is in trouble." She turned her bright, encouraging smile on Lizzie. "It will work. I guarantee it."

Lizzie had her doubts but Fannie was Teensy's concern, after all.

They waited several seconds until the door was opened

by a nervous-looking Fannie. She had on a shapeless beige T-shirt and beige capris. Gone was the classy-looking lady she'd met with before. It looked like Fannie was trying to disappear from view.

"I know why you're here," she blurted out and started to cry.

Teensy swept into the hallway and put an arm around Fannie's shoulder. "Oh, my goodness gracious, Fannie. What are you so upset about? We're here to help you, that's why we're here. Just tell us all about it and you'll feel so much better." Teensy glanced over at Lizzie and raised her eyebrows, almost triumphantly, Lizzie thought.

Fannie pulled a tissue out of her sleeve and blew into it, then looked from one to the other. "What do you mean?"

"Well, about your story," Teensy answered.

The tears started again. "You see, I was right." She pulled away from Teensy and wandered into the living room off the hallway to the left. Teensy and Lizzie were right behind her.

Fannie sat perched on the edge of the seat of a dark brown lounge chair. Teensy sat on the matching sofa beside it.

"Is your husband here?" she asked.

"No. Hammond is out of town for a couple of days, on business. He's an accountant and has this one client who moved away and still uses him."

"That's nice, dear. So, tell me about your story," Teensy demanded.

Fannie dabbed at her eyes and hiccupped. Lizzie remained standing at the doorway.

"Well, it all started because I was bored and I thought Hammond was fooling around on me. So I thought, I'll show him. I'll get a life of my own, become someone famous, and he'll regret tossing me aside." She looked at Teensy and then over at Lizzie. "That's why I did it."

Lizzie shifted from one foot to the other.

"Did what, Fannie?" Teensy reached over to pat her hand but Lizzie could hear the exasperation creeping into her voice. "Kill your husband?"

"What?" Fannie leapt up. "What did you say? I cannot believe you'd think that."

"But that's what all this is about, isn't it? Your story is about an abused wife who plots to kill her husband. That's you, isn't it? I've seen the bruises on your arm, the scarf you sometimes wear tightly around your neck even on a hot day."

"No, it isn't me. It's research."

"What?"

"I was doing what you said to do, getting into the head of my character."

Lizzie had to pretend to cough in order to cover her mouth and keep from laughing. The feeling of relief was immense.

"You what?"

Fannie nodded. "Hammond would never slap me around but I can tell you, I go through a lot of emotional abuse. Well, maybe not done in a mean-spirited way or anything. It's just like he's living in his own world except I'm here, too, and he doesn't know it most times. So that's my starting point. I used actor's makeup for the bruises. I used to do makeup with the local amateur theater, you know."

Teensy sagged back against the sofa but had to struggle upright when her feet left the ground. "Well, you had me convinced. You write a mean story, girl."

"Uh, that's what I have to tell you."

Teensy looked at her, one eyebrow elevated.

"Uh, it's not my story at all except for the feelings I was trying to inject into it. The story belongs to my cousin, Robin. She wrote it when she was off work taking care of her youngest, and I've always admired it so when I signed up for your course and couldn't come up with a single idea, I used it. She hadn't published it or anything. It's just sitting in her drawer."

"You plagiarized?"

"I guess. But you know, I wasn't really thinking about that. I was hoping to make it my own story and by pretending to be an abused woman, I thought I could become a better writer. But I got to feeling so badly about doing it because here you were spending so much time with me, encouraging me and all. I couldn't lie to you about it anymore. I've been a nervous wreck for days now, and when you seemed so concerned this morning at class, well I just couldn't get out of there fast enough."

"Humph. What about your telling Lizzie about how you get into the zone and all when writing a book?"

"Well, I hear lots of authors say that or something similar, all the time. You've even said it. And, I kind of experience it," she added sheepishly.

"What does your cousin think of this? Did she agree to it?"

"She doesn't know." Fannie dabbed at her eyes. "I just kept a copy when she asked me to read it. I guess I'll have to tell her, though."

Neither woman said anything for a few minutes. Lizzie eventually broke the ice. "Well, seeing as she hasn't published the story and hasn't tried to do so, I doubt there's any real harm done, in the literary world. On the other hand, spousal abuse is a very serious matter. I think it's a worthy topic to tackle but I don't approve of your methods, especially since it was a story just handed to you and not something you had any serious convictions about. Or so it seems."

Teensy shot her an icy glance.

"And," Lizzie continued, ignoring Teensy, "I do think you have a lot of apologizing to do to Teensy here. And we really are relieved you're not in any mortal danger, aren't we, Teensy?"

"Uh, yes. Yes we are." Teensy rallied. "And I do think you're on the right track, trying to write in some of your own emotions, although I've never seen anyone actually physically harm themselves in order to do that."

"Oh, I didn't. Mostly it was make-up. Well on purpose. I walked into the door, really honestly and truly."

"As I was saying, why don't you take those emotions and write your own story around them?"

Fannie's jaw dropped. "You mean it? I'm not kicked out of the class? Because I was so afraid that's what you were here for."

"You can stay in the class, but you have to work your butt off to get caught up, understood?"

Fannie nodded. Teensy smiled. "Well, that's very good then, girl. I'll see you in the next class. Lizzie, we must be going."

Lizzie followed Teensy out the door, after Fannie had given them both huge hugs. When they were back in the car, Teensy drove off quickly and then pulled over once they'd rounded the corner.

"I never for the life of me saw that coming." She turned to face Lizzie. "Did you? I mean, you read her work, too. Did you not think it was for real?"

"I did but I could have been influenced into believing that."

"But since it's her cousin's story, what if she's attempting to murder her husband?"

"I think we should just let it rest, Teensy."

Teensy looked like she might argue but instead broke out

into a smile. "I guess you're right and that's my author's imagination at work, also. Maybe I could make a story out of this. What do you think?"

"I think there's no stopping you when you put your mind to something, Teensy."

Teensy grinned and threw the car into gear.

Chapter Twenty-six

✧✧✧

"Let's go. I think we just made a bad thing worse."

A ROUX OF REVENGE—CONNIE ARCHER

"I have a thought," Lizzie said, as Teensy eased her car back into Lizzie's driveway.

"Something to do with Fannie?"

"No. Darla."

"You have my attention, sugar."

"I was just thinking about Fannie's symptoms of abuse. The bruise, easy to get if you walk into something, and the wearing of scarves. Does that remind you of someone?"

"Are you suggesting darlin' Darla was pulling those same tactics?"

Lizzie paused, wanting to be clear on just what she meant. "I know you didn't actually see her but you heard our accounts of what happened. We saw bruising on her arms and neck and she whimpered when touched on the shoulder. Her face was untouched, although I've read that serial abusers know just where to punch the victim so that it doesn't show. On the other hand, there is Fannie. I may be way out of line here, but it's got me wondering."

"As you know, I've always wondered about her. But what's her motive? Money?"

"Yes. She admitted that she needs money to pay off her gambling debt and also that Wade thought Molly would be willing to give them some if asked. I'm thinking she did, as did Bob. And Molly even paid them some to help with the organizing of the upcoming literacy book sale. But if that had run out, what could they come up with next?"

Lizzie thought a moment before going on. "He's abusing her, and Molly was going to train her to work in the bookstore, but with all that's been happening, that hasn't. So, to answer you, I don't know. It falls sort of flat here."

Teensy snapped her fingers. "The girl stole something valuable from Molly's house. They're going to sell it and run away."

Lizzie grimaced. She guessed anything was possible at this point.

"I always did think that girl was up to no good," Teensy continued. "And even her mama said she was always scheming. I'd say she got that from her grandmamma."

"You knew her?"

"Sugar, I knew everyone back then. We all went to school together—Molly, Bob, Sue-Ann and me. It didn't take much to see that Bob was really sweet on Molly." Teensy had a faraway look on her face.

"Why didn't anything come of it?" She was interested in hearing another take on the situation.

"Not in those days. Molly was well above Bob socially and he knew it. There's no way he'd make a play for her. Now Sue-Ann was more his class and she knew something good when she saw it. She went after Bob faster than greased lightning. They got married right after high school, as I heard tell. Of course, I'd married my John and moved away before that had happened."

"Did Molly know how Bob felt?"

"Didn't have a clue. She thought everyone was her friend. And they were."

"Well, I'd like to head over to the motel right now and see if we can maybe convince Darla to play show and tell. She shows us her bruises and tells us how she got them."

Lizzie took a good look around the parking lot at the Mountain View Motel, on the lookout for Wade's pickup. It wasn't there and she hoped he was with it, wherever that was. She took one last look over her shoulder as they approached the door. All clear.

Teensy tried knocking lightly on the door and when that didn't work, gave it a good pounding. She was just about to try again when the door eased open a crack. Teensy pushed it back and they heard a cry as someone bumped against the wall.

Lizzie flipped on the light as Teensy closed the door behind them. Darla had slumped down against the wall, her face bleeding from cuts to her mouth and the side of her eye.

"Oh my Lord, child," Teensy said, dropping down beside her.

"Did Wade do this?" Lizzie asked.

Darla tried nodding but grimaced instead. Lizzie and Teensy each grabbed an arm and helped her to stand, leading her to the bed, and easing her into a sitting position. Lizzie pulled out her iPhone and punched in Mark's number. After quickly explaining what they'd found, she locked the door as he suggested.

"I just called Mark and he'll be here in a jiffy. This time

it doesn't matter what you want, Darla. Charges are going to be laid against Wade. He can't just go using you as a punching bag whenever he wants."

Lizzie took a good look at the bruises on her left arm, fading at this point. Darla's neck looked clear. She'd leave it up to the doctor to find out if there were traces of ongoing physical abuse but that's what it looked like. *Guess I was wrong.* It took just a few more minutes before Mark was knocking on the door, telling them to let him in.

He took one look at Darla and spoke into his radio, asking for an ambulance. "I've got cars driving around and positioned close by in case Wade comes back." He walked over and kneeled before Darla.

"Do you want to tell me what happened?"

She shook her head ever so slightly but after a few seconds said, "Wade got real mad that I came back without getting any more money. He also doesn't want you hanging around here. He flies off the handle sometimes, you know."

Lizzie wanted to ask how she'd planned to get money but realized this wasn't the time for it. She'd fill Mark in on her suspicions and let him deal with it even though she wasn't entirely sure about them herself.

The ambulance arrived shortly and after an initial checkup, Darla was convinced by Teensy to go with them just to make sure everything was okay.

Mark looked around the room and then asked the two what they were doing there. After Lizzie had explained, he gave it some thought and then said, "So, you think the original claims of abuse were part of a con to get money out of Molly and Bob?"

"We do," Teensy answered before Lizzie had a chance to say she'd changed her mind.

"Well, seeing as this is now a crime scene, I'm going to

have my people search it top to bottom. Let's find out all that Wade had going on in town."

He held the door open for them and then waved in two police officers.

"We'd better go and break the news to Molly and to Bob," Lizzie said. She looked at Teensy, who nodded.

Mark squeezed Lizzie's arm and then went back inside to join the search.

"Let's grab Molly and then hightail it down to the hospital," Teensy said, backing out onto the street. "We can do our explaining in the car."

They reached Molly's house in no time. She smiled at them as she opened the door but that changed to a frown when she saw their faces. She held the door wider and they shuffled inside.

"Mopsy, honey, we've got some disturbing news." Teensy looked at Lizzie and then continued, "We've just come from visiting Darla and the girl's gone and gotten herself beat up. She's at the hospital right now getting checked over. We're here to take you there."

Molly said nothing but carefully put the vase of flowers she'd been holding down on a table in the hallway. It took but a few minutes for her to go upstairs and then return, handbag in hand. Once they were out in the car, Molly said, "Now, tell all."

Lizzie decided it might be better for her to explain but she left out a lot of the details. Molly seemed to accept what she said and didn't ask any more questions until they reached the hospital parking lot. "Did you tell Bob?"

"No. We thought we'd leave that to you," Lizzie admitted a bit sheepishly.

"We'll see how she is, then decide when it's best to call him."

They were ushered down the hall in emergency to a small examining room. Darla was alone in the room, perched on the edge of the bed. Molly rushed over and gently hugged her. "How are you, honey?"

Darla shrugged but then winced in pain. "All right, I guess. They say nothing's broken and I can go."

"They're not watching you for signs of a concussion or anything?" Molly turned to Lizzie. "That seems rather lackadaisical, wouldn't you say?"

"I'll go talk to them."

Lizzie returned a few minutes later confirming what Darla had said. "She's good to go but she should take it easy."

"All right then, let's head to my place."

When they arrived back at Molly's, she said, "Now, I'm going to insist that you go straight up to your room and try to get some rest, Darla. I'm going to give your granddaddy a call."

She shooed the others out to the patio while she phoned Bob. He arrived within ten minutes and joined them outdoors. His face looked pinched. He was wearing what he called his painting clothes, and Lizzie detected flecks of green paint on his arms and hands.

"That's it. That scumbag goes behind bars and they can throw away the key, if I have any say in it."

"Calm down, Bob. It's all in hand." Molly walked over to him and turned the wing of his collar over. "Darla's upstairs resting and I think this might be a good time for you to head on over to the motel and pick up her things. Surely the police will let you in to do that."

"I've already thought of that, Molly, and cleared it with the chief. He also said he'd have a patrol car keeping an eye on your place, so you're not to worry. But if you hear anything out of the ordinary, do not wait to see if you actually heard it, you get on the horn right away, Molly Mathews, and call 911. Do you hear?"

"Of course I do. And I certainly will do that. We know what this monster is capable of doing. Now you get going, Bob, and when you return, we'll all just have a settling glass of wine out back. Lizzie, you can stay for a while, can't you? And Teensy?"

"I'd be happy to, Mopsy, but I'm getting awful hungry," Teensy answered. "Why don't I just give a call and have some Tex-Mex takeout delivered." She looked at the other three hopefully.

"Sounds like a good idea. I'm sure by the time it gets here, we'll be able to eat something."

"Sure. You get yourself ready, Mopsy. I'm already set."

Lizzie grinned. Bob left and Teensy grabbed the phone, checking her smartphone for the number she needed.

Lizzie touched Molly's arm. "Why don't you pick out some wine and I'll get a tray and glasses. There's nothing else to do at this point." She wanted to keep her busy rather than sitting around worrying.

Molly nodded and led the way to the kitchen. "Do you think she'll be all right?" she asked, as she checked her wine cupboard and pulled out a bottle of Shiraz.

"I'm assuming you mean Darla and yes, I'm sure she'll be just fine. Her injuries aren't severe even though they look terrible. Let's just hope she sees Wade for what he really is, this time."

"That poor misled girl."

Or not. Lizzie realized she wasn't totally ready to give up her earlier suspicions.

Chapter Twenty-seven

◇◇◇

"Things you and I are going to need two long spoons
and a quart of Haagen-Dazs to talk about," I said.

THE LAST GOOD DAY—GAIL BOWEN

Lizzie was itching to get Darla all to herself and question her about her earlier bruises. There was no doubt that this time, the wounds were real and inflicted by Wade. But Lizzie was dithering, wondering again if maybe the earlier ones were pretty much for show. The problem was, she needed to speak to Darla and she knew that doing it while the girl was still vulnerable gave her the best possibility of learning the truth.

She also knew that Molly, especially after today's incident, would not be amenable to that. She no doubt believed everything Darla had ever said. What to do?

She glanced at Teensy and realized she was being watched. Teensy gave her a quizzical look and then took the final mouthful of her chicken enchilada. Lizzie answered with a slight shrug. She had no idea how to proceed. Tonight, anyway.

Darla provided the answer an hour later when she joined the others outside.

"How are you feeling, child?" Molly asked, standing at the same time as Bob, to escort Darla to a chair.

"I'm feeling light-headed from those drugs and a bit achy all over, but I don't want to stay alone up there." She spotted the tray of wine. "Could I have some wine?"

"Not with all that medication in you. I'll get you some iced tea. It's hibiscus sweet tea. It should hit the spot." Molly disappeared into the kitchen while Bob retrieved some of the remaining enchiladas and passed a plate to Darla.

"Are you hungry? This was real good earlier. I could heat it up for you if you'd like."

"No. Thanks anyway. I'm not really hungry. Just thirsty."

Molly was back in no time with a tall glass of tea. The others watched Darla take a sip before they settled back in their seats.

Teensy spoke first. "Well, you go right ahead and enjoy your flowery drink, sugar, and I'll do the heavy lifting for ya." She saluted Darla with her glass of bourbon on the rocks.

Molly shook her head but Bob started laughing. Soon, they'd all joined in.

Even Darla managed a smile. But not for long. Lizzie noticed her attention wandering over to the maze. *Perfect chance.*

"Have you walked the maze yet, Darla?"

"Uh-uh."

"It might be too wearying for her," Molly said.

Teensy jumped right in. "Of course not, Molly. Lizzie, why don't you go walking with her and make sure she comes right back if she looks tired." Teensy gave Lizzie a wink that no one noticed and then smiled at Molly. "Now tell me, Mopsy, are you planning on going to the Morgans' garden party at the end of the month?"

"What? You do flit all over the place, don't you, Teensy? I hadn't really thought about it but I guess I'll probably go."

Darla pushed herself gingerly out of the chair and Lizzie matched her pacing as they made their way to the maze.

"I just love walking this," Lizzie said. "It's been here as long as I can remember and it's just the greatest way to forget your troubles or sort out things that are troubling." She left it at that for a few minutes and they walked together in silence.

Finally, Darla said, "It is peaceful in here. I feel like the world is far away."

Lizzie nodded but didn't want to break the spell by talking. Not yet, anyway. Finally, Darla broke the silence again. "You must think I'm a real dork."

"Why would you say that?"

"My going back with Wade after what he'd done to me before."

"Oh, but you didn't really think he would actually beat on you, did you, Darla?" Lizzie stopped and faced her. "Those earlier bruises weren't because he hit you, were they?"

Darla gasped. She stared at Lizzie for a few moments and then nodded. "You're right, but how did you know?"

"Something someone said today triggered the memory that we never actually saw anything except for some bruises on your arm. They could have been caused by anything, even just walking into the door, couldn't they?"

Darla nodded again.

"But what I don't know is why."

Darla started walking more quickly this time. Lizzie caught up to her easily and then paced her until she was ready to speak again.

"For the money." Darla spoke softly and Lizzie had to strain to hear. "I needed lots of money to pay off my gambling debts and I also needed money to live on."

"And you thought Molly, even though she'd already given you some money, would be a good source of more? But why pretend to be beaten up?"

"Because I knew I couldn't just keep asking until I had enough, and I couldn't ask for the whole amount all at once. Wade came up with the idea. I bruise easily, you know? He only had to grab me hard or I would bump into the door-frame or something like that and I would have a bruise. He thought that Molly wouldn't hesitate to buy him off if it looked like he was beating on me."

"And you went along with it."

"Yes." She was quiet so long Lizzie thought she'd finished talking. "Don't you get it? I really needed the money. My life could be in danger. That was the only way to get it."

"Oh, I get it all right, but you sure don't. Molly and Bob also trusted you. They were worried sick to think you'd been hurt, as they are now. Tonight it was for real, though?"

"Yeah. Wade thought I'd changed my mind." She paused a few minutes. "And, I had," she added in a soft voice.

"Why?"

"Because I realized he wanted a lot more money than just to pay off what I owed. And also, I kinda feel bad about trying this scam on Molly and Granddaddy. They're nice, ya know?"

"Yes, they are. You know, all you had to do was ask and be honest about it. I'm certain they would have worked something out for you."

"You really think?"

"I know them. They care about you. But they do not take kindly to deceit."

"You can't tell them, Lizzie."

Lizzie stopped and waited until Darla had also. "No, I can't, but you can. And will."

"I can't," she squeaked out.

"Think about it, Darla. You have to start doing the right thing at some point in your life. It might as well be now when you're surrounded by friends and family."

Tears started flowing and Darla wiped her eyes on the hem of her T-shirt. Lizzie hadn't brought any tissue either. She waited until Darla had regained her composure, then suggested they walk back, which they did once again in silence.

Molly looked from one to the other as they reappeared and took their seats. After a minute, Darla pushed herself to a standing position again. "I'm really beat. I think I'll just go back in and lie down." She left, avoiding looking at Lizzie.

Lizzie sighed and avoided looking at Teensy.

Chapter Twenty-eight

◇◇◇

It was a good thing my hair couldn't actually stand
on end, because it would have at that moment.

THE DIVA FROSTS A CUPCAKE—KRISTA DAVIS

Sleepless nights can sometimes be a blessing. Well, that
might be an overstatement, Lizzie decided, but a sleepless night can help get things accomplished. In her own case,
the tossing and turning, the midnight prowl to the fridge, the
opening of the bedroom window and leaning on the sill to
watch the quiet night did eventually help Lizzie sort through
all that had been troubling her ever since Rafe Shannon's
body had been found.

Possibly even from before that, like when Darla Lyman
popped into their lives.

What she hadn't been able to wrap her head around was
why someone like Rafe Shannon, a lowlife from the big city,
would end up in Ashton Corners. Had he been tracking
Darla, it would have made sense, although Lizzie was the
first to admit she had no idea how these dealings between

bookies and payees went. But, Darla had stated he was surprised to see her in town, and only then did he put pressure on her to pay up.

Had said bookie sent him searching for someone else? If so, who? Their equally lowlife former mayor was already behind bars, and although there was no way Lizzie believed every citizen in Ashton Corners was upstanding, she couldn't quite imagine any heavy-duty gamblers living in town and being able to keep it under wraps. Someone would have spilled the beans by now, especially with all the questions being asked around town about the murder.

The only outsiders intersecting in this scenario were Rafe himself, Darla, and Wade Morris. She knew the connection between Rafe and Darla. What she suspected, but had no proof about, was a connection between Rafe and Wade. Both had arrived in town within days of each other. All three had, actually. They were all from Atlanta. Darla and Rafe were connected by gambling. And, Darla had a connection to both men. Wade had said he'd followed Darla to town to protect her. Would he have killed Rafe Shannon to that end? Probably. The only other dealings Wade had in town had to do with drugs. Granted, Lizzie admitted, she didn't know all about his wanderings about town.

How much of a coincidence could this all be?

Eddie Riser had not admitted to knowing either man but then, why would he? If Darla knew, she wasn't saying. In fact, it looked like she wouldn't be saying much of anything from now on.

Eddie had said something that hadn't really twigged at the time, though. Lizzie had woken from a short sleep, one of many throughout the night, with the memory of their conversation. Eddie had used the term "they" when talking about Rafe. *They who*?

What if Rafe and Wade were mixed up in something together? What was it, and did it lead to Rafe's murder? She liked Wade for this, but was that mainly because she so disliked the guy? Still, too many questions.

Her mind kept leading her back to Darla. She had to know something more.

Lizzie leapt out of bed at the sound of her radio going on and pulled on her running shorts and T-shirt. How wonderful is the mind at rest! Tasked with remembering, it usually comes through once all the clutter of being awake is removed. She'd stop by Molly's later in the morning and give it one more try.

She fed the cats and headed out for her run. Along the way back she veered over to Garrett Street and paused to have a look inside the window of a recently vacated store that was in the process of being renovated. She'd heard through the school grapevine that it was destined to become a teachers' supply store, but she didn't have any other details. She hoped for some sign of the progress or a contact name posted. If the rumor were true, Lizzie hoped to have a conversation with the owner early in the game, when shelves were being stocked, in order to have some specific literacy materials brought in. She hadn't been by for a week, and although she could manage to see through a tear in the kraft paper that lined the windows that progress had been made, she was no closer to finding the information she wanted. She'd have to keep asking around. Surely, someone knew the answer.

She slowed as she finally reached her street and was down to a walk when she arrived home. She looked over at Nathaniel's window as she passed by, remembering he'd wanted to talk to her about something. She'd been so busy over the past week, as had he. She hadn't even seen him around, so the meeting hadn't happened. She wondered what he'd wanted. Yet another unanswered question.

Lizzie slowed as she pulled into Molly's driveway. She'd just passed Wade's pickup parked on the street. And it was empty. She got slowly out of the car and looked around her. No sign of him. She tried knocking but there was no answer. That was strange. Molly was never known to go anywhere this early in the morning. Her heart started racing a bit faster.

Lizzie tried the door and it opened. She was getting a real bad feeling. Maybe she should call Mark. But she couldn't wait for him if Molly was in trouble. She flashed back to last summer when she'd found Molly unconscious on her kitchen floor. That spurred her through the door and down the hallway.

She paused at the kitchen door, listening. She couldn't hear a thing. She cautiously pushed it open and glanced in. Empty. She walked around the counter and looked down, just to be sure.

Lizzie let out the breath she'd been holding in. Maybe they were both upstairs. Lizzie went to the bottom of the stairs and called out. She could hear some banging and muffled sounds coming from behind her. She followed the sounds to the laundry room just off the kitchen. There definitely was banging coming from in there along with what sounded like Molly's voice.

"Molly, are you in there?" She rattled the doorknob but it wouldn't open. She pressed her ear against the door. "Molly?"

It sure sounded like her. She managed to make out the word "key" and "ledge." Lizzie stood on her tiptoes and just managed to reach above the door. She ran her hand along and knocked a key to the floor. Fumbling with it, she eventually got it in and opened the door. Molly came rushing out.

"Oh, thank goodness you're here, Lizzie."

"What happened?"

"It's that Wade. He forced his way in here and locked me in my own laundry room. I told Claydon that lock was ridiculous but he never got around to changing it and neither did I." She glanced out the window. "I'm not sure where he's taken Darla."

"His truck's in the front, although there are no police cars around. You call 911 right now and I'll take a look out back."

"You'd better wait here till the police arrive. He was meaner than a sack full of rattlesnakes."

Lizzie shivered at the image that conjured. "All the more reason to try to find Darla." She ran out before Molly could add anything, and stopped at the edge of the patio to listen. Nothing. No, that wasn't right. She could hear some whimpering and it sounded like it was coming from inside the maze. She knew this maze inside out. She started into it, approaching each corner with caution, walking steadily toward the sound until she could make out what was being said.

"I told you to shut up, Darla. I can't think with you making out like that." Molly was right. Wade sounded plenty angry.

The sounds stopped abruptly and Lizzie hurried as fast as she dared.

"I'll give you one more chance to tell me where you put that USB stick."

"You can punch me all you want, Wade Morris. I'm not saying."

"I think you're getting to enjoy being punched, Darla. I'm going to try something else." Wade's voice sent chills through Lizzie's body.

She knew she was close but not sure what to do. She paused to listen for sirens but couldn't hear any. The only thing to do was get Darla out of there. Lizzie rounded the next corner as Darla cried out in pain.

"Fingers are easy to snap, Darla. So are wrists. Shall we try that next? There are so many bones in your body I can freakin' break real easy. You'll be in so much pain you won't be able to see straight."

Darla whimpered. Lizzie hoped it wasn't because she wouldn't see her boyfriend again. Lizzie dropped to her knees and crawled a few feet, looking for the opening in the hedge. As children, they'd taken great delight in disappearing from one path to the other, something Claydon Mathews had added for Lizzie's enjoyment. Although the cuts were obscured by overgrowth these days, the basic openings were still there.

She found it and poked through just to be certain. It would do. Now, she'd have to keep going until she met up with Darla and Wade, manage to distract him and then get Darla to run with her. She knew her way through the maze blindfolded. She and Darla would slip through two of the openings and make their way back to the beginning before Wade could figure it out. It sounded easy. *Sure.*

Darla screeched, "No. I'll tell you. No more pain. Please."

"That's a good girl. Of course, no more pain. You give it up and I'll be out of here before you know it. You won't be seeing me again."

"I thought you said you loved me," Darla whined.

"I do, baby, but this is all about money. A lot of it. More than you realize. And since I can't trust you anymore, I have to make a choice. And guess what I choose. Now where is it?"

"I dropped it in Lizzie's handbag," she said with a sob.

Uh-oh. Time to make a move.

Lizzie rounded the corner and cautiously came up behind Wade. Darla gasped when she noticed her. Wade turned and grabbed Lizzie's arm.

"Why, right on cue. So nice of you to join us but I notice, no handbag. Where is it?" He gave Lizzie a shake. She winced and clamped her mouth shut. She refused to let him see she was also in pain.

"I didn't bring it. I had no idea Darla had hidden something in it. It's at home." She tried to signal Darla with her eyes, wanting her to be prepared to run.

"Well then, guess we'll all take a ride to your place." He stuck his gun in his belt and bent over to grab Darla's arm, too.

Lizzie brought her knee up and bashed him where it hurt the most. He let go of them both and doubled over, clutching himself. Lizzie grabbed Darla and pushed her ahead. When they'd gotten a bit of a lead, she heard Wade yelling and heading after them.

She shoved Darla toward the opening and made her crawl through, Darla crying out in pain. Lizzie followed and then grabbed Darla's good hand to help her up, and ran. They crawled through the next hole just as Wade fired the gun. Lizzie had no idea where the bullet had gone. It hadn't hit either of them though.

"You bitches. You'll really know pain when I get hold of you."

Darla whimpered but Lizzie kept her going. The start of the maze was just ahead of them. They could hear Wade gaining on them as they reached it.

Mark stood in front, gun drawn and pointed at them as they emerged. He waved them over to the side and Amber Craig grabbed them, pulling them to safety. Two officers flanked Mark, guns also drawn.

"Drop your weapon, Wade," Mark yelled as Wade skidded

to a stop at the entrance. He looked from one officer to the other and then slowly did as told.

"Hands behind your head and on your knees," Mark ordered. One of the officers holstered his gun and ran over to grab onto Wade and grabbed his wrists, forcing him down to the ground. The other two officers waited until Wade was flat on his stomach, hands handcuffed behind him.

"I wouldn't have killed them," Wade whined. "I'm not a killer. I just wanted that damned stick. Darla, baby, I love you."

Darla, still shaking and nursing her hand, spat out, "Too late, Wade."

Mark glanced at Lizzie and smiled.

Chapter Twenty-nine

◇◇◇

Time to call the locksmith.

DEATH IS LIKE A BOX OF CHOCOLATES—
KATHY AARONS

Lizzie had gone back home to change out of her torn jeans while Bob and Molly took Darla to the hospital. She grabbed her handbag off the hall table and brought it upstairs, emptying it on the bed. There was the USB stick, just as Darla had said. How did it get in there? She thought back to when she'd last used the handbag but wasn't sure. She shrugged, tossed everything back inside, and set it at the top of the stairs so she'd remember to take it along to Molly's.

It took just a few minutes to change into black cotton pants. She exchanged her long-sleeved T-shirt for a red-and-white-striped cotton pullover, just for good measure, then lingered, looking at her reflection in the mirror. She stared without seeing, processing all that had taken place in the past hour. She still felt shaken to the bone, despite the fact that Wade was in custody and could no longer hurt Darla. But he had said he wasn't a killer. Was that true? Of course, he'd deny it. But, he sounded desperate. What if he wasn't lying?

So, what about Eddie Riser? There was nobody else left on the suspect list. She knew it was out of her hands, the rest up to Mark and his team. But she couldn't get it out of her head. She'd wondered about him being the killer early on in the process, but he'd seemed to be just a middle guy, someone whose biggest sin was putting drugs in the hands of teens. Bad enough, for sure. But she hadn't taken him to be a cold-blooded killer. Wade had seemed the more likely suspect but that could have been because she didn't like the guy.

She finally shrugged, trying for a lighter frame of mind. She'd go back to Molly's and wait with Teensy for the others to arrive back from the hospital. The worst was over.

She wondered where the cats were. They'd usually be close by, keeping an eye on her, anticipating whether she was going out and therefore, time for a catnap, or maybe staying in and therefore worthy of stalking in case she sat down and a lap presented itself. Maybe they were sitting by their dishes, in need of a top up.

She ran lightly down the stairs and into the kitchen, almost doing a double take when she saw Riser sitting at her table. Her breath caught in her throat. Her eyes went directly to the gun in his hand.

"Nothing to say?" Riser asked, looking calm but sounding menacing.

"What are you doing here?"

Riser eyed her up and down. "Nice outfit. Is there a USB stick tucked in there somewhere?"

Lizzie gasped. "No. Chief Dreyfus has it."

"That's one lie. I allow only three, you know. Like in, three strikes and you're out." He grinned. "I'll let you in on a secret. I was with Wade Morris this morning when the three of you had that little talk in the maze. No one paid me any attention. Of course, you couldn't see me in back of it and when all that fuss happened with the cops, I made good my getaway. But I was close enough to hear you say your purse was at home and the USB stick is in it. So, give it to me. Now."

"Why do you want it? What's it got to do with you?"

"You don't get it, do you? It's my business and none of yours. However, I will tell you that Rafe Shannon was trying to take over my territory. And then he planned to do the same to some nearby towns. That stick is valuable. He's done all my legwork and made it easy for me to be the one expanding."

Lizzie gasped. "You're the head of the drug ring? I thought you were just a dealer."

Riser smiled again. "Nice cover, eh? The cops thought the same and kept watching me to take them to my leader. I had some fun planting clues that had them looking at someone else." He barked out a short laugh. "Shows how dumb they can be."

"You killed Rafe Shannon."

He didn't answer.

"Was Wade Morris in on that?"

"Wade wants to be 'the man.' He thought Shannon could make it happen, so now he thinks I'll bring him in on the operation. But he's wrong. He's proved he's a screwup and I just have to lay low until the law takes care of him. Now, get me that stick." He waved the gun at her.

She needed to stall him. For what she wasn't sure. Mark didn't know he was here. Mark didn't even know she was here. Lizzie needed to think of some way to save herself. She did know it was unlikely he'd release her after all he'd just admitted. Unless he meant to grab the stick and leave town. But that seemed like wishful thinking. He had his business established in Ashton Corners.

"But Wade will tell the cops all about you."

"Let him talk. There's no proof. Just his word. In fact, all the proof leads to him. I've been very careful about that."

"Why kill Rafe Shannon at Molly's house?"

Riser shrugged. "I was tailing him and just took advantage of a good opportunity. No one would ever connect me with that house, and besides, Wade Morris was not far behind me. I was sure he'd take the rap but he was smarter than I thought and got out of there real fast." He shifted the gun to his left hand and then back.

"Get me that USB stick. Now."

Lizzie couldn't think of anything but to do it. Maybe she could toss it in the corner and he'd go for it and she'd hit him over the head. She glanced around. Nothing handy to do that.

"Now. Or else." He waved the gun again.

"My handbag is on the stairs." She gestured to the hall-way but at that moment, noticed Brie sitting outside on the window ledge. Without thinking, she ran to the back door.

"My cats are outside. You let my cats out. You idiot." She pulled open the door as he stood and rushed to her.

"You stupid bitch. Shut that door." He grabbed her arm as the door swung open and the cats rushed inside.

She wrenched her arm from him, angry about the cats. "My cats could have gone wandering and gotten hurt." The gun was in her face. She took a deep breath. "All right, I'll get your dumb stick."

Lizzie stomped toward the hall.

Riser followed, continuing behind her up the stairs. The cats struggled to get to the top first, getting underfoot and tripping Riser. He fell back, hitting his head against the table at the bottom. The gun slid out of his hand.

It took Lizzie a few seconds to realize what had happened. She ran down the stairs, grabbed the gun and pointed it at the inert Riser. He tried to move, then groaned.

Lizzie sidled around him, reached for the phone, and dialed 911. She backed up against the opposite wall, willing Riser not to move. She knew she wouldn't be able to shoot him. She looked for something to tie him up with but couldn't see anything. Instead, she dragged the coffee table out of the living room and managed to get it over him. It would at least slow him down.

She looked up to the second floor but couldn't see the cats anywhere. She finally breathed a sigh of relief when the sirens grew louder and brakes squealed in her driveway. A few seconds later, Mark burst through the front door.

He took one look at Lizzie with the gun and Riser with the coffee table straddling him, and broke into a grin.

Chapter Thirty

◇◇◇

"That would be lovely. And on the way back, can
you bring me an itty bitty glass of something stronger
than tea?"

NONE SO BLIND—BARBARA FRADKIN

Lizzie had filled Teensy in on all that had happened before
the others made it back from the hospital. They were now
all seated outside on Molly's patio, lemonades in hand. Darla,
her right hand bandaged, held her glass with her left one.
Molly and Bob sat flanking her. Lizzie sat across from them.

"So, Darla," Bob was saying, "you'd better tell us all
about it. And I mean, all."

"Wait a sec," Lizzie said. "First of all, I want to know
how that USB stick got in my handbag."

"Your purse was just sitting there that morning I stopped
by to see you, so I dropped it inside. I thought it would be
safe and I could get it later."

"Why's it so important? What's on it?" Bob wanted to know.

Darla winced as she moved her injured hand. "It belonged

to Rafe Shannon. Wade stole it from him. I'm guessing that he killed him for it."

Lizzie kept herself from jumping in with the real story. She glanced at Teensy and gave a quick shake to her head. Teensy winked back.

"Do you know what's on it?" Bob persisted.

Darla shook her head. "Not really but I'll bet it had something to do with Rafe's drug ring."

"He had a drug ring going?"

"I heard he was trying to get one started." Darla bit her bottom lip and looked like tears would flow any second. "I didn't know anything about any of this when I came here, I promise."

"Why don't you start at the beginning?" Molly asked gently.

Darla looked at her a moment and then nodded. "Okay. The truth. When I came here it really was to try to find my granddaddy. I was real curious, you know? And I felt like no one wanted me. Mama had just kicked me out. And also, I was real scared because I needed to get money to pay off my gambling real fast. Last time Rafe and I had a talk"—she used her hands to provide the quotation marks, wincing as she flexed her bandaged hand—"he called it my last chance. He said next time I'd be real sorry if I didn't have the money. So I ran away."

She looked at Bob. "I admit, I was hoping you could give me the money. And then when I saw Molly's place and how much money she must have, I thought, this could be it." She glanced at Molly. "Sorry but that's how it was. I was desperate."

Molly nodded but her face remained impassive.

"How did Wade become involved in all this?" Lizzie asked.

"He followed me. He said he was real worried about me."

She started crying. Molly leapt up and got a box of tissue from the kitchen.

"Now you just take your time, honey. We want to help you."

Darla nodded and dabbed at her eyes, and blew her nose. She shifted in her seat.

"When did he really get here?" Bob asked.

Darla gulped. "He got here the same day as me but later that night. I'd phoned him to say where I was staying and he just appeared."

"So he'd been here the whole time?" Molly asked. Lizzie could tell she was trying hard not to let any emotions show.

"Uh-huh. He stayed in the room because he said he didn't want it to get back to either of you. But then he saw Rafe Shannon coming out of one of the rooms next morning. He knew him but I'm not sure if he knew he'd be here or not. Wade says not but I think he really did, because he knew what Rafe was doing here."

"Drugs," Bob said.

"I guess."

"Did Wade want a part of the action?" Bob asked.

Darla nodded. "He said that Rafe had hired him."

"When did he say that?"

Darla shrugged. "I don't know. It was last week. Maybe the same day I saw Rafe in town. That's it. I was so upset and I told Wade all about him and he said it would be all right because Rafe and him were now partners."

"Then why did Wade kill him?"

Darla shook her head and the tears started flowing again. "I don't know. That's all I know, honestly."

Again, Lizzie didn't volunteer what she knew. There was more that needed telling and she wondered if Darla would do so. Mark said when someone used the word "honestly," it usually meant the opposite. What was she hiding?

So she asked. "What aren't you telling us, Darla?"

"Lizzie." Bob's voice held a bit of a warning.

"Oh, come on now. Surely, you can tell she's holding something back." Bob might have a plan to ease the information out of her, but Lizzie was losing patience very quickly. A lot had gone down in the past couple of hours and the realization of just how dangerous the entire situation had been was finally sinking in. She hugged herself and bit her bottom lip so that she wouldn't say any more just now.

Darla stared at her, tears forgotten. "Okay. Wade did tell me that Rafe was starting up a drug network and that Wade would be his right-hand man. The USB stick had all the contact information on it. After that beating he gave me, I took it to keep him away. If Wade swore to leave me alone then I'd give it back to him."

"And you think he'd stick to his word?" Bob asked, sounding as skeptical as he looked.

"What else could I do? After the last time he beat me up and all." She glanced at Lizzie with pleading in her eyes, and Lizzie realized she would be sticking to that story. No talk about the plan they'd hatched. No mention of there being only one true beating.

"I wanted nothing more to do with him especially after all he'd done, but there's something that just keeps pulling me right on back to him," Darla continued. "Ya know? I had to make him stop doing that to me. I know I'm too weak to stay away. And then there's the part of me that wonders, like, what if he's the only chance I get?"

"At what?" Molly asked.

"At love," Darla whispered through fresh tears.

Lizzie couldn't help rolling her eyes. She glanced around. Fortunately, no one had seen her do it. She realized there wasn't anything she could do to make Darla tell the entire truth.

Molly moved over to sit beside Darla and put an arm around her shoulders. "That's not true, Darla. You'll have a lot more chances if you just let yourself be open to them. I promise."

Darla hiccupped just as Mark came around the corner of the house.

"I see you've already gotten the story out of her," he said to all.

Bob stood up and walked over to pour another drink. "Not all of it. And it's not a pretty story."

Mark shook his head. "I sent someone over to the hospital to escort her to the station to give her statement. It's customary to tell the police first." He looked pointedly at Bob, who held his gaze. Mark sighed. "Okay, let's hear it from the start."

"Again?" Darla sniffed.

"Yes. And then you'll be doing the same thing at the station."

"Maybe I can bring her in tomorrow to do that," Bob stated.

Mark exchanged another look with him. "That will work. But I want to hear what you have to say while it's still fresh in your mind." Mark pulled out a small tape recorder from his pocket. "And, I'll just tape it in case you need refreshing tomorrow." He leaned over and put it on the wicker patio table in front of Darla.

Darla looked at it and then at Bob, who nodded. She went through what she'd already told them in a much stronger voice this time. The story remained much the same, Lizzie thought.

When she'd finished, Mark shut off the recorder and accepted a glass of lemonade from Molly.

"I need to use the restroom," Darla said and hurried inside.

Mark waited until she disappeared from sight. "That pretty

well fits in with what Wade told us. There are some parts she doesn't know, or doesn't want to admit to knowing."

"That's hardly a fair comment," Bob said.

"That's how I see it. You're thinking as a granddaddy, not as a cop. Now, do you want to hear or not?"

Bob settled back and crossed his arms over his chest. He obviously didn't like being reminded he wasn't a cop anymore.

Mark nodded and took a long drink before talking. "It seems Rafe Shannon, among his many other jobs, has been running drugs for one of his bosses in the Atlanta area. I guess he had bigger plans and had been buying up drugs for some time now, hoping to start his own little drug kingdom throughout some of the smaller towns here. He found out about Eddie Riser and arranged to meet him and sell him some drugs at a better rate than Eddie's old supplier."

"I wonder what made him choose Ashton Corners?" Molly asked.

Mark looked uncomfortable but finally answered. "Apparently Rafe had told Wade it was because of the cops here and having family in the right place when the going got hot."

Bob looked puzzled. Lizzie knew better than to say anything. Let Mark handle it.

"It's a long story and one that doesn't need to be told here. Wade was pretty willing to talk to us. I think he's realized it can't get any worse for him. For starters, that USB stick holds the plans for Rafe Shannon's new drug ring. He saw himself as quite the drug lord and Ashton Corners was to be his first foray into a network. He brought Wade on board as his second in command."

"But I still don't understand why Wade killed him," Bob said again.

"He swears he didn't do it. What he will admit to is having gotten into an argument with Shannon the day before over Wade's cut. So Wade was already mad at him, when Rafe said he was coming over here to talk to you, Molly, and get you to pay off Darla's debt. Wade got angry and followed him. But he found Shannon already dead so he got out of there in a hurry."

"Eddie Riser had beat him to it," Lizzie added.

Both Bob and Molly looked shocked.

"Do you believe him?" Bob asked.

Lizzie filled them both in on what had happened at her house. Molly reached over and gave Lizzie's hand a squeeze when she'd finished. "I'm so thankful you're okay, honey. And, you had no idea, Mark?"

Mark shook his head. "I can't believe that guy. He sure had us fooled, although we had begun wondering how the guy in charge could be so slick and keep such a low profile."

"You mean, it was Eddie Riser's business? That punk?" Bob asked.

"Right. He even had the other guys on his team believing they were all answering to someone else. Pretty smart, actually. Until Rafe Shannon wanted in and then there was only one way this would play out. And once Wade tried dealing himself in with Riser and told him about the USB stick with all of Shannon's business info on it, Riser saw a way of making even more money."

Darla came back outside at that point. She looked at Molly. "Wade said he didn't want Rafe screwing up a good thing. Wade had already decided I should ask you, even beg you, to pay the debt and maybe even get a bit more out of you." She started to cry again.

Molly looked stunned. Even Bob didn't seem sure what to say.

Darla sniffed and blew her nose. "Am I in any trouble with the law?" she asked Mark.

He shook his head. "Not unless it turns out you were really involved with the entire plot."

She blanched and cried out.

"I'm not saying I believe that, Darla. Seems to me your biggest trouble is here with your granddad and Molly."

Darla lowered her head, which made it difficult to clearly hear what she next said. "I know. I'm really, really sorry. I wouldn't blame you two if you kicked me out right now and never spoke to me again."

No one said anything for a few minutes. Lizzie had a feeling that this was the real Darla speaking, not someone trying to play an angle. She wondered if Molly and Bob felt the same thing. She was still upset with her, though, for not telling the entire truth. But who knew, that might eventually come out, once Darla settled into a new life. She could only hope so. Secrets were not a good basis for any relationship. But she also knew it wasn't hers to tell.

Bob cleared his throat. "I'm not saying I'm not disappointed in you, young lady. But I do understand where you're coming from. But you know, you can't go around playing the 'poor me' card all the time. You have to take responsibility for your life. So, I'll make you a deal." He waited until Darla looked at him before continuing.

"You go on home to your mama and I'll come with you. It's time I got to know my daughter, after all. And I want you to find a job, a real job and to put some effort into doing it real good."

"You said you wanted to work in a veterinary office, didn't you, Darla?" Lizzie asked.

Darla nodded. Bob looked surprised.

"Okay then, that's a plan. You find that job and I'll pay

off your gambling debt. Then you make regular payments to me out of your paycheck until the debt is settled." He held up his hand before she could say anything. "It's strictly a loan and we'll draw up the papers all legal like. You have to take responsibility for this, Darla, but I'll be there for you."

Lizzie pulled some more tissues out of the box and handed them to Darla just in time. She flung herself into her granddad's arms.

"I will. I promise. I promise," she mumbled into his shoulder.

Molly wiped away a tear from her cheek as she stood. "I think I'll go see about some supper."

Chapter Thirty-one

✧✧✧

She laughed. "You know something? I am, too."

CHRISTMAS MOURNING—MARGARET MARON

Lizzie brought the final bowl of salad outside, this one a sweet potato salad, and placed it on the serving table next to the others. She looked over all the food waiting to be enjoyed. For a supper called together at the last minute, this one looked like the planning had gone on all week. Maybe that's what they should do for the Easter Sunday dinner Molly had insisted on hosting on the weekend. She looked over to the grill, where Bob, Mark and Jacob were discussing the merits of splashing beer on the burgers.

Molly had been persuaded to sit and enjoy her cold glass of white Sauvignon Blanc while Sally-Jo set the table. Stephanie, Andie and Darla sat on a blanket on the grass, playing with baby Wendy.

What a contented-looking scene, Lizzie thought. And to think that just a couple of hours before it was turmoil. Molly had thought to invite the book club over to help celebrate the wrapping up of the case and also, to help divert Darla's mind from what had gone on that day. Everyone had eagerly accepted and come bearing gifts of food. Lizzie was sure the deli counter at the Winn-Dixie had been emptied by now.

"Yoo-hoo. I hear there's a party going on," Teensy called out as she stepped out of the kitchen.

"I'm so glad you got my message," Molly answered. She pointed to the bottle of wine on the table. "Help yourself."

"Oh, Mopsy. You can be sure. I just wanted to bring this little dessert to the celebration."

She placed a glass cake container at the end of the table with the other desserts and popped off the cover. "Voilà!"

Molly, Lizzie and Sally-Jo gathered around.

"Why, Teensy, how sweet," Molly said, and waited until Teensy had poured her wine before clinking glasses with her.

Sally-Jo elbowed Lizzie as she read the message atop the cake. *Go hog wild.*

"Anybody hungry?" Bob called out. He looked over at Darla, and the relief on his face was visible. She looked carefree and as young as Andie as she lay flat out on the ground, playing with Wendy.

"I surely am," Teensy replied, grabbing a plate and easing up to Bob. "I know you have fish-cooking skills but I haven't tasted your burgers yet."

"You are in for a treat, ma'am."

"I'm always ready for a treat." She laughed as she headed back to the table to fill her plate with the salads.

When they all had their food and drinks in hand, Bob called for everyone's attention. "I'd just like to say something quickly. A small toast." He held up his glass. "To family and friends. Which really are one and the same."

Molly squeezed his hand and Teensy kicked Lizzie under

the table, motioning toward the two with her head. Lizzie grinned and shook her head.

"So tell me, Sally-Jo, is everything all settled in the mama department for the wedding? Or should I be asking?" Teensy looked across the table at Sally-Jo as she asked.

Sally-Jo swallowed before answering. "It is, Teensy. And it's safe to talk about it. Mama turned out to be sort of reasonable after all was said and done."

"You got the dress of your choice?"

"Yes'm, I did."

"And the trade-off? She gets to keep her limbs intact?"

Jacob laughed and answered for Sally-Jo. "I don't even think they came to blows, Teensy. Mama gives on the dress and gets to take over the food."

Teensy rolled her eyes. "Oh boy, you kids are such suckers."

Lizzie kicked Teensy under the table and gave her head a quick shake when she looked at her.

"Just kidding," Teensy said quickly. "I'm so glad there's peace in the family. In all families," she added, looking over at Darla.

"Well, it might be short-lived," Jacob said, getting up to refill his plate.

"How so?" Molly asked.

"Can I tell them?" he asked Sally-Jo, who nodded. "Mama doesn't yet know that we've decided to elope. And the date is going to be a secret. We'll still go ahead with the church ceremony and all the reception plans so that there's all the hoopla. But it's turned into such a circus and we want this to be a very special time, just for us."

"Does that sound mean or selfish?" Sally-Jo asked.

Lizzie reached across and touched Sally-Jo's arm. "I think you have to do what's right for you two. It is your special time."

"You can say that again," Jacob agreed, sitting back down beside Sally-Jo and putting his arm around her. "It's been an emotional roller coaster for Sally-Jo, who always tries to please everyone. I think she's entitled to please herself this time."

"Whoo-hoo," Teensy shrieked, clapping her hands.

The others didn't know what to say but their smiles said it all.

Mark put his arm across the back of Lizzie's chair and leaned close to her ear.

"They may be onto something," he whispered.

Reading Lists

Lizzie Turner

1. Victoria Abbott—*The Wolfe Widow*
2. Julie Hyzy—*Grace Against the Clock*
3. Eva Gates—*By Book or By Crook*
4. Jacklyn Brady—*Rebel Without a Cake*
5. Ellery Adams—*Murder in the Mystery Suite*

Sally-Jo Baker

1. Rosie Genova—*The Wedding Soup Murder*
2. Nancy J. Parra—*Engaged in Murder*
3. Beverly Allen—*Bloom and Doom*
4. Cleo Coyle—*Espresso Shot*
5. Leann Sweeney—*A Wedding to Die For*

Molly Mathews

1. Jacqueline Winspear—*Leaving Everything Most Loved*
2. Rhys Bowen—*Heirs and Graces*
3. Susan Wittig Albert—*The Darling Dahlias and the Texas Star*
4. John Curran—*Agatha Christie's Secret Notebooks*
5. Carolyn Hart—*Death at the Door*

Bob Miller

1. John Sandford—*Storm Front*
2. Bill Pronzini—*Strangers*
3. Craig Johnson—*A Serpent's Tooth*
4. Randy Wayne White—*Deceived*
5. Carol O'Connell—*It Happens in the Dark*

Stephanie Lowe

1. Carolyn Hart—*Ghost Gone Wild*
2. Kylie Logan—*The Legend of Sleepy Harlow*
3. Daryl Wood Gerber—*Stirring the Plot*
4. Lisa Spellman—*Spellman Six: The Next Generation*
5. Catriona McPherson—*Dandy Gilver and a Bothersome Number of Corpses*

Andrea Mason

1. Janet Evanovich—*Top Secret Twenty-One*
2. Leigh Perry—*The Skeleton Takes a Bow*
3. Heather Blake—*One Potion in the Grave*
4. Dawn Eastman—*Be Careful What You Witch For*
5. Victoria Laurie—*No Ghouls Allowed*

Jacob Smith

1. Paul Christopher—*Secret of the Templars*
2. Stuart Woods—*Standup Guy*
3. David Rosenfelt—*Hounded*
4. Robert Rotenberg—*Stray Bullets*
5. Christopher Buehlman—*Those Across the River*

Turn the page for a preview of the first book in
a brand new series from Erika Chase writing as
Linda Wiken,
available soon from Berkley Prime Crime

"Let's see: Canadian, French, Greek. Here we go, Italian," J.J. said softly to herself as she walked along the aisle at the nearby Barnes & Noble. She had stopped by after work on her way home. She needed that cookbook tonight.

She scanned the titles and authors, pulling out the ones that looked of interest to flip through. She liked looking at the pictures. That was her downfall. While she loved the whole idea of cooking elaborate meals, her forte was in the reading of cookbooks. She had an entire, although small, bookcase at home filled with cookbooks, but only those with large and colorful photos of the dishes. And, although her friend Evan Thornton had persuaded her to join the Culinary Capers dinner club, she secretly believed she would never have caved if it hadn't been for this one weakness. The one obsession that cost her money but was not a vice: cookbooks. Now she could really indulge it without a twinge of guilt.

She grinned as she started flipping through the pages of *Nigellissima* by Nigella Lawson. Great photos, easy-to-read recipes—although she had no idea how complicated they might be—and best of all, Italian foods. She quickly scanned the rest of the cookbook section and then made her way to the checkout clutching her prize. It would be an Italian night at Casa Tanner.

She drove home quickly, unlocked the door to her apartment and slid through before Asia, her two-year-old Bengal cat, could dash out into the hallway. That had happened on more than one occasion, the test of wills: one demanding to be outside and on the prowl, the other insisting that Asia was an indoor cat. J.J. had compromised by setting up a portion of her large wraparound balcony as a cat playground complete with a large patch of real grass. Of course, the mesh blocking the sides and top were what gave J.J. peace of mind. Asia didn't seem to mind too much, except when trying to catch a bird midflight.

She checked her phone messages—nothing important— and then dished out some canned food for Asia and tossed a green salad for herself.

As she ate, she eyed her briefcase on the floor by the kitchen counter. No, she wouldn't go over that budget tonight. She didn't even know why she'd brought it home. She'd made herself a promise when she left her old life behind—no more working days and nights on a project. Her own life was as important as her job. She would be kinder to herself.

She found herself thinking back to her days as an account executive with the high-profile advertising agency McCracken and Watts in Montpelier, Vermont. Just before she got bogged down, once again, in thoughts about Patrick Jenner, her ex-fiancé, she shook her head and reached over to pull her new cookbook out of its bag. She ran her hand gently over the cover before opening it. She had to admit, she was a cookbook junkie. She loved the colors, the travelogue that accompanied her favorites from overseas, and the feeling that she actually knew her food. She did realize, though, that loving cookbooks did not a good cook make. Oh, what she'd give for osmosis. She sighed and finished eating her salad. She couldn't wait to share *Nigellissima* with the others.

J.J. sipped her espresso while watching the dwindling lineup of people ordering their coffee and hopefully, for the staff, something sweet to go with it. Beth Brickner kept smiling although J.J. bet her feet hurt by now. It was eleven A.M. and the Cups 'n Roses coffee bar had opened at seven. J.J. knew that Beth tended the front counter with the help of one barista for the first couple of hours. After that, the part-timers started their shifts but Beth held her ground at the cash. She enjoyed the customers, as she'd once said.

As if she realized she was being watched, Beth looked over and smiled, transforming her face from looking its sixty-two years to about twenty years younger, J.J. thought. She smiled in return. Her attention shifted to the front door and the two people walking through it: Connor Mac and Alison Manovich, two more of the Culinary Capers members. When Evan Thornton arrived, Beth would slip away from her duties and join the four others for their monthly planning meeting.

Connor, after collecting his usual mochaccino, slid in beside J.J. in the group's regular booth, which formed a semicircle in the right corner of the shop, mostly facing the street. It was J.J.'s favorite spot, allowing her to watch the passersby and, admittedly, leading to distractions at times, especially when the discussion focused on cooking techniques.

"You're looking great, J.J.," Connor said, reaching over to squeeze her hand. "I've been meaning to call you but the week just slipped by. Are you free for dinner tonight?"

J.J. gave about two seconds' thought to playing hard to get. After all, Connor was gorgeous and was probably used to women falling all over him. And what self-respecting single gal would admit to being available at the last minute on a Saturday night? But she felt comfortable with Connor and she knew that after about six months of dating, this was as exciting as it would get between them. Dinner would be good and she said so.

"Great. I'll pick you up at six? Thought we'd try that new spot downtown, the Hidden Keg." He leaned closer and lowered his voice. "In fact, I second-guessed you and already made reservations. Hope you don't take that the wrong way."

J.J. shrugged. "Of course not. They'd be easy enough to cancel if I said no and you couldn't find another date." She was teasing him and he knew it.

"Okay. See this spot over here on the bench?" He pointed beside him and slid over the few inches. "I know my place."

"And I know my place is in this chair," Alison said, setting her plate with two sour cream twists down beside her mug of regular coffee. "Hey, J.J. How's it going?"

"Good although hectic. What about you, Alison? Keeping the bad guys in their places?"

Alison sighed, took a long sip, and sat back in the chair. She looked like a teenager when she went casual, like the jeans she wore with a T-shirt and hoodie over it. Her police uniform seemed to add several years along with that necessary air of authority. "Tell me about it. For a small village, Half Moon Bay does have more than its share of looneys, I sometimes think."

"As long as they're not dangerous," Connor muttered.

"No, they're usually not. They seem to leave their weapons behind. Or they're saving them for downtown Burlington. Thankfully."

J.J. hadn't noticed Evan entering until he slid in beside her on the other side, placing a medium cappuccino in front of her. "Beth says this'll save you having to get up and fetch your own. She'll be right over. Howdy, all."

"Wow, Evan. Is that a swath of gray I spy in your hair?" Alison asked playfully.

Evan ran his right hand lightly over the spot in his short red hair. "It is. Do you think it makes me look more worldly?"

Alison took a closer look. "Not really, sorry."

"All right, how about more scholarly? I'll settle for that."

"Oh, definitely," Alison agreed and took a quick sip, almost covering her grin.

"Huh."

"Well, I think it makes you look worldly, scholarly and older, which translates into trustworthy, even with the freckles," Beth added, taking the empty chair beside Alison. She missed Evan's grimace but knew it would be his response. "Keep it, Evan. It really looks good, whatever the adjective."

Evan smiled. "Why, thank you, Beth, arbiter of good taste."

"Oh, boy. Before we get carried away with the niceties," J.J. interjected, "can I say good morning to you all and introduce you to Nigella Lawson?" She flipped over the cookbook she'd had sitting on the table in front of her, and balanced it upright. "*Nigellissima* is my choice for the next Culinary Capers dinner."

She glanced around from one club member to the other,

hoping to see her own excitement mirrored in each of the
faces. Okay, that might have been asking too much. No one
ever leaped up for joy right at first. She started flipping
through the pages. "Great photos, aren't they? I'll pass it
around and you can all have a more thorough look. I bought
it just last night so I haven't had time to really read it through
carefully but I might go with the beef pizzaiola. So, if I do
the meat dish, we need a pasta to start with, and after my
pièce de résistance—I know I'm mixing my countries here—
two side dishes, and dessert."

Beth looked at the index in the back of the book, running
her finger slowly down the names of the dishes. "This looks
like it could be fun."

She passed it to Alison, who did the same. After the book
had made its way around the table, J.J. leaned forward,
crossing her arms on the table. Her desire that they should
all buy into this choice had intensified as the others had
checked it out. "So, what say you? Is it a go?"

Connor laughed. "You are into this one, aren't you? As
I remember, last time you winced and shrugged your way
through our checking out the book."

J.J. sighed. "You're right. Last time I just chose something I thought would be doable. This time, I'm enthralled
looking through the cookbook and I'm hoping that will
translate into a delectable meal."

"Well, if that's the vibe you're getting, then I'd say we
should all be on board," Evan said. "I vote yes." He looked
around the table and the others nodded their agreement.
"There. A done deal, J.J."

"Great. You don't mind getting your own copies of this
book even though it's at the upper end of the price range
we set?"

Alison finished her cappuccino before speaking. "I'll

probably just borrow it from the library again. But I'm happy to try out a side dish."

"Dibs on dessert," Beth added.

"Guess I'll take the other side dish and we'll confer, Alison," Connor said. "What does that leave for Evan?'

"How about the pasta?" J.J. suggested.

Evan thought about it for less than a minute. His eyes lit up as he announced, "I've been thinking lately about buying a pasta machine to make my own fresh pasta. This is the kick in the pants I need to do just that. Besides, Michael can't object to the expense if it's for the dinner club." He grinned.

"I can't picture Michael objecting to anything you decide to do." Beth had taken on that motherly tone she sometimes used with Evan. J.J. wondered if he noticed it. If he did, he never let on. Or maybe he enjoyed it.

Even though Beth was at least two decades older than the others, retired from being a high school music teacher for five years and now the owner of the Cups 'n Roses for two years, the difference in ages wasn't a big deal.

"That's great. So, *Nigellissima* it is, and we feast on these wonderful recipes at my place in four weeks."

Heaven help me.